## "It's a Lesson We All Have to Learn."

"To be a cynic, you mean?" she challenged. "The way you are?"

"To be clearheaded and see life as it is, not through rose-tinted glasses." He moved toward her, and Shelley felt the familiar quiver of excitement. "You've got to face up to things and not run away from the truth."

"What truth?" she asked, trembling.

"The truth about yourself."

He slowly raised his hand, and she felt herself go rigidly tense. She knew one truth, and it was the only truth that really counted. She knew that she wanted this man. . . .

---

**NANCY JOHN**

is an unashamed romantic, deeply in love with her husband of thirty years. She lives in Sussex, England, where long walks through the countryside provide inspiration for the novels that have brought her a worldwide following.

Dear Reader:

During the last year, many of you have written to Silhouette telling us what you like best about Silhouette Romances and, more recently, about Silhouette Special Editions. You've also told us what else you'd like to read from Silhouette. With your comments and suggestions in mind, we've developed SILHOUETTE DESIRE.

SILHOUETTE DESIREs will be on sale this June, and each month we'll bring you four new DESIREs written by some of your favorite authors—Stephanie James, Diana Palmer, Rita Clay, Suzanne Stevens and many more.

SILHOUETTE DESIREs may not be for everyone, but they are for those readers who want a more sensual, provocative romance. The heroines are slightly older—women who are actively invloved in their careers and the world around them. If you want to experience all the excitement, passion and joy of falling in love, then SILHOUETTE DESIRE is for you.

I'd appreciate any thoughts you'd like to share with us on new SILHOUETTE DESIRE, and I invite you to write to us at the address below:

Karen Solem
Editor-in-Chief
Silhouette Books
P.O. Box 769
New York, N.Y. 10019

*Twila Chiesi*

# NANCY JOHN
# So Many Tomorrows

*Silhouette Special Edition*
**Published by Silhouette Books New York**
**America's Publisher of Contemporary Romance**

SILHOUETTE BOOKS, a Simon & Schuster Division of
GULF & WESTERN CORPORATION
1230 Avenue of the Americas, New York, N.Y. 10020

ISBN: 0-671-53517-X

First Silhouette Books printing April, 1982

10 9 8 7 6 5 4 3 2 1

May by Tony Ferrara

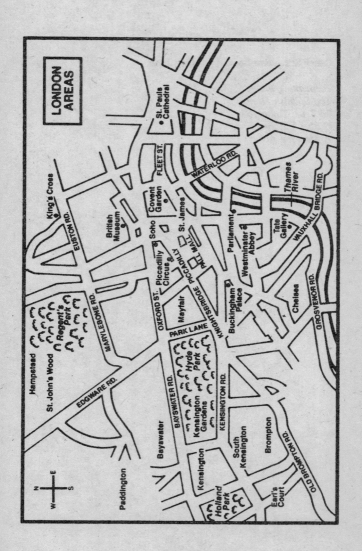

# Chapter One

It was a gray, dismal April evening, with a bone-chilling rawness in the air. Snow had fallen earlier in the day, and wet mush still lay in the streets.

The girl on the airport bus to Kennedy, booked through on an economy flight to London, glanced back at the Manhattan skyline and wondered how long it would be before she would see it again. She was small-boned and delicately built, with a silken mass of warm chestnut hair that fell to her shoulders and an oval-shaped face. It was a beautiful face, yet in her clear amber eyes there was a look of indefinable sadness. She was remembering when she had made this same journey eleven months before as an excited and deliriously happy bride. She and her husband had driven to the airport in a chauffeured limousine, with the pampered luxury of a Concorde awaiting them.

Aboard the crowded DC10, her hand luggage stowed, she sat down and fumbled awkwardly with the catch of her seat belt. At once her neighbor on the aisle side leaned across to assist her. He was a smooth type of around thirty, and though a bit too fleshy to be called handsome, he seemed brashly confident about his appeal.

"Marvin Benchley," he introduced himself, treating her to a brilliant smile. "I'm in computers. And you?"

"Shelley Armitage." She gave him her name politely but coolly, and left it at that.

With a glance at her platinum wedding band he inquired, "Traveling to join up with your husband, honey? Or are you leaving him home this trip?"

"My husband is dead," Shelley explained before she could check herself.

"Gee, that's real tough, losing your husband so young!" Quickly discarding the sympathetic expression, he went on brightly, "So you'll be on your lonesome in Britain? Maybe we could kind of get together, huh?"

Shelley cursed herself for a fool. Why hadn't she learned the lesson yet, in six whole months, that a young widow is considered to be an easy target? She gave a noncommittal mutter and pointedly leaned back and closed her eyes.

"Guess you're tired," he said, sounding disappointed. Then he added with a meaningful laugh, "You go ahead and have yourself a snooze, honey. We've got the whole long night to get acquainted."

Shelley was more than just tired. Now that it was too late to turn back, she was suddenly stabbed with doubt. How crazy to have imagined that in London her heartache would be easier to bear. London was Rex's city, where she had lived during those five brief months as his wife. Now, without Rex, she would just be an unattached female in a place where she didn't belong.

Shelley's roots were in a small town amid the apple orchards of Maine. Her father had owned the neighborhood pharmacy there until his fatal coronary the week before her fifteenth birthday. Five years ago, having graduated with a major in English lit, she had arrived in New York determined to make her career in one branch or another of the communications business.

Her determination had ultimately paid off when she found a job with a Madison Avenue advertising agency. At Prescott and Liedermann she made an early hit with a catchy slogan for a new baby food, and under the benevolent eye of Ed Braine, the agency's copy chief, she was given more and more challenging work to tackle. She rapidly became respected as a young copywriter with a highly original slant to her thinking. The job was immensely satisfying to Shelley, and thoughts of romance and marriage were deliberately held at bay in favor of building her career. Her relationships with the men she now and then dated were kept on a casually friendly basis, with no risk of any lasting involvement.

Until, a week after her twenty-fifth birthday, Rex Armitage erupted into her life.

Rex was a senior account director with the London subsidiary of Prescott and Liedermann, and he'd come to the corporate headquarters in New York for discussions about the British launch of a new fabric softener. By the third day of his visit, which was when he made his first appearance in the copy room, he was already a legend to the entire female staff of P&L. A tall, dark Englishman with breath-robbing good looks, stylishly attired in Italian hand-tailored suits and expensive silk shirts, he was said to be charming, witty and devastatingly sexy. All of which Shelley had heard with only the mildest interest—until that fateful moment when the man concerned was brought across and introduced to her by Ed Braine.

Rex had to be called magnificent. Superbly proportioned, his well-knit frame carried not an ounce of surplus flesh. His skin was healthily bronzed, and his crisp curly brown hair was styled fashionably between long and short. Moving with easy grace, he came forward and took her hand, holding it caressingly while his intent hazel eyes smiled down into hers.

"Why has it taken me three whole days to get around to meeting you, Shelley Bowyer?" His voice was rich and deeply resonant. "Luckily, though, I'm here for another two weeks at least, so we haven't lost too much time."

That first day they lunched together at an exclusive French restaurant on West Fifty-fifth Street—for Rex to wise up, as he put it, on the copy room's thinking about the Derrydown account. After a superb meal and the sort of attentive service she was to discover that Rex commanded everyplace he went, they lingered over coffee at their corner table until well after three o'clock; yet not one word of business was discussed. Shelley listened enthralled as he expounded on London and Paris, Vienna and Rome, Madrid and Athens—he seemed intimately acquainted with all the exotic cities that were only names to her.

In the cab back to the office, she gasped in dismay when she noticed the time. "Ed will have a fit that I've taken so long over lunch."

"I'll square Ed," Rex said confidently. "Now, about this evening. . . ."

Not only that evening, but the next and the next and the next . . . dinner, dancing, seats for the hit Broadway shows that nobody could get tickets for at any price. Saturday night it was the Rainbow Grill at Rockefeller Center, where they could look out at the lights of Manhattan.

Rex held her hand, and with his thumb began to stroke the inside of her wrist erotically. "You'll have to say good-bye to all this, my sweet American girl," he murmured.

"Say good-bye . . . How do you mean?"

Rex smiled gently at her confusion. "When I return to England, you're coming with me. Now that I've found you, I don't intend to let you escape. We're going to be married at once."

With Rex there were no ifs and buts, no hassles, no delays. He swept her along with him, and Shelley was only too happy to let him. Prescott and Liedermann released her at once and promised her a comparable job in London. A tenant was instantly found to take over the lease of her studio apartment in a renovated Murray Hill brownstone, and every loose end of her life was neatly tied off. The day before they were due to leave for London, she became Mrs. Rex Armitage. After the ceremony, there was a big celebration party in Rex's hotel suite, and Shelley was amazed at how many friends he already seemed to have collected in New York.

Her marriage became all that mattered to her, and she gave herself to it with total commitment. She felt lost and lonely when the demands of Rex's job took him away from her for an evening, a night, or even, on two occasions, a whole weekend. . . .

A hand touched her arm and Shelley jumped into startled awareness. Her neighbor, Marvin Benchley, was turned toward her with a solicitous smile.

"Sorry if I woke you, honey, but it's suppertime. Shall I fix your table for you?"

"Er . . . yes, if you would, please." Marvin Benchley clicked the folding table in position, and the waiting stewardess slid her supper tray onto it.

"You could do with a little snifter, by the look of you," he went on. "You missed the drinks when they came around, but I saved a bit. Care for a drop? There's still some ice left in the glass."

Shelley decided that she needed something to get herself together. The unaccustomed whiskey was raw and burning on her throat, but it did help calm her jangled nerves.

"Thanks, Mr. Benchley," she said, returning the glass.

"Call me Marv," he reproached her, as he dug his fork into the chicken pâté. "So what are you going to England for, Shelley? A vacation? To see the sights and have yourself a ball?"

As if stung, she overreacted. "It's only six months since my husband was killed, so I'm hardly in any mood to have myself a ball. As it happens," she went on in a less ferocious tone, "I'm returning to London to take up the job I had while I was married. Rex and I both worked for the same international advertising agency. We met when he came over to New York on a business trip. We got married right away and they transferred me to London, but after Rex was killed . . . well, I guess it was only natural for me to want to return home."

"It figures," Marvin agreed. "But now you're heading back to London again. How come?"

Shelley shrugged helplessly. She had no real answer to give him. "It's just a feeling of being unsettled, I guess. And the firm made no objection when I asked to be transferred again."

"What agency are you with?"

"Prescott and Liedermann. Maybe you've heard of us?"

"Of course I've heard of you." Marvin looked pleased. "You're the agency my own firm uses, Cosmos Computers. I guess you must know us very well?"

"Yes, I do! I never worked on that particular account, though, and it wasn't one that Rex handled." As they proceeded to trade names of people they each might know, Shelley reflected ruefully that Marvin Benchley had managed to trap her into conversation after all. Thank goodness she was being met at Heathrow Airport, otherwise the man might be difficult to shake off.

She wasn't sure who would be coming to meet her, but guessed that it would probably be Clare Royston. She and her husband both worked at the agency; Clare was an assistant in the media department and Nick was one of the art buyers, responsible for commissioning photographs that were to be used in advertisements. Shelley had Clare to thank for fixing her up with a small apartment at the same address where the Roystons themselves lived. It was a little house overlooking the Thames, she gathered, in a district called Putney. This was on the outskirts of the city and no more than a name to Shelley, though she figured that she and Rex might have passed through it when dashing off on a weekend at some friend or client's country place in his sleek white Porsche—the car that had eventually killed him.

Shelley only managed to peck at her supper tray,

and then leaned back and closed her eyes once more. Again, scenes of the life she'd so briefly shared with Rex came flashing into her mind. Their luxurious penthouse apartment had been just off Knightsbridge, with views across the rooftops to St. Paul's and Big Ben. In those five months they must have thrown at least a dozen big parties, and she could never hope to remember all the notable people Rex had invited. It had been a dazzling, exciting new world to Shelley.

"That little shindig went like a bomb, sweetheart," Rex chuckled delightedly on one such occasion, after the last guest had gone. "It always pays dividends to think big and spend big. I reckon we've done ourselves a real favor this evening. That chap Jeremy Carstairs has the placing of a six-figure advertising budget in his pocket, and it'll be coming my way before the year's out, you'll see. You're a big asset to me, Shelley, did you know that? All the men fall in love with you, even if the women do hate your guts for being so attractive."

"They don't need to worry," she joked. "I've already got the only man I'll ever want."

"We'll drink to that," he said with a wink, and went off to fetch champagne from the fridge. On the tray beside the bottle and cut-crystal glasses, when he came back, Shelley saw the glitter of gemstones, a bracelet of sapphires and diamonds set in a twisted rope of silver.

"Oh, Rex, how lovely!" she gasped, picking it up. It must have cost . . . what? Shelley couldn't even begin to hazard a guess. With a glance around that included the luxurious room, the whole super-deluxe apartment, their extravagant life-style, she said uneasily, "It's a sweet thought, darling, and terribly generous of you, but you don't have to keep giving me presents. Sometimes . . . well, I guess I feel that we go through too much money."

Rex threw back his head and laughed. "We have an English proverb that goes, 'Money is round and meant to roll.' Not to worry your head, there's always plenty more coming to me. In point of fact, I've got a piece of good news that I was saving up for this moment. Today I finalized things with Le Français Cosmetics, and the account is definitely in the bag for P&L. They're budgeting a million-pounds-plus for the first year's advertising, so my commission will be enormous! Enough to cover that trinket and a dozen more like it. What say you and I pop off somewhere special for the weekend to celebrate?"

"Oh, Rex, how exciting!" Her amber eyes sparkled with delight. "The way you make things happen at P&L, goodness knows where you'll end up."

"In the managing director's chair, sweetheart," he said with blithe confidence. "And that can't be long delayed now, considering Henry Firth's state of health."

After a moment's hesitation Shelley said, "I heard a whisper that Jason Steele is in line for managing director."

"Jason Steele?" Rex's voice was scathing with contempt. "He hasn't got a hope."

"Are you sure? He seems to be very highly thought of as media director."

"What does that job amount to, for heaven's sake?" Rex demanded. "Sitting on your backside all day phoning around to book slots for TV, and for advertising space in newspapers. What counts in the advertising game, my love, is style and flair and mixing with the right people. Take it from me, Jason

Steele will never rise to anything more than he is right now."

Her husband's dislike of Jason Steele amounted almost to a personal vendetta. Shelley had always felt uneasy about this until a recent incident made her realize that Rex had some justification for his attitude. One day when her boss in the copy room was out with the flu, she had deputized for him at a weekly think-tank meeting. One of Rex's accounts, Baxter's, the vinyl-flooring people, had been on the agenda. Rex made it clear that he thought the provisional media schedule was quite hopeless, a feeble and uninspired advertising program. Jason Steele, who happened to be chairing the meeting, remained adamant. With a maddeningly superior air he refuted every objection Rex made and extolled the virtues of his own department's proposals. Shelley had been obliged to sit there and listen to it all, while inwardly she boiled with fury.

The moment the meeting broke up and she and Rex got a chance to talk, she burst out sympathetically, "I can see what you mean about Jason Steele now, darling. He had to go and make a big display in front of everybody of how clever he thinks he is. He's insufferable!"

Rex's handsome features were still flushed with anger. "He seems to think he can throw his weight around these days, with old man Firth half out of action. Mr. Jason-Bloody-Steele needs cutting down to size, sweetheart. And I shall enjoy doing just that when I'm running things here."

But fate never gave Rex the opportunity. Less than six weeks later, her husband had been killed outright in a car accident. And when Henry Firth's deteriorating heart condition finally made his resignation inevitable—by which time Shelley was back in

New York—it was Jason Steele who had been instated in the managing director's vacant chair.

Jason Steele! Time and again since her return to New York she had remembered with a flush of shame those incredible moments of madness just a few days after Rex's death. Jason, who'd been assisting her with all the inevitable formalities, had found a tenant to take over the lease of the Knightsbridge apartment, its sky-high cost now way beyond her means, and one evening he came around to discuss the agreement he'd had drafted by a lawyer. Somehow Shelley had found herself in Jason's arms, as if he were comforting her in her grief. For long, drawn-out moments the atmosphere was charged with tense emotion, and then they were kissing passionately. Shelley longed to erase the incident from her mind, but she knew it was indelibly imprinted. At least, in New York, there had been three thousand miles of ocean separating her from the scene of that embarrassing memory. Yet here she was hurtling back across the Atlantic to London. To the selfsame agency where Jason Steele was now the man in charge.

Insanity! But it was all arranged now, an irreversible *fait accompli*. Her immediate boss, Ed Braine, had pulled strings on her behalf to fix the transfer. In London she would just have to keep a low profile and hope that Jason Steele would be so busy in his new position of power that he would never deign to notice a mere assistant copywriter on the agency's staff.

At Heathrow Airport the plane landed in a drenching April shower. But even before the passengers had set foot inside the terminal building, the sun burst forth and everything was sparklingly bright. Going through passport control, Shelley thought

that she had successfully shaken off Marvin Benchley, but he caught up with her again while she was
waiting to collect her baggage.

"Are you taking the subway to London, or the
bus?" he asked.

"Neither," she was glad to tell him. "I'm being
met."

He finally gave up, pulling a rueful face. "Lucky
you! Oh, well, take care, Shelley. Maybe we'll meet
up somewhen over here. You never know. *Ciao!*"

Once through customs, Shelley glanced around at
the people waiting. There was no sign of Clare
Royston, and she felt an exaggerated sense of let-
down. Okay, she told herself, so the plane had
arrived dead on schedule and Clare was maybe just a
few minutes late. It was nice of her to be coming at
all in the rush of Monday-morning traffic.

"Hello, Shelley," said a cool male voice from right
beside her. "Have a good flight?"

She spun around quickly and, with a shock of
surprise, met the inquiring dark-browed gaze of
Jason Steele. He was taller than she remembered—
taller by a couple of inches than Rex had been, with
angular features and a thick mass of springy peat-
brown hair. His disconcertingly keen eyes were a
deep charcoal gray in color.

"Oh . . . hello, Jason."

"You don't seem very pleased to see me," he
observed laconically as he reached down for her two
suitcases.

"It's just . . . well, I guess I didn't figure on your
being here to meet me. I thought that maybe Clare
Royston would come."

Jason began leading the way through the throng.
"Since the airport happened to be right on my route
back to town, I decided I might as well pick you up

myself. I've been staying in Windsor over the weekend, at Sir Mortimer Cleveland's place." He wanted it clearly understood, Shelley noted, that he had not put himself to any special trouble in coming to meet her this morning. Well, that was fine by her; it meant that she wouldn't need to feel overly grateful to him.

They walked in silence until they reached Jason's car, a blue Mercedes. He stowed her cases, then unlocked the door to let her get in. It wasn't until they entered the airport tunnel that Jason spoke again.

"Actually, Shelley, it seemed a sensible idea for us to have a preliminary chat before you turn up at the office. You see, I've decided not to put you back to working in the copy room. I think you'll be more useful on my personal staff, directly answerable to me."

# Chapter Two

Shelley was in the pint-size kitchen of her new apartment when the telephone rang. She had to think for a moment before remembering where she'd seen the phone—on a small table beside the bed. Switching off the hot plate and licking her fingers, she hurried through to answer it.

"Hi, Shelley! This is Clare. Jason just arrived at the office and says that he met you okay and dropped you off at the house. I thought I'd give you a quick ring to say hello and welcome."

"That's nice of you, Clare! Say, I love this flat; it's got everything I could possibly want. And the view across the river is out of this world."

"Isn't it just? How're you feeling? Jet-lagged?"

"A bit. I've more or less unpacked my stuff, and at the moment I'm fixing some scrambled eggs. It was swell of you to stock up the fridge for me, Clare.

And those daffodils are lovely—a real homey touch."

"All part of the service. Listen, I'm up to my eyeballs right now, so I'd better not chat. But I'll see you this evening when I get home—that's usually around six-thirty. Oh, by the way, you're eating with us tonight. Nick and I can put you in the picture about what's happening at P&L. Though I suppose J.S. has already done that?"

"Somewhat. It came as quite a shock to learn that he's putting me on his personal staff."

"A nice shock, though," laughed Clare. "Me, I'm green with envy. It looks like you're all set to go places."

It would have been ungracious, Shelley thought as she put down the phone, to tell Clare that she would greatly prefer to return to her old desk in the copy room. She really was pleased, though, about the little furnished flat. Consisting of living room and bedroom, kitchenette and bathroom, it occupied the top floor of a small and very attractive terrace house that fronted the curve of the Thames where the famous annual Oxford-and-Cambridge boat race started. Clare and her husband occupied the two floors below her, an apartment with its own separate entrance off the downstairs hall.

This flat would be her haven, her safe cocoon, where she could keep the world at arm's length while she worked through her emotional problems and came to terms with herself. But at P&L, she was not to be given the chance she'd expected to coast along quietly in a job that was safely within her capabilities. Instead, before she felt ready, she was being pitchforked into a tough, challenging job that would make heavy demands on her. And what was infinitely worse, it was a job that involved working right alongside Jason Steele.

"I don't quite understand what I'll be expected to do as a member of your staff," she had protested on the drive from the airport. Her voice had carried an aggressive note she'd not intended, but having to sit beside Jason in the close confines of his car had made her nerve ends raw.

"It's simple enough. Your directive will be to assist me in whatever way I decide."

"But doing what? I'm a copywriter, not an administrator."

"Which is precisely why I think you might be useful. With you directly answerable to me, I shall expect unprejudiced opinions on the output of the creative departments."

"But why *me?*" Shelley demanded.

"Because I think you can do what I require . . . with guidance. First of all, you're female, and I want someone who can look at our campaign presentations from the woman's viewpoint. Second, your coming in as an outsider is an advantage."

"How's that?"

"If I were to pick someone from one of our existing teams here in London—from the copy room or studio or wherever—there might be an element of personal loyalty toward former workmates which would impair good analytical judgment. It's in the very nature of creative people to come up with some pretty wild flights of fancy now and then, and they need to be restrained."

Shelley felt her indignation rising. "In other words, I'm to be your hatchet man. I'm to be the one to kill off any of the ideas that tend to go a bit over the top, while you sit back and let me take the rap."

"Like hell I intend to sit back!" Jason shot her a

dangerous look from beneath his dark brows. "I was appointed by New York to run the London end, and that's precisely what I shall go on doing. Don't get any inflated ideas of your importance in the scheme of things. You'll be nothing more than an assistant whose comments I shall listen to before making my decisions. Of course, if you don't feel capable of doing the job, Shelley, you'd better say so right now and save me a lot of wasted time and trouble."

She was silent, taken aback by Jason's sudden anger. But he wouldn't let her off the hook. "Well?" he demanded. "I'm waiting for your answer."

"It just seems a bit . . . underhanded," she muttered. "I mean, telling tales to the boss."

He sighed impatiently. "All that will be required of you is to show loyalty to the organization that pays your salary. It's the good of P&L as a whole that we should all keep in mind. That, and nothing else. Your job as a member of my personal staff will be perfectly straightforward and ethical. I might add, Shelley, that there are several people who would dearly have liked to land it for themselves."

"So why choose me?" she asked again.

"I've told you why. You already know the setup here, but you're coming to it as an outsider."

"Not exactly an outsider," Shelley demurred. "I've only been away a few months."

"A lot has happened in that time," he said. "A great many changes have been made at P&L."

"I bet!" Shelley couldn't conceal her bitterness. They had turned off the motorway and were driving over Kew Bridge.

"Shelley, what made you decide to return to London?" Jason asked when the silence had lengthened uncomfortably.

It was the question she had been dreading from

him. She lifted her shoulders in an elaborate shrug. "Somehow I couldn't seem to settle down in New York. I thought that maybe back here I . . . I . . ."

His voice was surprisingly gentle. "You realized that you'd been running away? Is that what you're trying to say?"

"I wasn't running away when I went back to New York after Rex's death," Shelley denied, and put up her hands to hide the color rushing to her face. Because it was a lie. She *had* been running away . . . running away from emotions which she despised. How much did Jason understand that? she wondered. She tried to put forward the best explanation she could muster for her sudden return to London. "After I'd been back in the United States for a while, I came to realize that it was the wrong decision. I mean, when I married Rex I was anticipating that this country would be my home in the future. I guess you could say that I'd kind of made the mental adjustment."

Jason grunted, but made no comment. She was left with a feeling that he found her rationale less than convincing.

When they reached Putney, he halted the car on the riverside road outside the house. It was built of warm red brick, with fretted gables and a fancy iron-railed balcony up which some kind of creeper was twining itself. And there were little pointed conifer trees set out in green tubs on the tiny front patio, and spring bulbs and polyanthas growing in the window boxes. Another fierce shower was peppering the turgid surface of the river, and they were obliged to wait in the car for a few moments for it to slacken off.

"D'you feel like starting work straight away?"

asked Jason. "Or do you want a day or two to settle in first?"

Shelley was sorely tempted, but the unpalatable wasn't going to become any less so by postponement. "No, I'll be at the office tomorrow morning," she said decidedly.

"Fine. You'll be sharing an office with my secretary, Beth Kirby. She'll look after you."

The shower petered out, and across the river a slant of sunshine gilded the trees of what looked like a park. Jason carried in Shelley's baggage, taking her heavy suitcases up the two flights of stairs with no visible effort. In the living room of her flat—which had white walls and furnishings in bright modern colors—he glanced around and nodded his approval.

"You'll be all right here, Shelley." It was a statement of fact rather than a question.

"Yes, I'm sure I shall." She wished Jason would go away. It had been disturbing enough sitting beside him in the car, but here in the intimate surroundings of the small flat it was ten times worse.

He still hesitated, watching her intently. "You'll be okay, then, if I leave you now?"

"Sure, why not?" How glacial she sounded! "I mustn't keep you, Jason."

A shadow crossed his face, and with a curt nod he turned and walked out. She heard him on the stairs, and went to stand at the front window, a hand at her throat where a pulse was throbbing. Jason came into view as he emerged from the front door and strode to his car, a forceful, determined figure. Getting in behind the wheel, he drove away briskly without an upward glance.

Shelley opened the door to Clare's ring just before seven o'clock, and they exchanged smiles. Warm

25

smiles, yet just a wee bit cautious. Gauging one another's measure, Shelley thought. They had not exactly been friends before, just office acquaintances. She'd always sensed that Rex didn't care for her getting close to people on her own, so her friendships had to be found among his own circle.

Clare Royston was an attractive woman who had just turned thirty, a tall brunette whose willow-thin figure was echoed in the high cheekbones and dramatic hollows of her face. She had a flair for the dramatic in her clothes, too, and presented a slick, sophisticated image that was right on target for the glittering world of advertising.

"Hi, Shelley! How're things going? Look, why don't you come right on down and have a drink? I need one, it's been a lousy day! Nick isn't home yet, so we can have a girls-together natter while dinner's cooking. I thought we'd eat about seven-thirty, if that's okay with you?"

"Sure."

Shelley followed her downstairs and into the Roystons' apartment. Their large living room ran from front to back of the house, with windows at either end and an open-tread staircase rising to their upper floor. The space was broken up with screens of smoked-glass shelving from which trailed a variety of potted greenery. In the fading daylight the room was subtly lit by a converted oil lamp that stood on a small hexagonal bamboo table, and ceiling-mounted spots picked out two large photo-montage murals. Clare had already switched on the stereo, and muted music eddied pleasantly in the background.

"Take a pew," she told Shelley, waving at a big white leather sofa with billowy hand-embroidered cushions. "What's your poison? Will a dry vermouth on the rocks suit your American palate?"

"Great! But make it a small one." Shelley looked around appreciatively. "You've got a lovely home, Clare . . . so spacious and comfortable."

"Yes, I have to count myself lucky there." Clare handed her a glass and toasted her. "Mud in your eye, Shelley. I hope you don't find your place too midgety. But when Jason asked around if anyone could possibly think of somewhere for you to live, it seemed a godsend that the upper flat here had just fallen vacant. I phoned our landlord and clinched it right away. Living space in London is at a premium."

"Same in New York!" So it was Jason, she mused uneasily, who had first set the wheels in motion about finding her a home. She hated the thought of having to feel obligated to him. Perhaps, when he had hesitated before leaving this morning, he'd been waiting for her to say thank you. But words of thanks to Jason Steele would not come easily to her. "Anyway, Clare," she added hastily, "I'm terribly grateful to you for fixing me up. The flat is just perfect for me, honestly. I couldn't hope for more. It's really charming."

"Still, it's not quite what you were used to when Rex was alive, is it? From what I heard, that ritzy penthouse you had in Knightsbridge was really something else."

Shelley felt oddly on the defensive. "Rex always maintained that if you can afford the best, why not have it?"

"I couldn't agree more!" Clare laughed ruefully. "I only wish that Nick and I had that sort of money."

"You're doing okay, though," said Shelley, glancing around again. "I just love that tapestry on the wall there. And these cushions. Your work?"

"Guilty." Clare laughed aside her talent. "I'm

really hooked on needlework. The trouble is, there's a limit to what you can accommodate in one home without overdoing the arty bit. Nick says I'll be wanting to embroider a cover for the loo before I'm done."

"How is Nick, by the way?"

There was a tiny pause. "Okay. I already told you he might be a bit late home, didn't I? These photographic sessions he has to set up do tend to run on sometimes."

"What's he working on at present?"

"It's a pilot scheme for the launch of a new product. Starglow Paints. That's yet another division of Cleveland Enterprises, so it's hardly astonishing that J.S. has landed the account for P&L."

"How do you mean? Does Jason have an especially good contact with Cleveland Enterprises?"

Clare smiled enigmatically. "You could put it that way."

"I seem to remember meeting Sir Mortimer Cleveland once," said Shelley, her clear brow wrinkled in thought. "It was at a press party Rex took me to. A rather distinguished-looking man with iron-gray hair and a little Vandyke beard. Is that him?"

"Bang on! And did you also meet the glamorous Naomi?"

"His wife? No, I don't think so."

Clare gave a merry laugh. "Not his wife, Shelley. His adored and pampered-rotten daughter! Quite a power behind the throne, is Naomi Waterton, now that she's divorced. She's moved back into the stately home with dear daddy, who's a widower, and he lets her do exactly as she likes . . . businesswise and otherwise, if you get me."

"So that's how the brilliant Jason Steele operates," Shelley said scathingly, feeling a curious sense of disappointment.

Clare shrugged. "It's the way things happen, for heaven's sake . . . you of all people ought to know that." She drained her glass and stood up. "I'd better go and get the dinner started. It's steak and chips. Come through with me, so we can talk."

Following Clare out to her Scandinavian-style kitchen, Shelley was tempted to ask what she meant by the remark *you of all people ought to know that*. But something restrained her; a wish not to sound naive, maybe. Instead, she inquired, "How is Jason making out in the top spot?"

"Things have certainly changed since he took over." Clare made a wry face. "He's a hard taskmaster and he expects top performance from everyone on the payroll. But it's no more than the standard he sets for himself. And he's not stingy with praise if and when it's due. Or a raise."

"Rex always maintained that Jason had no flair for the advertising business," Shelley remarked thoughtfully.

"There's flair and flair! That husband of yours was a totally different type from J.S. Rex was absolutely brilliant as an account director, of course. No one would deny that. One way or another, he had what it takes!"

Shelley nodded. "You know something, Clare? I still find it difficult to think of Rex as being dead. He was the most totally alive sort of person I ever met. Living with him was always . . . unpredictable. Exciting. I never knew what was going to happen next."

Clare glanced at the kitchen wall clock and muttered with a frown, "Time's getting on!" After a tiny pause she said, "Is it wise, Shelley, coming back to London?"

"Jason asked me the same question."

"So what's the answer?"

Shelley lifted her shoulders helplessly. "It's hard to say why I came back. I just felt somehow that I belonged here in London. Where I'd been happy, I guess."

Clare swung around and looked at her curiously. "Okay, so your husband was killed, and that's a shattering blow for any woman. But you can't spend the rest of your days in mourning the way Victorian widows did. You've got to forget about your life with Rex now, and look to the future instead."

"It's easy enough to talk!" objected Shelley with a surge of resentment. "But how would you feel, Clare, supposing you were to lose Nick?"

She went pale. "What made you say that?"

"I just meant that you should try to put yourself in my position and you'll begin to understand. Rex's death has left me so . . . so unsettled. Somehow I just don't seem to know anymore what I want from my life."

Clare gave her a distracted look. "Will you keep an eye on things while I go and make a phone call? I won't be a minute."

Shelley heard Clare dialing, then her voice, sounding agitated. Surely, she thought, what I said couldn't have scared her so much that she had to phone at once and check that Nick was still all in one piece. When Clare returned to the kitchen, her face was somber, and she carefully avoided meeting Shelley's eyes.

"I suppose," she said gloomily, "that when dinner's ready we'd better go right ahead and eat. Whether or not Nick is home by then."

"There's no rush as far as I'm concerned," said Shelley. "I guess he won't be all that much longer, will he?"

"How should I know?" retorted Clare. "Oh, by the way . . . you remember that baby Fran Artis in Consumer Research was expecting? Well, she got bigger and bigger and it finally turned out to be triplets. Quite a shock for her and Don, but they're very happy about it now."

Okay, thought Shelley, we'll stop discussing Nick's late arrival if that's the way you want it. She let herself be steered into a question-and-answer session about what had been happening in the lives of various other people at the agency. It carried them right through dinner and coffee afterward. At around nine o'clock Shelley diplomatically yawned and got to her feet, claiming that she was pretty tired after a night spent on the plane. She saw the relief in Clare's eyes as they said good night.

Much later, Shelley roused from an uneasy sleep to hear the sound of voices raised in anger coming from below. So Nick had arrived home at last!

Jason's secretary, Beth Kirby, was already at her desk when Shelley arrived at the executive suite on the twelfth floor of the steel-and-glass office building in Mayfair. She was a well-groomed and briskly efficient woman of about fifty who'd been around at P&L for a long time. The greeting she awarded Shelley was distinctly short on warmth. Shelley guessed that she was viewed as an interloper, a threat to Beth's own closeness to the boss.

"I'm looking forward to working with you, Beth," Shelley said brightly and insincerely for openers.

Beth gave a cool, unrelenting nod. "Although we

shall be sharing the same office, I doubt if our work will overlap to any extent."

An inauspicious beginning! Shelley, settling herself at the desk across the room, decided that she'd have to work determinedly for a better relationship with Beth Kirby if she was to stick it out at this job.

An inner door was flung open and Jason stood there, his tall, big-boned frame almost filling the space. He wore a light gray suit with a blue-spotted necktie, appearing effortlessly well-dressed. Shelley knew him to be no more than thirty-four, but he carried the air of authority of a considerably older man.

"'Morning, Beth!" His glance came to rest on Shelley. "So you've arrived, then?"

Was he mad at her for being late? She took a furtive peek at the digital clock on the wall. It was only 8:56, so what was wrong with that for a nine-o'clock start?

"Nick Royston drove me in, with Clare," she said.

Jason clearly wasn't interested in her mode of transport. "You'd better sit in with me this morning, to get the feel of things," he told her brusquely. "Okay, Beth, I've been through my mail and I'm ready to dictate."

"Right away, J.S.!" Beth gathered her notebook and pen. "Er . . . have you remembered that George Turner is coming upstairs at nine-thirty to discuss those Heyday Holidays visuals you didn't like?"

"I've remembered. We should be through by then." He held the door open for his secretary, and threw Shelley a sharp glance. "Well, come on!"

Halfway to the door she realized that she had nothing on which to make any notes that might be necessary, so she dodged back and fished in her shoulder bag for a ball-point and pad. That would have to do for the time being.

Shelley had been in the managing director's sanctum only once before, to receive a pat on the back from Jason's predecessor for a neat copyline that a client had commended specially. It was a large room with windows looking over the treetops into Hyde Park, and had been redone in a tasteful combination of café-au-lait, cinnamon and olive green. The massive steel-and-leather desk was uncluttered, except for a few opened letters and a green manila folder. This latter Jason slid in Shelley's direction after gesturing her to bring up one of the chairs set against the wall.

"These are the Heyday Holidays visuals we'll be discussing in a minute," he told her. "Take a look through them and decide what's wrong."

While he rapped out replies to his morning's mail, a series of staccato sentences which no doubt Beth was expected to translate into more diplomatic language, Shelley opened the folder and glanced through its contents. There was a collection of roughs—swiftly but expertly executed pencil sketches of ski scenes at various European resorts. Some were of snow-clad slopes, and others of *après-ski* activities. She liked the general theme, which was echoed in each one—"Ski Lift to Paradise." She read through the typed copy which was attached to each sketch, and thought she recognized the crisp, sparing style of Steve Hinton, the deputy copy chief.

"Well?"

The barked-out remark was addressed to her, Shelley realized. Jason had finished with Beth, who was departing.

"These visuals are very good," she commented. "They should make an effective series of ads."

"You think so? Despite the fact that I've said they're off target?"

"I understood that my job was to give you my honest opinion," she countered.

"Granted. But I was rather hoping that you might spot the wrong thinking in this case."

Shelley took a steadying breath and edged her chair a fraction of an inch farther away from him. "It seems totally pointless for me to do a job which entails giving you my evaluations. I'm not qualified for that sort of thing. It would be much better all around if you put me back in the copy room where I really belong—and where I expected to be put when I asked for a transfer to London."

"As long as you're working for this agency," he retorted, "I shall be the one to decide where you work and exactly what you do. Understood?"

She shrugged again. "You're the boss."

"At least," he said ironically, "that's one point we can agree on."

Why was he doing this to her? Shelley thought miserably. She wondered just how long she would be able to stand working for him before being forced to look for another job.

A buzzer sounded and Jason pressed a key on the intercom. Beth's voice came over. "George Turner is here, J.S."

"Okay, send him in."

George was a quiet, modest sort of man, immensely proud of his plump wife, who grew prize roses, and his three brainy daughters, who were all doing terribly well at school. He gave Shelley a friendly smile as he entered the room.

"Sit down, George," said Jason. "You two know each other, don't you?"

"Sure. How are you, Shelley? It's nice to have you

back with us—though naturally it won't be the same for you now. I mean, with Rex. . . ." He faltered to a stop, his amiable face screwed up with embarrassment.

Jason brushed aside the social niceties. "George, about these Heyday visuals . . ."

"Er . . . yes, J.S.?"

"Shelley has glanced at them, and she thinks they're damned good."

George was obviously gratified and darted her a nervous thank-you smile before Jason went on to say, "However, she isn't yet in a position to judge precisely what we're aiming at in this campaign. When you sent this stuff up to me yesterday, George, I tried to look at it through the eyes of a couple spotting a Heyday ad in one of the up-market glossies. Especially the wife's eyes, knowing that she's likely to be the one to make the final choice of where they go. The way it came through to me was that these ads just miss the impression that Heyday should be giving. When people pay top rates for their holiday, they automatically expect all the little routine touches of luxury as part of the package."

"Isn't luxury exactly what these visuals are offering?" Shelley objected. But George immediately chimed in, "I think I see what J.S. is driving at."

She sighed. Was she about to discover that Jason had surrounded himself with yes-men, eager to agree with the boss the instant he clued them in to his way of thinking?

Her sigh wasn't lost on Jason. "Perhaps, George," he said dryly, "you'd better give Shelley the benefit of an explanation."

"Well, don't you see, Shelley, we've been stressing the wrong points in these mock-ups. Luxury bedrooms with baths *en suite,* first-class cuisine, indoor swimming pools and squash courts, live music and cabaret for *après*-ski, and so on. But such things are what people who pay this sort of price take for granted. We've got to try to find a unique selling proposition. Right, J.S.?"

"Right."

Shelley felt a grudging respect for Jason. She had to agree that this criticism made a lot of sense. There were a number of cases on record of an ad campaign failing because the inherent message of the advertisements appealed to the wrong people. So Jason's perception might have prevented a very costly blunder for the Heyday firm.

They talked around the subject for another five minutes and then George departed, fired with enthusiasm to come up with an entirely new slant to lay before the client.

For the next half-hour Shelley had a chance to sit back and observe Jason in action as he made a series of brisk phone calls: to the agency's associate in Zurich, to a merchant-banker client about some prestige advertising, to a TV producing company because P&L was missing out on prime-time slots and he wanted to know what the devil they thought they were playing at. Her grudging respect increased. He certainly knew how to handle people—with firmness or tact, anger or flippancy, depending on the individual and the circumstances. Shelley found herself watching him through her silky lashes. His was a craggy, chiseled face, not the least degree handsome in the way Rex's had been, yet its irregular planes and hollows had a strange fascination. As he leaned back in his swivel chair talking into the phone, he appeared to be totally relaxed. Yet Shelley could sense his acute concentration as he skillfully developed his arguments. There was an assured strength in the angular thrust of his chin, the determined set of his mouth, and no one could doubt the intelligence behind those intensely dark gray eyes. Reluctantly she conceded that Jason Steele might well be a man to inspire enthusiasm and loyalty in the staff he controlled. And no doubt every woman in the firm found him deeply attractive, too.

As Jason slapped down the phone, Beth's voice came through again. "J.S., just to remind you about the departmental meeting in the conference room in ten minutes. You're chairing it."

"Hell, yes! I'm not getting a minute this morning to devote to Shelley." He glanced at his wristwatch and frowned. "Look here, Beth, you'd better cancel that working lunch with Bill Saunders, and book a table for Shelley and me at the Bienvenue. One o'clock, okay?"

"If you say so, J.S." The disapproval in her cool voice couldn't have been plainer, but Jason ignored it and flipped off the intercom.

Shelley felt dismayed at the prospect of sharing a meal with him. Was she to spend the entire day in this state of jangled nerves, unable to relax for a single instant?

"I can't see the point of your taking me out to lunch," she muttered ungraciously.

"But I can," he retorted, "so perhaps you'll allow me to be the judge! And for heaven's sake, Shelley, equip yourself with a decent-sized notebook before we go along to the meeting."

Shelley seethed. She had scarcely been allowed thirty seconds to settle at her desk this morning before being summoned to his presence, yet Jason was blasting her for not being property equipped. Her mind raced feverishly.

"You didn't ask me whether I was free at lunch-time today," she said, trying to hide the tremor in her voice. "As it happens, I'm afraid I won't be."

Jason's dark gaze sliced right through her ploy. "You've been in this country scarcely twenty-four hours and already you've got a lunch date?"

"I . . . I didn't say that."

"So what prevents you from lunching with me?"

"I . . . I have some shopping to do," she floundered.

"You can do that after you finish this afternoon; there'll still be shops open. Or, alternatively, you can send one of the juniors out for whatever you need. I'll be grateful, Shelley, if you don't waste my time on trivialities."

# *Chapter Three*

*D*affodils were dancing in a warm breeze as Shelley walked with Jason through the formal gardens of Grosvenor Square. Above the imposing facade of the United States embassy, a massive golden eagle glinted in the sunshine. Skirting the Franklin D. Roosevelt memorial, they soon reached Brook Street. A few yards along, they came to the Bienvenue Restaurant, a discreet sign over the narrow doorway the only indication of its existence.

"Did Rex ever bring you here?" asked Jason as they went inside. When Shelley shook her head, he added, "Not his sort of place, I suppose."

"Why should you say that?" she protested, bristling. "Rex knew how to eat well."

"I'm sure he did." The remark was delivered dryly.

It was a small and unostentatious place, with crisp white linens and gleaming glass and silverware. The headwaiter greeted Jason with a smiling bow and escorted them to a table in an alcove.

"I hope you like French food," said Jason as they were handed menus.

"It would be too late now to say that I didn't."

He looked faintly surprised at her tart comeback, but made no comment. "The rack of lamb *en cocotte* is particularly good here," he recommended.

"I might as well have that, then."

Shelley knew that she was being churlish, but Jason's reference to Rex had been meant as a snide criticism. She wanted to challenge him for an explanation, but something held her back. Perhaps a fear that he might go on to say things about her husband that she wouldn't want to hear.

While they were eating their meal, which was excellent, Jason outlined the changes he'd made at Prescott and Liedermann since he'd taken command.

"Fundamentally, it's a matter of pace," he explained. "Henry Firth in his prime was a terrific ad man. He built up the London end of P&L from nothing and put us right in the big league in Britain. But when his health began to fail, the poor chap couldn't maintain the necessary thrust. In the advertising business you can't just coast along. Inaction is death."

"I can't say that I noticed any signs of inaction when I was here before," Shelley commented.

"The trouble was largely a collective attitude of mind among the staff. A sense of complacency about past achievements which was far from healthy. There needs to be real impetus behind everything that's done in an ad agency. That's the only way good advertising is produced. An ever-present sense of urgency. Hustle!"

"An ever-present fear of getting the chop?" she suggested.

"I certainly don't intend working at P&L to be a meal ticket for anyone," Jason said bluntly. He set down his wineglass with a deliberate movement and looked at her across the table. "If you're so unhappy about my regime, Shelley, I wonder why you applied to be transferred back to London. You knew that I was in charge here now."

She couldn't meet his steady, penetrating gaze. "I . . . I didn't expect to have any direct contact with you."

"Otherwise you wouldn't have come?"

Shelley was silent, not knowing the true answer to that. But Jason obviously expected some sort of reply, and in the end she murmured, "I had a curious feeling that England was where I belonged."

"Yet you had spent only a few months here."

"The five happiest months of my life," she said unsteadily, and added on the spur of the moment, "There's something else, too. I guess it could have to do with having English ancestors. My father's folks came from Gloucestershire, way back."

Jason's dark eyes lit with interest. "Whereabouts in Gloucestershire?"

"Oh, it's just a tiny place. You wouldn't know it."

"Try me."

"Lower Rillington."

He laughed. "I know it, all right! I was born and raised in Bourton-on-the-Water, which is a small town only a few miles from Lower Rillington. My sister still lives there, as a matter of fact. She married the boy next door, who's a doctor now. Did you manage to trace any of your ancestors from headstones in the graveyard and old church records?"

"I haven't had a chance to look yet."

"Didn't Rex take you? I'd have thought it would be one of your first excursions when you came to live over here."

"Actually, Rex did talk of taking me there, but . . . well, somehow the time flew by so quickly and we never quite got around to it."

"Pity!" he said, lifting his dark eyebrows. "So you'll be making your pilgrimage to Lower Rillington anytime now?"

"I guess so. That is, if I stay in England long enough."

Jason's expression changed quickly to a frown. "I'd advise you, Shelley, to hang on for a while. They're certain to take a poor view on the other side if you ask to be transferred back to New York again. You'd begin to look like a Ping-Pong ball, bouncing back and forth across the Atlantic."

"You're very hard."

"I'm merely being practical."

"Why won't you let me go back to the copy room, Jason?" she asked. "With all this talk of expansion and new clients I've been hearing about this morning, there must be a job for me there."

"True. But as managing director I have to take an overall view and arrange the disposition of the personnel to the agency's best advantage. *You* might prefer to hide yourself away in the copy room, but I happen to think that, with your capabilities and potential, you're a darn sight better placed on my personal staff."

It was flattering in a way, Shelley granted, but all the same . . . Before she had a chance to weigh her thoughts, Jason switched the subject.

"Is the flat okay? You've not discovered any shortcomings as yet?"

"Oh, yes . . . I mean, no. It could hardly be

better." She made herself add, "I understand that it's thanks to you."

"To me?"

"Clare told me that you asked her if she knew of anywhere suitable for me."

Jason shrugged it off casually, picking up his fork again. "When I knew that you were coming over, I inquired around among the staff for somewhere for you to live. Clare was the one to come up with an answer. Just a timely stroke of luck."

"All the same," Shelley said awkwardly, "it was good of you to bother."

As he had been good to her before, she recalled with a pang. It was Jason's organizing hand, in those first traumatic days after Rex's death, which had helped her get through. Jason had simply stepped in and taken charge. With no delay, he came around to see her at the Knightsbridge apartment the morning after the news of Rex's fatal accident had been broken to her by the police in the early hours. A neighbor had stayed with her for the remainder of that night, and Jason arrived before ten A.M.

"We've just heard, Shelley! I'm very sorry. I've come to see what I can do for you."

Sitting with Jason over lunch in this quiet restaurant, she could remember the tortured ambivalence of her feelings toward him on that terrible morning. She felt immensely grateful for his dependable support, yet she also felt a sort of hatred for Jason Steele. It was as if, barely concealed by a veneer of fake sympathy, he had been triumphantly rejoicing that his rival for the managing directorship was dead and out of the running.

Jason had guided her smoothly and surely through all the necessary formalities: accompanying her to the coroner's inquest, attending to the funeral arrangements, taking bothersome details off her shoulders. Then, on the fateful evening that she would never be able to forget, he came to arrange assigning her lease on the apartment to the new tenant he had found. Shelley had sat at the snakeskin-topped writing table while Jason stood beside her, drawing her attention to the various clauses in the lawyer's document. The typewritten pages seemed to swim before her eyes and Jason's succinct words of explanation failed to register in her benumbed brain. Her whole body felt rigidly tense; there seemed to be an aching constriction around her heart, and she had a sensation of being sucked into dangerous rapids.

Had she herself risen, without conscious volition? Or had Jason drawn her into his arms? It was impossible to be sure. Her only clear memory was of finding herself cradled close against him, finding the comfort she so desperately needed in the solid warmth of his body, the strong beating of his heart, and the wafting of his breath upon her hair. Slowly, as if impelled by a force quite beyond her control, she lifted her face and met the deeply intent gaze of his dark eyes. There were long, pulsing seconds in which neither of them moved, neither spoke.

His lips, when they came to meet hers, sent quivers of hot fire darting through Shelley's veins. She felt a dizzying sense of exhilaration as she became aware of Jason's surging, throbbing desire. The kiss deepened and he crushed her against him, his hands sliding sensuously over her body while Shelley's arms crept up to twine about his neck. She pressed herself even closer, and her fingers dug convulsively into the crispness of his peat-dark hair.

How long she would have permitted this madness to continue Shelley could not be certain. Perhaps for only the briefest time. But the fact remained—a painful fact which lay like a heavy shadow on her conscience—that it had not been she who had ended the embrace, but Jason.

Releasing her, he had gone at once to stand by the window, his back turned. She was aware of him speaking, but in her haze of shocked bewilderment she missed the first few words. Something prosaic about her having sufficient time in which to look around for a cheaper place to live. "You're all paid up here until the end of the month, so that gives you more than a fortnight to find a flat you like." His voice was even and controlled, cool and distant. "I'd advise you, though, to return to the office before that. In fact, as soon as possible. It will be better for you than being on your own."

Shelley shook her head. Her mind, which until now had been in a state of utter chaos, was suddenly made up.

"I won't be coming back to the office. Or finding another apartment. I'm going home."

Jason wheeled around to stare at her. "New York, you mean?"

"Where else?"

He hesitated. "Do you think you'll be any happier there?"

"Of course I won't be happier," she choked. "But here in London . . . everywhere I turn, every street, every building, will remind me of Rex."

"Running away isn't the answer," Jason said quietly. "Somehow you've got to come to terms with what has happened, Shelley. You've got to *want* the pain of Rex's death to pass. It will, you know, given time."

"No, it won't. And I *do not* want it to! But here in London there's just too much pain for me to bear. I'm going home."

Jason had looked long and steadily at her. She was terrified that he would come and sweep her into his arms and start kissing her all over again. If he did, she would be lost. But mercifully he just nodded and asked, "Do you want to return to your old job in New York?"

"I guess so . . . if they'll have me." She would need to find work somewhere—and soon. Rex had earned big and spent big, and when everything was wound up—the salary and bonuses due to him set against the bank overdraft, the debit balance on his various credit-card accounts set against what the furniture was fetching—there would be precious little left over for her to manage on. Though Rex had talked a lot around the time of their wedding of taking out a large insurance policy on his life, it emerged now that no premium was ever paid. Altogether, there was no more than a few hundred pounds to cover her fare home and get herself settled in New York.

"Okay, then," said Jason. "I'll ring Ed Braine and talk to him. I'm sure he'll manage to fit you in again."

That same day she'd had a transatlantic call from Ed to say that sure she could come back, and welcome. "We're all so sad for you, honey. Gee, it must be terrible! Rex was a great guy, and I can guess what you're going through right now."

So Jason had fixed it. Over the next few days he rapidly tied up the remaining loose ends so that she could leave London without delay.

The news of Jason's formal appointment as managing director in Britain came just five weeks after she was back in New York. Nobody seemed in the least surprised. It was apparently taken for granted in all of Prescott and Liedermann's worldwide subsidiaries that Jason Steele should step into Henry Firth's shoes. And Rex Armitage was a forgotten man.

The sun had vanished behind threatening black clouds when they recrossed Grosvenor Square, and the daffodils drooped in anticipation of another sudden April shower.

"We'd better look sharp," said Jason. "It'll be bucketing down in a couple of minutes."

They were caught by the first few drops just before they reached the spacious foyer of the office building. A porter in braided uniform touched his cap to Jason and pressed the button to call the express elevator that went straight up to the twelfth floor.

Up in the executive suite, they entered Jason's office directly from the lobby. A woman was seated at the big desk, negligently at ease in Jason's own chair. Dressed with throwaway chic in a suede safari jacket and culottes, she was, without doubt, a stunning beauty. A gleaming curtain of raven-black hair fell to her slender shoulders, framing her ivory-pale face. Her eyes were magnificent, a vivid green-gold, large and lustrous. But at the sight of Shelley in Jason's company, those eyes narrowed to angry pinpoints, all at once giving her face an ugly expression.

"What kept you, darling?" she demanded. "More than fifteen minutes ago Beth was assuring me that you'd be back at any moment. I thought you told me that you only take an extended lunch hour with people who rate the treatment businesswise."

Jason's smile was enigmatic. "Shelley is a new

assistant on my personal staff, Naomi, just arrived from New York."

"So Beth said!"

Even before Jason called her by name, Shelley had figured out that this was Sir Mortimer Cleveland's divorced daughter, the apparent power behind the throne at Cleveland Enterprises. From what Clare had hinted, she'd gotten the dumb idea that Jason's relationship with this woman was totally calculating, in order to clinch for P&L the huge advertising budget of her father's business empire. But the heavy sensual promise that exuded from every pore of Naomi Waterton's body would be quite sufficient to attract Jason, never mind the incidental commercial advantages.

"This is Naomi Waterton, Shelley," explained Jason; then added, as if warningly, "We handle a great deal of business for her father, Sir Mortimer Cleveland."

Shelley nodded a coolly polite greeting. "I remember. Cleveland Enterprises, isn't it?"

"Of course, you were here for a short time before, weren't you?" drawled Naomi, twisting the gold bracelet on her left wrist. "About six months ago?"

So she and Beth had been thoroughly discussing her! But what, Shelley pondered, could have emerged from their conversation to cause the hostility which Naomi Waterton was transmitting loud and clear? Or was it merely that her lover had been lunching with another female at a time when she had taken the whim to drop by and see him?

Having no wish to stick around, Shelley crossed to the inner door, murmuring, "I'll just go and . . ."

Jason frowned and glanced at his watch. "I'll need you back here in fifteen minutes. I've agreed to see a chap from one of the independent TV production units who reckons he's got a brilliant idea for a KrackaKrunch commercial."

"Just give me a buzz when you want me," she said as she slipped out.

The TV man arrived in good time for his appointment. However, he and Shelley had to cool their heels for a further quarter of an hour before Naomi Waterton deigned to depart. She swept through the outer office with a bright smile for Beth and a very offhand nod in Shelley's direction.

On the way into Jason's office, Shelley caught a tiny smirk of pleasure on Beth's face. More than rooting for Naomi, she decided, Beth is anti Shelley Armitage! She thinks I'm bad news for her much-admired boss. But you're mistaken, Beth, she thought dejectedly. You've got it the wrong way around. It's Jason who is bad news for me.

Each morning Shelley got a lift to the office with the Roystons. In the evenings, though, since she couldn't be sure what time she would finish, she made her own way home, fighting for space on one of the crowded rush-hour buses. As Rex's wife, she had never used buses.

The morning journeys to work were always uncomfortable, due to the bad feeling between Nick and Clare. Shelley suspected that they'd been bickering right up to the moment she joined them and would resume again the first chance they got. She had half a mind to opt out, perhaps inventing a need to match Jason's habitual eight-thirty-A.M. arrival at the office. But they would know it was just an excuse, and she didn't want to seem unneighborly. Shelley felt sad about the situation, because she had always thought of the Roystons as a particularly happy couple. Like Clare, Nick was striking in appearance. But these days a sulky, mulish expression marred his dark, handsome features. He wasn't exactly rude to Shelley, but neither was he more than barely civil.

On Friday morning, stuck in a traffic jam outside Harrods department store, Shelley tried to keep the edgy silence from getting to her by chatting brightly about some photographs Nick proposed using for the Slikfit jeans campaign, which she and Jason had been discussing the day before.

"They're really fantastic, Nick. I thought you'd chosen the models dead right . . . especially that young blond girl. She's got a terrifically sexy figure, and she sure can wear hip-hugging pants. Wherever did you find her?"

The tension in the car was suddenly electric. As the lights changed and the traffic nosed forward again, Nick muttered, "Oh, she's from one of the agencies. We've used her before."

Clare, sitting beside her husband in the front seat, stared rigidly ahead as though she were turned to stone. Sighing inwardly, Shelley mused that if Nick had something going with the pert little piece in those photographs, he needed to have his brains checked out. She was scarcely eighteen from the look of her, and not a thought in her silly head beyond how devastatingly sexy she was. Poor Clare!

As soon as they pulled up in Prescott and Liedermann's underground car park, Shelley jumped out, hastily thanked Nick and Clare and made a dive for the elevator.

By Friday evening Shelley decided that she must start making a social life for herself. At the office, Jason had kept her busily occupied every moment, but the evenings seemed very dead. Clare and

Nick, the way things stood between them, were quite ruled out as company. Now the weekend lay ahead of her: a long, lonely stretch of time.

The people she knew in England outside work, all being Rex's friends, tended to be slightly older than she was, mostly in their thirties. But until she got around to making some new acquaintances, it seemed sensible to spread the word that she was back in London. She sat right down at the phone with the directory on her lap.

Inevitably, there were disappointments. No answer from the first number she tried; another couple were away on a Caribbean cruise, according to the maid. After twice getting a busy signal, she finally got through to Blanche Farleigh, whose husband, Ludovic, was the chief executive of a magazine-publishing group. Blanche was a marvelous hostess and the dinner parties at their Chelsea home were always spectacular.

"Oh, yes . . . Shelley! How goes it? Sweet of you to ring. I'm afraid that I'll be up to my eyes for the next week or so, but maybe later on we could fix something. Look . . . sorry, but I simply must dash. . . ."

Shelley felt like giving up, but that would be stupid. Things changed in six months, she reasoned with herself. She couldn't expect their former friends to be waiting around for her to call. She decided to make just one more attempt this evening, and if that came to nothing . . . well, she'd leave it for now.

She chose the Traffords, Janie and Clive, a childless couple in their mid-thirties. Janie ran a smart boutique in Notting Hill Gate, and Clive was the publicity manager of a firm whose advertising was handled by Prescott and Liedermann. They lived in Kensington, not far from Putney.

It was Clive who answered. "Who is this? Oh, *Shelley!* Great to hear your voice, love. It's terrific news that you're back in this country. Of course, you must miss poor old Rex . . . don't we all? But life has to go on, huh?"

"How are you both, Clive?"

"Couldn't be better, sweetie. Janie's got herself a second shop now. She'll be making more money than me before she's done."

"I was wondering, Clive . . . maybe we could meet sometime? It would be marvelous to see you both again."

"Sure, why not? Love to!" Shelley let herself breathe once more, aware that she'd been making the Traffords a test case. It was wonderful that Clive followed through by saying after only a momentary pause for thought, "How about coming round this evening?"

"Oh, but I didn't expect . . . not at such short notice."

"No time like the present, that's my motto. Have you eaten yet?"

"No, not yet."

"Come for dinner, then. Can you manage eight-thirty?"

"Sure I can, if it really is okay. I mean, I wouldn't want to mess up your plans."

"Don't give it a thought. It'll be lovely to see you."

"It's really great of you," Shelley said warmly. "Give my love to Janie. 'Bye for now."

As she put the phone down she felt happy out of all proportion. Blanche's brush-off a few minutes ago seemed unimportant. Shelley caught herself humming cheerfully as she showered and debated what to wear.

She rang for a cab to take her to Mentone Court, and arrived a few minutes after eight-thirty. How it brought back memories—and pangs of sadness—to cross the pink marble foyer and ascend in the gilt-caged elevator, as she had often done with Rex. The door to the Traffords' eighth-floor apartment opened at once to her ring and Clive stood there beaming at her, his arms outstretched in welcome. She greeted him with a kiss on the cheek, and he gave her a fond hug.

"Marvelous to see you again, and you're looking as beautiful as ever. Come along in . . . here, let me take your coat."

Clive looked exactly as she remembered him, except maybe just a couple of pounds heavier. He had a squarish face with carefully styled brown hair and a mustache; his wide, ready smile showed teeth that were sparkling white against his suntanned skin.

He ushered her through to the opulently-furnished lounge, where music with a Latin American beat was playing softly. "What's your poison, Shelley?" he asked, waving her to a seat on the enormous yellow sofa.

"Oh . . . some white wine would be nice."

Clive pulled a face. "Have something with a bit more kick? A Bloody Mary?"

"Okay, then . . . but be stingy with the vodka, please."

He fiddled at the elaborate onyx-and-gilt bar. "Actually, I'd already heard that you were back in London. It was that chap Mike Austin who told me. He's been P&L's contact with our firm since . . ." Clive brought her a cut-crystal goblet with her drink. "Mike mentioned something about your going up the ladder these days. The boss's right-hand man, he said."

"Well, not quite. But it's true that I'm on Jason Steele's personal staff. Unfortunately," she added.

"Why unfortunately, for heaven's sake? What's wrong with a spot of promotion?"

She could have told Clive that she didn't happen to fancy working directly under the man who had personally benefited by Rex's death. Because that *was* true, even if there was a deeper cause for her disquiet. But since Clive's firm was a client of P&L, it would be indiscreet to mention anything that might sound critical of the agency's top management. Taking a sip of her drink—which she realized at once was much stronger than she wanted—she said with an offhand shrug, "Copywriting is my particular thing, so naturally I expected to be put back in the copy room."

"But if Jason Steele reckons you have potential for bigger things, Shelley, you ought to feel flattered. The word is that he's a guy who doesn't make mistakes. He's impressed our top brass no end since he took over the agency. I'll tell you this for free, our chairman is seriously considering letting P&L handle the advertising for our other division, too. And that's something Rex could never get his hands on, even with my help, though he pitched us hard enough for it."

She had not come here this evening, Shelley thought ruefully, for the pleasure of hearing Jason Steele praised to the skies. She tried to sound enthusiastic as she said, "That would be nice for P&L, Clive. I hope it works out for us." She broke off, glancing around. "Er . . . where's Janie?"

"Oh, she's not here. Didn't I say?"

"Not here?" Shelley gasped in dismay.

"No, she's popped over to gay Paree for a few

days." Clive gave her a grin. "Janie shoots me a line that the occasional trip to Paris or Rome is necessary in the boutique business. Which is as maybe! Still, I don't begrudge my better half the odd spell off the ball-and-chain if it helps to recharge her batteries."

"But, Clive . . . why didn't you tell me when I called?"

"Does it matter, sweetie? You're here now, and we can have a nice cozy little dinner together and spend a pleasant evening."

Shelley felt sick for having walked into this tricky situation. She wanted out, but it would be too absurd to bolt off here and now like some nervous teenager. Besides, she must stick with the thought that Clive was publicity manager for one of P&L's clients, with the prospect of an additional account in the offing. Obviously he'd been at loose ends this evening, and when she called out of the blue, he'd grabbed his chance. Okay, so he felt a bit devilish inviting another woman around for the evening while Janie was away, and maybe he'd even make a pass at her when he'd downed a few more Scotches. But she ought to be able to handle him, for goodness' sake, without any hard feelings.

"If I'd known that Janie wasn't here," she said, keeping it light, "I never would have put you to the trouble of fixing dinner for me. Or is that one of your hidden talents, Clive?"

He grinned. "I have many talents, but *cordon bleu* cookery isn't one of them. Not to worry, though, I've got it all organized. A very handy aspect of living at Mentone Court is that there's a restaurant right here on the premises, and they'll send up a complete meal anytime you want." He glanced at his watch. "It should be arriving any minute now."

Right on cue there was a ring at the door, and when Clive went to answer it, an elderly white-jacketed waiter wheeled in a laden trolley. With a bow of acknowledgment to Shelley, he plugged in the electric hot plate, flipped a white damask cloth over a small table and laid out two settings.

"Shall I open the wine, sir?"

"Yes, let it breathe, eh?" That done, Clive added, "Right, you can leave things to me now, Alf." A banknote flickered between them and was deftly pocketed.

The food was very good. They began with wafer-thin smoked salmon, and then a delicious *boeuf Stroganoff* with whole-grain rice. The red wine was smooth and mellow to the palate.

"It was a surprise to hear that you'd come back to England," Clive said when they reached the dessert stage. "What prompted that?"

The inevitable question once again, and she had no better answer to give than when she'd tried to explain her reasons to Jason and Clare. "Somehow I just couldn't seem to settle in New York, and I thought that maybe it would make more sense to return here."

Clive nodded sympathetically. "It must be bad on your own, especially after having been married to a chap like Rex. Things really hummed when he was around."

"It *is* bad," she confirmed sadly. "I still can't really accept the fact that he's dead. I keep thinking that it must all be a ghastly nightmare from which I'll wake up . . . that any minute he'll be calling me to say he's sorry about being late but that he's on his way home right now and simply can't wait to see me."

There was a brief hesitation; then Clive asked, "Any plans for getting hitched again?"

"For heaven's sake, Clive!" she protested.

"Bit too soon for you, eh? You've hardly had a chance to look round and see what's available." Clive helped himself to more wine. "You know, Jason Steele might be worth having a shot at. You've got the looks and the brains, Shelley, so you could be in there with a fighting chance."

"That . . . that's a ridiculous thing to say," Shelley stammered.

"Oh, I don't know. He must be giving serious thought to the idea of getting married. A wife like you could give the right sort of respectable background to a chap in his position. A lot depends, though, on whether Naomi Waterton has wedding bells in mind—or if not, whether she'd let any other woman get her hooks into him. Have you met the glamorous Naomi yet? I bumped into them together the other week at some TV shindig, and I must admit I envied him, the lucky devil! She really is some luscious piece of woman."

"As far as I'm concerned," Shelley asserted forcefully, "Jason Steele is welcome to her."

Clive grinned disbelievingly. "Mind you," he went on with a chuckle, "Steele may reckon he's got it made, the way Naomi can twist Daddy Cleveland around her little finger. But my guess is that he's walking a knife edge with her. What happens if she gets bored with lover-boy and seeks greener pastures? How long would you rate P&L's chances of hanging on to the Cleveland accounts then?"

"Really, Clive," Shelley stammered, "can't we please change the subject?"

"Anything you say." He raised the coffeepot. "Want some more?"

"Er . . . I've still got some, thanks."

With a soft click the tape ran out, and Clive went across to change it. He came back to the table and held out his hand. "Let's dance, huh?"

"No, Clive, I don't think so."

He grabbed hold of her and pulled her out of the chair. "Come on, loosen up a bit. You only live once."

Shelley protested again and tried to drag herself away. But Clive was surprisingly strong, and she found herself locked in a fierce bear hug as he swayed to the beat of the music.

"I always fancied you like mad, Shelley darling," he murmured thickly. "It had to be hands-off while old Rex was around, of course, but there's nothing to stop us now, is there?"

Revolted even though she had expected something like this, she struggled wildly to free herself. "Clive, don't be a fool. Let me go!"

He laughed, holding her firmly. "You young widows are all the same . . . real dynamite when you get going."

In a fury of anger, Shelley found the strength to jerk herself away. "Will you stop this, Clive! It's ridiculous! I haven't given you the smallest reason to think that I . . ."

He was momentarily shaken by her explosive vehemence. "Listen, sweetie, you're quite safe with me. I won't talk out of turn, if that's what you're scared of. I mean, it's in my own interest to keep mum. Janie wouldn't expect me to be pure while she's away, but she'd rather be spared the lurid details. So I won't spread it around, no chance."

"There'll be nothing *to* spread around," Shelley said grimly. "I'm leaving right this minute!" She headed for the door, but Clive was quicker and got there first, standing with his back to it. His face was flushed and ugly.

"Look, if you don't feel in the mood, what stopped you saying so right at the bloody start?"

"I tried to. . . ."

"Like hell you did! There wasn't a squeak out of you when you realized that we were here on our own. You went through that intimate little dinner party without batting an eyelid. You don't imagine that you can get me all wound up and then turn cold on me at the last minute?"

She stared at him miserably. "I was in love with my husband, Clive, and he's only been dead six months. Six months! You can't really think that I would . . ."

"Why not? Okay, so keep your lovey-dovey memories of Rex, but that doesn't mean you've got to live like some damned nun. Why deny yourself one of the few pleasures that make life worth living?"

"It's not a matter of *denying* myself—" she began, and was interrupted by his scornful laugh.

"You mean that you don't really like it at all?"

"You're hateful, Clive. Just because your carefully planned seduction scene misfired . . ."

"Heaven only knows why Rex ever married you; he was a hot-blooded man by any standards. I wonder how long you two would have lasted together if he'd not been killed."

"Rex loved me very much," she cried, fighting back tears. "You can't take that away from me, Clive, however hard you try. Okay, I'm not so naive as to imagine that Rex didn't have quite a few other women before he married me . . . more than most men do, I guess."

"You can say that again!" said Clive in a sneering drawl. "And not only *before* he married you!"

Shelley caught her breath in a stab of agony, then whispered, "You'll never make me believe that."

"I don't care whether you believe me or not. It just happens to be a fact that the whole time I knew Rex, right up to the day he was killed, he could never be satisfied with just one woman."

She backed away from Clive and stumbled against an armchair. "You . . . you're lying!"

"Okay, so I'm lying." He shrugged indifferently, but there was a gleam of triumph in his eyes.

"Rex loved me," she said again.

Clive shook his head in mock sadness. "You must have been a big disappointment to a man like him, Shelley. When I think of all the other birds Rex dated in his time . . . and he had to get himself saddled with a frigid one for his wife."

"I am not frigid!" she said between clenched teeth.

"No? But then, it's not a thing that any woman would admit to."

Shelley felt an urge to shout and scream at Clive, but she couldn't. There had been little things . . . hints. She had tried to ignore them, but she had been aware, all along, that she had rushed into marriage with far too little forethought. What had she really known about Rex? And later, when she began to suspect, she couldn't admit the truth, couldn't humiliate herself that way. To have admitted that she'd made a ghastly mistake would have destroyed all the dreams she had cherished since childhood of finding wedded bliss with Prince Charming, and so she had stubbornly clung to an illusion that Rex had loved her as she had loved him, and that, given time, he would have settled into marriage.

Though trembling in every limb, she succeeded in facing her tormentor with cold dignity. "You're vicious, Clive! You're just trying to hurt me because I won't go to bed with you. But you haven't succeeded. You haven't succeeded in the least. Now, let me pass."

Clive stepped aside from the door. "Willingly! I'll be glad to see the back of you. You've wasted too much of my evening already, curse it!"

She snatched up her coat as she went, but she didn't stop to put it on until she was in the elevator.

# Chapter Four

From Monday morning on, all week, Shelley was kept hard at it by Jason. This was something of a blessing, she had to admit, leaving her no time to brood—at least during office hours.

Each day she still took a lift to work in the Roystons' car, but the atmosphere between Clare and Nick had become so thick that she wondered how much longer the arrangement could continue. Often she could hear their clashing voices coming up from the apartment below, and a couple of times she had been disturbed from sleep by the sound of a bitter quarrel. She wondered sadly if marriage was ever the idyllic fusion of hearts and minds and bodies that had filled her romantic dreams since teenage days.

Friday afternoon, when she was hurrying to get a report finished, Jason called her into his office.

"Have you anything planned for the weekend?" he demanded crisply.

"Nothing special." She added guardedly, "Why do you ask?"

"I think you'd better come to Cheltenham with me."

Shelley was taken aback. "What do you mean?"

"I've just had a call from the chairman of Cosmos Computers asking me to attend the last evening of their sales conference there. Lord Carfax wants me to give his reps a rousing pep talk about the ad campaign we've got lined up for the autumn. I think it would be a good idea for you to come along, too, Shelley. It's an opportunity for you to learn something about client relations."

"Oh, but . . . but I don't really think . . ."

"This is important! My talk to the reps is scheduled for six-thirty. And then I'll be expected to stay on afterward for the final dinner and general socializing. So we'll drive down to Cheltenham after lunch, and stay overnight at my sister's place. I told you she lives in Gloucestershire."

Shelley was seized by a feeling of acute alarm at this prospect. Working all day so close to Jason was difficult enough, but at least in the office his usually brusque manner helped her to keep her wayward emotions in check. But driving to Cheltenham with him, spending an entire weekend in his company, staying overnight at his sister's house—all that was something else entirely.

Jason claimed that this was a necessary business trip. But was that really true? Or had he recalled those electric moments after Rex's death—moments that she herself would never be able to erase from her mind—when he'd held her in his arms and kissed her passionately? Had he regretted not taking his chance to seduce her that evening? He must have felt pretty confident, in those tense, spun-out seconds, that if he had followed through she would have succumbed to his lovemaking. Was he now thinking that he would try his luck with her again this weekend?

The thought of Jason making love to her sent shivers rippling through Shelley's body, and she felt a sudden stab of longing. She was a free agent, she argued to herself, and there was no reason why she shouldn't give in if Jason still wanted her—as he had so obviously wanted her that other evening. And yet she rebelled at the thought of being just another woman in Jason Steele's free-and-easy love life. Second to Naomi Waterton . . . and how many others besides?

Shelley raised her chin defiantly. If Jason was entertaining any ideas like that about her, he could think again! "If I do go with you to Cheltenham, there would be no point in my staying over. I'd get a late train back to London."

He firmly shook his head. "It wouldn't be safe for you to arrive at Paddington station well past midnight and be wandering around in search of a taxi. No, we'll do it my way." Without waiting for Shelley to agree, he buzzed through to Beth and told her to get his sister on the phone.

When he was connected, Jason said briskly, "It's me, Hilary. How're things with you and Paul? Good! And the offspring?" He laughed. *"Of course* they fight all the time. Just like we did! Listen, the reason I called you is to cadge a couple of beds for tomorrow night, okay? There's a do at Cheltenham I've got to be at, and I'm bringing one of my assistants with me. Shelley Armitage, who's recently arrived over here from New York." The voice on the line crackled a moment; then Jason said, "Yes, that's the one. Right then, Hilary, see you. Expect us at some ungodly hour tomorrow night,"

As he rang off, Shelley said uncomfortably, "You make me feel terribly awkward, being thrust on your sister like this."

"Forget it. Hilary loves having visitors. I'll pick you up tomorrow at two o'clock sharp. Be ready! Now, to get back to these research findings on food processors . . ."

Saturday morning Shelley shopped in Putney High Street for next week's groceries. As she walked home again beside the river, she felt a surge of rebellion against Jason Steele. Why was she letting him push her around? There could be no justifiable business reason for her to accompany him to Cheltenham.

The moment she arrived back in the flat, she looked up his number in the telephone directory. He lived, she knew, in a converted mews flat somewhere near the Chelsea Pensioners' Hospital where the famous Royal flower show was held each year. She dialed his number and after a moment the receiver was lifted.

"Jason Steele."

Shelley's nerve suddenly failed her and she banged the phone down without saying a word. She immediately reproved herself for being so cowardly. Yet she could not summon the courage to call him again. It would be so much simpler, she reasoned, to go along with Jason's plans than to get involved in a hassle with him. But she would be very much on her guard not to give him the slightest excuse for thinking that she was available.

Jason arrived to collect her at two on the dot. When Shelley went to answer his ring, there was a mildly irritated look on his lean face, as if he'd expected her to be meekly waiting on the doorstep for him, baggage in hand.

"All set?"

"I'll only be a moment." She felt a sense of satisfaction in keeping him waiting momentarily. She went through to the bedroom and took her time about slipping into the russet velvet jacket that went with a pleated brown skirt and cream silk blouse. When she emerged, Jason was standing by the living-room window, staring thoughtfully across the river. He turned and gave her an unhurried appraisal.

"Very nice, Shelley! Like most American girls, you know how to dress."

She muttered an embarrassed thank-you. Paradoxically, she half-wished that she'd not taken such care over choosing what to wear, yet at the same time she felt gratified to have drawn the compliment from him.

"I'm ready now," she said.

As he came forward to take her overnight bag from her, his fingers brushed against hers. Shelley recoiled instinctively, then cursed herself for letting her feelings show. Following Jason downstairs, she could still feel her skin burning from that fleeting inadvertent touch. In the car she caught herself sneaking glances at his craggy features and firmly molded mouth. She was acutely, disturbingly conscious of his nearness, of the warm, husky tang of his after-shave. Unobtrusively she edged closer to the door.

Jason restricted their conversation to business matters. He put her fully in the picture about the

Cosmos Computers advertising program, which was rated a major account at P&L. "This do in Cheltenham is quite a big affair. Cosmos have regularly held conferences at different sites, but this is the first time they've brought their international sales force all together in one place. Reps are attending from all over the world."

Shelley recalled her companion on the plane. What was his name? Marvin Benchley, that was it. This conference, of course, was the reason for his visit to England. He'd been telling her all about it, but she hadn't really listened. She resolved to keep a weather eye open for the pushy Marv.

"What shall I be expected to do?" she asked Jason.

"Look, listen and inwardly digest. Socialize as much as possible. You can parry any questions you aren't able to answer by explaining that you've only just come over from the New York office. Act friendly, and altogether be a good advertisement for Prescott and Liedermann."

It was sunshine and April showers all during their two-and-a-half-hour drive. Cheltenham, historically a fashionable spa town to which people of wealth and high society flocked to drink the purifying waters, looked graciously beautiful in the soft golden light of late afternoon. They drove the length of the famous promenade with its double avenue of horse-chestnut trees that were just unfurling their tender green leaves. Beneath the trees, formal beds of spring flowers made a bright tapestry of color. On one side of the broad thoroughfare were elegant shops, and on the other, a fine terrace of Regency houses, their pastel-painted facades gleaming immaculately.

The conference hotel was a large modern building

near a leafy park. Shelley, wondering where she could change into the dress she had brought for the occasion, was surprised to find that Jason had engaged a bedroom for her temporary use. It was a thoughtful gesture, she conceded, then immediately wondered if he had some ulterior motive. But apparently not, for he added, "Why don't you order some tea to be sent up, and relax for a while? We'll meet again down here at six o'clock."

With forty-five minutes to spare, Shelley decided to take a leisurely bath before ringing room service for tea. She welcomed this period on her own to unwind after the tense strain of the drive.

Back in the bedroom, wrapped in a huge fluffy bath towel, she realized with dismay that too much time had slipped by. She would have to skip the tea and get herself ready as quickly as possible. She was thankful that, as a last-minute decision before leaving New York, she had splurged on some new clothes, including the dress she'd brought along to wear this evening—a lovely floaty creation in mauve chiffon silk, with a Java-print design of exotic birds.

More than ten minutes after the appointed time she left her room and hurried toward the elevators. A man who was already waiting there gave her a look of startled surprise.

"Hey, Shelley! You of all people! Remember me—Marv Benchley?"

Oh, no! It just wasn't fair to run into him when she'd had no time to prepare a line of retreat. "Hello, Marv!" she muttered with a grudging smile.

"You look great, Shelley, really terrific. You've come along to represent your firm, I guess? Say, isn't this England a peculiar place? The folks here are so darned uppity."

"Oh, I wouldn't say that," she protested. "They're not really, when you get to know them."

The doors slid open and they stepped into the empty car. As they were riding down, Marv grinned at her meaningfully. "I just thought, Shelley . . . what if the elevator got jammed? Then you and I would have to spend another whole night together. How about that, eh?"

Marv was still chuckling when they reached the ground floor. He slid his hand under her elbow to steer her out to the lobby, where they very nearly collided with Jason.

"I was just about to ring upstairs to see what had happened to you," he snapped. He'd noted Marv's possessive grip on her elbow, Shelley realized, and she quickly pulled away and moved out of range, then wished that she hadn't acted so guiltily.

"I bumped into Mr. Benchley, whom I met on the plane coming over," she told him with a defiant glare. "Marv, this is my boss, Mr. Steele, the managing director of Prescott and Liedermann. He's here to give you Cosmos people a talk about the advertising program."

"In precisely eight minutes' time!" said Jason, pointedly glancing at his wristwatch. "Come along, Shelley."

Marv grinned ruefully. "Too bad there's no chance to talk now. But maybe we can get together later on tonight, Shelley? I know your room number, don't forget."

"Oh, but I won't be staying . . ." she started to explain, but Jason was already hurrying her away. "Marv didn't mean any harm," she protested. "You had no cause to be so rude."

"Rude?" Jason dismissed her charge as unimportant. "I want you to meet Lord Carfax before we start. He's the chairman of Cosmos."

Lord Carfax was a surprisingly benign-seeming man for a high-powered industrialist. His wife, tall and distinguished-looking in a moiré silk outfit that matched her silver hair, seemed rather reserved at first, but Shelley soon realized that this was caused by shyness. She was invited to sit with them both in the front row of the packed conference hall.

From the word go Jason seized his audience's attention. Kicking off with a joke about computerized advertising, he launched into a brief, concise account of the extensive sales promotions lined up for the months ahead, which included a number of brand-new incentive schemes. He wound up with a challenging call to the Cosmos reps to go out and do their utmost to make this coming year the best ever for themselves and their company.

During the course of the evening, Shelley was introduced to more people than she could mentally index. With a big effort, she made herself carry out Jason's instructions to act friendly and be a good advertisement for Prescott and Liedermann.

Soon after eleven Jason came and murmured into her ear, "It's okay for us to leave now. Come with me and say our duty good-nights. Then pop upstairs and fetch your things."

Dread caught at Shelley's heart. Up to this moment they had been surrounded by other people, but now she was to drive off into the unknown alone with Jason. Why hadn't she found the courage to put her foot down and refuse to come on this unnecessary trip?

"Er . . . shall I change?" she muttered.

"No need; it's quite a short journey to Hilary's."

While doing the rounds with Jason, she saw Marv Benchley chatting to a group of men. She had managed to avoid him all evening, but in a strike for independence, she excused herself and strolled over to Marv.

"I'm afraid I've got to leave now," she said, with a warm bright smile, aware that Jason was watching. "Are you heading right back to the States?"

"'Fraid so. First thing tomorrow morning."

"Oh, well, I hope you have a good flight, Marv."

He flashed a knowing glance at his companions, and laid a hand on her arm. "Pity you're not staying here tonight, or we could've got together again." He hesitated a split second; then, before she guessed what he was about to do, he leaned forward and planted a kiss on her lips.

It was her own fault, Shelley fumed, for putting on an overfriendly act for Jason's benefit. She might have figured that a pushy type like Marv would take advantage and do a bit of showing off in front of his pals.

"A touching little farewell scene," Jason commented sarcastically as she rejoined him.

In the car, they soon left the lighted streets of Cheltenham behind and drove through a landscape magically silvered by moonlight. Jason seemed to be preoccupied with his thoughts, and Shelley felt grateful that he didn't expect her to talk. Presently they turned off the main highway onto a winding secondary road. After driving for a few more minutes, Jason drew the car to a stop halfway up a hill. He cut the engine and headlights. In the sudden silence Shelley could hear the whisper of a night breeze, and an owl's hoot came from somewhere nearby.

71

"See that lane to the right, Shelley? It would take us down to the village your ancestors came from, Lower Rillington. We'll go tomorrow."

She glanced at Jason in dismay. So he was not planning to return to London first thing! She ought to insist here and now that she had to get back, invent some plausible reason for doing so. But, weakly, she remained silent. Visiting Lower Rillington was something she'd always wanted to do, and in some strange way the thought of going there with Jason was appealing.

"Everywhere around here is steeped in history," he went on. "This ridge is part of a medieval 'saltway,' one of the packhorse routes that were used to bring sea salt for preserving autumn-slaughtered meat through the winter months. It's probably more than a thousand years old. And going back even further there are Stone Age forts and burial grounds to be found hereabouts."

"It makes one feel . . . sort of insignificant."

Jason answered slowly, so unlike the brisk, forceful boss she knew at the office. "It certainly helps one to gain a proper sense of perspective. We're just a couple of dots on the immense surface of time."

She shivered, as if a chill wind had suddenly sprung up. "Are you saying that nothing in our lives is important? Nothing matters?"

"People get so emotional about their petty human relationships. It's never worth it."

"You're just a born cynic," she flashed.

"In point of fact, that's not true. Believe it or not, Shelley, I started out with my head full of romantic dreams. Thankfully, I saw the light before I made a complete hash of my life."

Wondering, Shelley turned to look at him. But

Jason was staring ahead, his dark eyes smoldering in the moonlight. She choked back an urge to ask what had happened to give him such a twisted view of things. A woman, for sure.

Jason seemed to become aware that she was watching him, and turned his head. There were long moments of silence; then slowly, irresistibly, she was drawn into the circle of his arms. Shelley trembled, then became very still. She could feel the vibrant warmth of his body through their clothes. When Jason bent his head to claim her lips, she felt a lovely golden sensation flooding her veins. It was like the long-awaited ending of an agony of loneliness, and her heart was thudding with excitement.

At long last Jason drew back a little, but only to murmur her name against the silky chestnut softness of her hair. The sound of his voice, deep and husky with the urgency of his longing, snapped Shelley back to her senses. With her palms flat against his chest, she thrust herself away from him, still too dazed and confused to feel anger.

"No . . . no, you mustn't. . . ."

"Yes," he said, drawing her close again. But Shelley resisted him fiercely. She was appalled by what had happened, filled with bitterness and resentment—against herself even more than against Jason. This was a repetition of that other occasion, when he, not she, had ended the embrace. Whatever had prompted him to draw back that time, he clearly thought she was still amenable. So, fighting off the treacherous instincts that made her long to yield to him, Shelley redoubled her struggles. At length, reluctantly, Jason released her.

"That was unfair of you," she stammered, finding her voice with difficulty.

"Why unfair? You were ready enough to be kissed. That coy maidenly protest came a bit late to be convincing."

"You . . . you took me unawares."

"Okay, let's not make a big drama out of something so unimportant," he clipped in a cold, angry voice. Leaning forward, he flipped on the lights and ignition and drove off with a roar.

Dazed by the storm of emotion Jason's kiss had unleashed in her, Shelley sat listlessly silent as they raced through the narrow country lanes. It came as a shock when Jason stopped the car again, after a sudden swerve to the left, and announced tonelessly that they had arrived.

Glancing up, Shelley made an effort to get herself together. The outline of a long, low house was etched against the dark sky, with warm light spilling from its windows.

# Chapter Five

Shelley wakened to a deep night silence. The moon had set by now, and outside her bedroom window it was densely dark. She felt chilled, somehow, though the soft bed was cozily warm.

Hilary and Paul Hawthorne had been warmly welcoming when she and Jason had arrived at a little past midnight. In the charming lounge of their converted Cotswold farmhouse, with the flames of a crackling log fire reflected in the polished oak furniture and shining brassware, Shelley had sipped a hot drink while they chatted. That Jason and Hilary were brother and sister was unmistakable. She had the same keen, penetrating eyes and thrustful chin, but in a softer, more feminine form. Her fair-haired husband, looking a somewhat stocky figure compared with Jason's tall, big-boned leanness, cast his discerning doctor's eye over Shelley.

"I prescribe bed for you now, my dear, just as

soon as you've finished that drink. You've had a long day, from the look of you."

Shelley had escaped gratefully up an oaken staircase whose polished treads were worn from centuries of use. There were oak beams across the ceiling of the bedroom, and rose-patterned chintz at the window. Hilary switched on a bedside lamp.

"I hope you'll be comfortable, Shelley."

"I will. I'll be fast asleep in thirty seconds flat."

And she had been. But now she was awake again, and tossing restlessly. She could feel the imprint of Jason's lips on hers, the thrilling promise of his kiss. A treacherous wave of longing swept over her that made her blush in the darkness. Wild, unbidden thoughts chased through her mind. . . . Yet despite her almost unbearable longing for Jason, she must never let anything happen between them again. For Jason, taking possession of her would be an act of contempt. The easy conquest of a woman who, he would think scornfully, had no standards of decency. He would be remembering how, within days of her husband's death, she had shown herself ready to respond to him.

Shelley must have slept again, for she wakened to the crowing of a cockerel somewhere across the fields. And later she heard a church bell ringing out for early communion. There were various muted sounds about the house, and she caught the appetizing aroma of coffee.

Rousing herself, she dressed and made her way downstairs. She found Hilary in the kitchen, perched on a high stool and leafing through the Sunday paper. She glanced up with a smile.

"Hi, Shelley! Help yourself to some coffee. Did you sleep well?"

"Beautifully," she lied. "Am I first up, apart from you?" she asked, filling a mug.

"Lord no! A doctor's house is an early-rising house! Paul and the kids are out in the paddock seeing to the ponies. We've got one each, you know. As for Jason, he's taking a stroll round the village. He always does that when he visits us. I think it gives him a nice nostalgic feeling. My brother enjoys the advertising battlefield, but when all's said and done, his roots are here."

"Yes, he was telling me."

"How are you making out with Jason?" Hilary asked.

Shelley hesitated. "Being on his personal staff wasn't what I anticipated when I came back here."

"So I gather." Hilary's voice was dry. "If you think he drives you hard, Shelley, always remember that he drives himself twice as hard. Too darned hard, if you ask me. But what I really meant was, how do you two get along on a personal basis?"

"We don't."

Hilary raised her eyebrows. "What does that mean?"

"Simply that your brother and I have a work relationship. Nothing more."

"Not even good friends?" said Hilary jokingly. Then she became serious. "I'm a bit surprised, Shelley. I was imagining—hoping—that Jason bringing you here this weekend meant that . . ."

"Purely work," said Shelley, too quickly.

"Pity!" With a single practiced movement Hilary slid off her stool and swung open the fridge door, reaching inside for a package of bacon. "It's time Jason dropped his obsession with work and relaxed a bit."

Desperate to get off the disturbing topic of Jason, Shelley said hastily, "I'm dying to meet your children, Hilary."

"You won't have long to wait, then. My keen maternal ear detects the sound of their dulcet tones coming across the garden."

A minute later the kitchen door burst open and two small, very similar bejeaned figures came rushing in, wrangling over some petty disagreement. They stopped short when they saw Shelley.

"Meet the Hawthorne Horrors," said Hilary. "You can tell them apart, Shelley, by the fact that Guy is half a head taller than Gemma. Nine and seven years old respectively, and more trouble than a cartload of baboons. Say hello to Shelley, you two!"

"Hi there!" said Shelley.

The little girl, with corn-gold hair and blue eyes, dimpled a delightful smile at her. The boy, with equally fair hair and even brighter eyes, stepped forward with all the dignity of manhood and gravely shook hands.

"You might at least have rinsed your dirty paws first, Guy," his mother observed, spoiling the effect. "Off upstairs with you both and get cleaned up. Breakfast in six minutes. Countdown starting now!"

The two men entered together. Paul greeted Shelley, then went to wash his hands at the sink. Jason inquired if she'd slept well, and she lied a second time; unconvincingly, to judge from the question that remained in his dark eyes.

They all assembled around the scrubbed wood table in the big farmhouse-style kitchen. The bacon was crisp and flavorful, and Shelley found herself eating with a keen appetite. The children kept chattering about their two ponies, arguing which was the faster.

"Do you ride, Shelley?" asked Paul.

She made a rueful face. *"Did* would be a truer answer. I haven't been on horseback for years, not since I first went away to college."

"You won't have forgotten how," Hilary predicted. "It's like riding a bicycle."

Guy broke off mid-sentence from contradicting his sister, and snorted. "You should have seen Mum trying to ride my bike the other day. She was wobbling all over the place!"

"Well, it's too small for me. And I'm not used to the modern gears."

"Excuses, excuses!" chorused both children together.

"I was thinking, Jason," said Paul, "why don't you take Shelley for a ride? It's a beautiful morning, and you're welcome to use Daemon and Brandy."

"Oh, but I don't think—" began Shelley, but Jason cut across her as if she hadn't spoken. "Great idea, Paul! Thanks. A breath of clean Cotswold air will do us both a world of good after the polluted atmosphere in London."

Every objection that Shelley could invent was briskly demolished. Hilary would fix her up with jeans, an anorak and a hard hat. And Brandy, though a spirited gelding, was beautifully well-behaved really, and infinitely patient.

She had one last try. "Jason promised yesterday to take me to the village my father's people came from. Lower Rillington. I'd like to see if there's any trace left of the Bowyers."

"After lunch will be a better time for that," Hilary asserted. "You might be able to get hold of the vicar then, and look through the parish records."

The day was stretching before Shelley alarmingly. She had expected to head back to London *before* lunch. With an inward sigh, she decided there was nothing she could do about it, so she might as well quit worrying and try to enjoy herself.

An hour and a half later, after a leisurely breakfast, Shelley and Jason clip-clopped at walking pace through the peaceful little country town. Its ancient houses, built of local Cotswold stone that had mellowed with time to a lovely tawny gold, glowed against the blue April sky. Running right alongside the leafy main street was the River Windrush, a shallow stream spanned by a number of picturesque footbridges with tiny parapets only a few inches high.

Jason was greeted by almost everyone they passed, while Shelley, as his companion, came in for many a speculative glance. Her pony was a lovely palomino, light-stepping and gentle, needing very little control, just as she'd been promised. Jason's mount was a bay, marked with a white diamond blaze down its face. Daemon was larger and friskier than Brandy, but Jason rode him easily, firmly in command.

Leaving the town, they climbed a quiet lane that ran between tangled hedges of hawthorn and wild rose to higher ground. Here a breeze blew across the meadowland, swirling the long grasses and buttercups.

"I know every inch of these hills from when I was a boy," Jason told her.

"I'm not surprised that you love it here," Shelley commented, letting her eyes drink in the glorious, sweeping landscape. Her remark clearly pleased him. For the next few minutes they rode without exchanging a word. Shelley found the lengthening silence too disturbing, and sought around for something to say.

"I do like your young niece and nephew, Jason. They're a really nice pair of kids."

He grinned. "To hear Hilary talk sometimes, you'd think they were the worst two imps of Satan ever born, their sole aim and object in life to drive their poor mother berserk. But if the truth's known, she's immensely proud of them."

"With good reason."

After a moment's pause, Jason asked with a searching glance, "Are you fond of children, Shelley?"

"Well, yes . . . sure I am. Though I can't say I've had all that much to do with them."

Another pause, longer this time. "Somehow, it's difficult to imagine Rex ever having wanted any. I wondered if perhaps you felt the same way."

A thrust of pain stabbed at Shelley's heart. It was perfectly understandable and reasonable that, in those all-too-few months of their marriage, she and Rex had made no immediate plans to start a family. But for the future . . .? Whenever she had tentatively raised the subject, he had put her off, asking if she wasn't happy as she was.

At such moments she would cling to Rex and tell him that *of course* she was happy, but had that really been true? Or was her vehemence a way of stemming the doubts that were even then sneaking into her mind? In the first weeks after Rex's death she had thought desolately that if only he had left her pregnant, life without him would have been a little more bearable. She was thankful now, though, that she hadn't borne Rex's child. She wondered bleakly if she would ever be able to trust any man enough to want to bear his child.

Staring straight ahead of her, she flung at Jason bitterly, "How can you possibly know how Rex felt—about children or anything else?"

"Okay, I shouldn't have said that."

"It's a bit late to apologize."

"I'm not apologizing! I was merely agreeing that it's pointless to discuss what's over and done with."

They were following a track as it dipped steadily downhill, and the grass beneath them was embroidered with dog violets and creamy white windflowers. At the foot of the valley the track forded a stream. Shelley halted Brandy there, and turned to face Jason defiantly.

"Maybe we should get something straight," she began, steadying her emotions. "I accept that you're my boss, which means that you're entitled to comment on my work, and criticize it where necessary. But that's it! My private life is strictly off-limits to you. Agreed?"

Jason returned her gaze steadily and without expression, letting the silence hang.

"Did you hear what I said?" she demanded, jerking her head so that a tendril of hair whipped against her cheek.

"I heard."

"Then you've got the message that from now I'd like things between us to be entirely professional."

"A very commendable attitude," Jason said dryly, a faint smile touching his lips.

"Do you imagine that I don't mean it?" Shelley flared.

"We'll have to see." Again Jason was silent, his dark eyes watching her face intently. Daemon scraped the ground with an impatient hoof, and Shelley heard a trout break the surface of the nearby stream. She felt the strangest sensation, as if these were precious seconds stolen out of time. The past and the future dimmed, held back by the sheer intensity of the present moment.

Unhurriedly Jason slipped down from the saddle and left Daemon to nibble sweet grasses along the bank. He held up a hand to Shelley in unspoken invitation, and as though mesmerized, she allowed him to help her dismount. Standing beside him with her hand still in his, she was achingly conscious of his nearness, of the virile, dynamic strength of his body.

"Why fight it, Shelley? The attraction is there between us."

She shook her head, trying to refute this, but the words wouldn't come. Jason's hand came up to touch her cheek gently, then moved around to caress her nape. There were long moments of tense, throbbing silence before he slowly drew her nearer. All Shelley's resolution to resist, all her strength of will, fled in an instant as Jason held her close against his lean body and met her lips in a drowning kiss. Without conscious volition her arms slid upward and clasped about his neck. The seconds pulsed by as the kiss intensified, and Shelley was swept away on a tidal wave of longing. She pressed herself even more closely against him, thrillingly aware of his kindling desire.

Suddenly the quiet was shattered by a clattering of horses' hooves and the sound of voices. They hastily broke apart and Shelley glanced around in confusion to see a string of young riders emerging from the woods to ford the stream. Their instructor, a stocky middle-aged man with a small black mustache, greeted Jason jovially and gave Shelley a look of slow appraisal. As the riders started to climb the track which led to the high meadows, she could hear the teenagers giggling among themselves.

"It'll be all over town by this afternoon," said Jason, his lips twitching in amusement.

"I can hardly imagine you objecting to that."

"I don't. . . . Shelley . . ." He reached out to her again, but she jerked away from him before he could touch her.

"We'd better get back," she said crisply, turning toward the ponies.

"No, wait! We've got to talk."

"There's nothing to talk about."

Jason's eyes slitted. "Running away again?"

"You're always accusing me of that," she blazed. "Is just wanting to be left alone, just wanting to be left in peace, running away?"

"It would be much better if you faced facts, Shelley."

She squared up to him. "Why don't you start facing a few facts about yourself? All your high-toned talk about needing me with you this weekend for business reasons was so much garbage, wasn't it? This was your real motivation."

"For heaven's sake, do we have to have a deep psychological discussion of motivation? A kiss is a kiss is a kiss. Just a natural impulse between a man and a woman who find each other attractive."

"Are your kisses ever as simple as that?" she cried.

Jason looked at her measuringly. "You seem to be making some point. Do explain yourself."

"Sure I will," she said defiantly. "The way I hear it, you use sex to bring in business and keep your clients happy."

Anger flared in his eyes. When he spoke, though, it was with lazy indifference. "The trouble with your argument, Shelley, is that you yourself can't be categorized under one of those headings. So what's your theory about my attitude toward you?"

Shelley wavered, wishing to heaven she'd never started on this. But if Jason wanted an answer, he could have one! "Maybe you think it would be pleasantly amusing to seduce me, having so fortuitously stepped into the job that would have gone to my husband."

There was a moment of startled silence. Then Jason asked quietly. "Are you saying that you seriously believe Rex was in the running for the managing directorship?"

"I happen to know it."

"Indeed? I'd be interested to know how you came by such a piece of information."

"Rex told me so himself."

"Rex told you so himself! I see! That clinches the matter, I suppose?"

"It sure does!" Shelley retorted, hating him for his sarcastic tone and for forcing her to defend a man of whose weaknesses, despite her love for him, she was all too aware. "Rex getting killed meant that you scooped his job. Now, I guess, you figure that it would neatly set the seal on your triumph to make a conquest of his widow, too."

Jason's voice was chilling. "There is something I should make crystal clear to you, Shelley. The fact that you were Rex Armitage's wife is most emphatically not a plus in my eyes. In fact, I see it as a major disadvantage."

Shelly steeled herself to remain calm. "Okay. Having established your near-to-zero opinion of me, perhaps now you'll reverse your decision and agree to what I've wanted ever since day one."

"If you mean putting you back to work in the copy

room," Jason rapped, "not a chance!" He clucked to the waiting ponies. "As you said, we'd better be getting back. Hilary mentioned that lunch would be at one o'clock sharp."

Shelley nodded stiffly. "After lunch, maybe we could return to London right away."

"I'm taking you to Lower Rillington."

"I'd rather skip that, if you don't mind."

"But I do mind, Shelley. You said you wanted to see the village, and it would be silly to miss the chance when you're so near."

She held back an angry protest. What was the use of arguing with the wretched man when he was so utterly dedicated to getting his own way? This weekend had been a terrible mistake, and she longed for it to be over. But even then, she would have to face Jason again tomorrow at the office.

The church of St. Mary Magdalene stood on a small knoll a little apart from the village of Lower Rillington. Its square Norman tower had a gilded weathercock that swiveled to and fro in the playful breeze. Neatly clipped yew trees flanked the pathway leading to the porch.

Shelley and Jason spent several minutes wandering among the graves in search of the name Bowyer, but many of the headstones were so encrusted with lichen that they were indecipherable.

"I wonder if I can be of any assistance?"

Neither of them had heard the man approach. Elderly, with white hair and smooth pink cheeks, he wore a clergyman's collar. "Humphrey Blair," he introduced himself. "Vicar of the combined parishes of Upper and Lower Rillington."

Jason explained that they were looking for the graves of any members of the Bowyer family. "Mrs.

Armitage is from the United States, and an ancestor of hers named Bowyer originally came from this village."

"Now let me see . . ." the vicar mused. "The last member of that family died at a very great age some forty years ago. Miss Grace Bowyer. I remember her well, even though it was so long ago. I had recently come to this parish as a curate, and I have to confess that I found her a rather formidable old lady. In her youth, I understood, she had been a prominent voice in the suffragette movement. It's a pity that you can't see the cottage where she used to live . . . such a charming place, next door to the old forge. But alas, they were both demolished a few years ago when the road was widened."

"She sounds an interesting person," Shelley said eagerly. "Can you tell us any more about her?"

The vicar gestured toward the church. "Perhaps you would care to come inside with me and see what information we can extract about your ancestors. In addition to the official parish records, we are fortunate in having the personal reminiscences of my predecessor, the Reverend Oswald Dillon, which relate the achievements of some of the notable personalities in this district. I am sure that you and your husband would find them of great interest."

"Oh, but we're not . . ." Shelley began awkwardly. The Reverend Humphrey Blair was a trifle deaf, however, and clearly he thought that she was demurring against putting him to any trouble.

"It's a pleasure, Mrs. Armitage, I do assure you. I am always happy to do whatever I can to assist those from overseas wanting to trace their English ancestry. A pride in one's family history is something to be encouraged."

As they accompanied the elderly vicar into the

church, Jason made no attempt to correct him about their relationship. So what, Shelley thought with a shrug, did it really matter? In a couple of minutes they would be gone, and she doubted that she'd ever be back.

In fact, she and Jason stayed rather longer than she had expected. When the vicar went off to conduct a christening ceremony at the font, he left them in the vestry studying various old records. A fascinating picture emerged of the Bowyer family as fighters against injustice of one kind or another—not only Grace, who had been a stalwart in the women's movement, but her father, John Bowyer, a doughty campaigner against the employment of young children in mills and mines. And his father before him, Thomas Bowyer, had been a supporter of Wilberforce in his fight to end the slave trade. Thomas, figured Shelley, must be her direct ancestor, father of the young railway engineer William Bowyer who in 1849 had sailed for the New World as the land of greater opportunity. It was all very exciting for her, and a matter of pride to find that she belonged to such a right-thinking family. Even if the name had died out now, she thought with a tilt of her chin, at least something of the Bowyer spirit must still exist in her.

At length the Reverend Blair rejoined them, still in his vestments. "If you have finished in here, Mr. and Mrs. Armitage, you might care to come outside again and I can show you the Bowyer graves." He beamed warmly. "This will be something to tell your children, will it not?"

Shelley couldn't allow his misapprehension to continue. Flushing, she said quickly, "But we're not married. This is Mr. Steele. As I happened to be staying overnight in the district, he offered to bring me here to see what I could find out about my family."

The vicar looked disconcerted. "Oh, dear! I'm afraid that I jumped to quite the wrong conclusion."

"Mrs. Armitage's husband is dead," Jason explained. "He was killed in a road accident six months ago."

"Is that so? How very sad." He touched Shelley's arm sympathetically. "Remember, my dear, that time is a great healer. You are still young, and I am sure that you will find happiness again in the future."

The three of them filed out through the north door of the church, and spent a few minutes looking at the final resting places of eight members of the Bowyer family. The epitaph for Grace Bowyer—which happily was quite legible—read: *"Courageous to the last!"* It brought a lump to Shelley's throat.

At last they took their leave of the vicar with many thanks, and Shelley offered him a donation to the church funds.

"How generous! Most kind! Every penny will be put to excellent use, Mrs. Armitage, I do assure you."

She and Jason had already said their good-byes to Hilary and her family after lunch, so now they took the London road. But after a few miles they left it again, Jason turning off at a sign for Oxford city center.

"Oxford is worth a visit while we're so close," he told her.

"I don't want to be late getting back," Shelley said in instinctive protest.

"Any special reason?"

"Not really, I guess." Admittedly, she felt glad now that she'd let Jason persuade her to visit Lower Rillington. So they might as well stretch the day to include a tour of the famous university city, she thought resignedly. Her interest stirring, she asked, "Who wrote those celebrated lines about Oxford's dreaming spires?"

" 'That sweet city with her dreaming spires.' It was Matthew Arnold. Not that I could quote him at length," he confessed with a disarming grin.

It very quickly became apparent, after they'd parked the car and set out on foot, wandering through picturesque alleyways and traversing ancient quadrangles enclosed within creeper-clad walls, that Jason knew the city like the back of his hand.

"So I ought to," he said when Shelley remarked on it. "I spent several years of my life here at the university."

"Oh, I see. What did you major in?"

"Both English and economics. By some fluke, I managed to scrape a double first."

"Scrape a double first!" she echoed ironically. "That's a typical British understatement. You must have been a brilliant student."

He shrugged dismissively. "For all my brilliance, I could never write inspired advertising copy the way you can, Shelley."

"When I'm allowed to!" she riposted.

Jason sighed. "You're not still on that tack, are you, after this afternoon?"

"What do you mean, 'after this afternoon'?"

"After learning about the Battling Bowyers. I can't imagine Grace Bowyer ever seeking an easy option. She'd have grasped eagerly at a challenge like the one I've given you, Shelley, and what's more, treated me to the sharp edge of her tongue, whenever she felt I deserved it!"

"Huh! I can just imagine what you'd have to

say if I dared to give you the sharp edge of *my* tongue."

"I rather thought you had—on more than one occasion," he countered, and there was laughter in his voice.

Odd, that the atmosphere between them was suddenly so much less tense. As if they had tacitly agreed on a truce, Shelley mused, and she decided that it was the most sensible course to adopt. If they were going to continue working in such close proximity, they had to lay off this constant sniping.

"Look, I don't know about you, but I for one am darned hungry," Jason went on after a moment. "Hilary's roast beef and Yorkshire pudding was almost six hours ago. I'll take you to a restaurant I used to go to in my student days whenever I felt particularly flush—which wasn't all that often!"

The idea appealed to Shelley, and she smiled. Well, she was hungry, too!

The date 1620—the year of the *Mayflower*—was carved into the keystone of an archway through which stagecoaches would have passed in olden days. Jason and Shelley strolled through into the cobbled courtyard and up a flight of external steps to the restaurant above. Inside, the fading daylight hardly penetrated the diamond-leaded windows, but shaded lamps on each table shed little pools of warm light. Great oak beams, black with age, supported the ceiling, and a blazing log fire robbed the evening of any chill.

They were shown to a table which overlooked the courtyard, with a glimpse between sloping roofs of one of the "dreaming spires" etched softly against the evening sky. Conversation from other diners murmured around them.

"The food is good here," Jason broke into her thoughts. "At least it used to be, and this is the sort of place where nothing changes in the span of a mere ten years or so. I can still recognize some of the waiters."

She sighed, wishing that this evening could just go on and on. "What a pity most things have to keep changing."

"You think so? Remember your ancestors. They were the sort of people who spent their lives fighting for change."

"But that was different, that was progress. Rejecting what was wrong and substituting something better."

Jason nodded, the lamplight making fascinating shadows across the planes of his face. "We'll have to see where you can get more information about the Bowyers, Shelley. Folks of their caliber must have hit the news from time to time."

As they talked over possible sources, it suddenly became an exciting quest in Shelley's mind. The local weekly newspaper which covered that district had been founded way back in the 1830's Jason told her, and its files might produce something of interest. Then the archives of the Rural District Council could be consulted. "I'll mention it to Hilary and see if she can come up with anything."

"Great!"

"Before we're finished, you'll be able to write a book." Jason smiled. *The Bowyers of Rillington.*"

They lingered for a long while over their coffee. Shelley was feeling strangely at ease, almost happy, as if the evening was cushioned from true reality. When they finally left the inn, Jason chose a quiet route back to London. Their conversation was the kind of easygoing talk of two people getting to know each other, trading likes and dislikes. They both confessed to finding most grand opera a bit too heavyweight to take, and both of them had wide-ranging taste in music.

"I especially adore good jazz, though," Shelley put in.

"There's plenty of that in London, if you know where to find it. I'll sort something out."

Later, when Jason swung his car onto the river embankment at Putney Bridge, it seemed the natural, friendly thing to invite him in for a cup of coffee, to round off the day.

Shelley left him in the living room while she got busy in the kitchen. When she returned with the tray, he was standing by the window. She had the impression that his attention was not really focused on the river, though. He turned slowly to look at her, his dark glance questioning.

"Shelley—" he began, but she cut across him in sudden panic. "I'm afraid it's only instant, Jason. I haven't gotten around to buying any real coffee yet."

"Oh, yes . . . that's okay," he said absently.

But the coffee remained untasted. As she sat down in one of the armchairs, Jason came to stand in front of her.

"Shelley . . ." he murmured once more, his voice deep and husky. With his hands he cupped her face, his thumbs gently caressing her jawline and the sensitive hollows of her throat.

The silence was intense,. accentuated by the faint chugging of a Thames police launch and the distant rumble of a late suburban train on the railway bridge farther downriver. Shelley waited for what she knew was coming with a feeling of inevitability. When Jason took her by the shoulders, drawing her slowly to her feet, she offered no resistance. She felt weightless, adrift in a limbo where everything beyond the two of them had no relevance or meaning.

Jason's arms slid around her, and Shelley was crushed against the length of his body. With exquisite awareness she felt desire soar in him, and she responded with a matching leap of longing. His embrace became more insistent, more demanding, and his lips sought hers in a deeply passionate kiss. Her mouth parted willingly, eagerly, when his tongue probed through to the dewy inner sweetness. As his hands roamed her body, she was suffused with the most wonderful, rapturous feelings. Never before in her life, it seemed, had she felt such a breathless sense of yearning.

Jason's fingers were at the neck of her silk blouse, tugging impatiently at the bow. With the buttons undone, his hand slid inside her lacy bra to cup the soft roundness of her naked breast, and Shelley moaned in delirious delight.

"You're so beautiful!" he whispered huskily. "No man could be blamed for wanting to make love to you."

When his lips found hers again, Shelley knew that she was ready to let him take possession of her, to sweep her along in a glorious act of love.

As Jason swung her off her feet to lay her on the sofa, by some odd trick of the lamplight she found herself staring straight into the eyes of her dead husband. Rex's photograph in a silver frame stood on top of the TV set. There seemed to be scorn in his expression, and bitter reproach. "You dare to criticize me," she imagined him saying, "but take a good look at yourself, Shelley. Within days of my death you were locked in this man's arms—a man, moreover, whom you knew I despised. You were ready for him to possess you on the spot if he himself hadn't held back. And now you're chasing after something that is no more meaningful than any of the little affairs you condemn me for."

It was an accusation against which she had no defense.

Shelley shuddered violently, icy-cold shivers snaking down her spine. Jason immediately sensed the change in her, and asked, "What is it? What's the matter?"

"Put me down," she said in sharp protest.

He hesitated, as if debating whether to ignore her request and try to recapture the passionate mood of a moment before. Then, with a reluctant sigh, he set her on her feet.

"Well?" he demanded, impatience in his tone. "What have I done wrong this time?"

"You must go!" she said. "At once!"

"Go? For heaven's sake, Shelley, what on earth has brought this on?"

She shook her head in a confusion of misery. "Please go. I want you out of here."

Jason's face was dark with anger. "I don't get this. You were ready enough just now. You *wanted* me. You can't possibly deny it."

She stepped back farther from him, unable to meet the stark condemnation in his eyes. "Haven't you got enough decency to leave when I ask you to?"

"I'm damned if I'm going to leave yet. Not until we've talked this through. You needn't worry, I don't propose to touch you again. But I think I'm entitled to a few answers."

"What gives you the idea that you're entitled to anything from me?" she asked bitterly.

"Aren't I? If I needed any evidence about how you react to me physically, I've had plenty these last two days. So I reckon you owe me an explanation for suddenly turning cold on me."

"This whole weekend has been a disastrous mistake," she said, sick with guilt. "You had no right to insist on my going to Cheltenham and staying over with your sister. Just because you're my boss doesn't mean you can order me to jump into bed with you."

His eyes sparked fire. "Damn you, Shelley, this has got nothing to do with being your boss! It's because of what there is between you and me."

"What there is between us?" she echoed, almost in agony.

"I'm talking about chemistry. When two people want each other as much as we do, they might as well be honest enough to admit it."

"And that's how you view the relationship between a man and a woman, is it? Just a matter of crude body chemistry and satisfying a physical craving?"

"And what's wrong with that?" he demanded. "The giving and receiving of mutual pleasure. Why should we deny ourselves?"

"That's a horrible outlook," she protested. "Mere gratification of the immediate sexual appetite." Like Rex believed in, she thought wretchedly, her eyes drawn back to his photograph.

Jason followed the direction of her gaze. "I see! So he's the cause of your emotional hang-up. I suppose that you're feeling disloyal to his memory or something? But there's not the slightest need to be, you know. Rex—"

"If you're going to break it to me," she interrupted breathlessly, "that Rex's memory isn't worth it because he was unfaithful to me, you needn't bother. I know the sort of man my husband was. And you're no better, Jason Steele!"

His dark eyes flared with anger. "Whatever low opinion you may have of me, Shelley, I'm not such a heel as to throw Rex's infidelity at you. I could see at the time how much you loved him, how much you wanted to make a success of your marriage. And I reckoned that Rex was a prize bastard for cheating on you the way he did. I don't expect you to believe this, but I'm really sorry you had to find out the truth about him since his death. It must have hurt like hell." Jason drew a rapid breath. "As for your accusation that I'm as bad as Rex was, I'll remind you that I don't happen to be a married man. I've never cheated on a woman, and I've never offered anything that I wasn't ready to deliver."

"But you won't allow any involvement," she said bitterly. "Isn't that your philosophy?"

"On the contrary," he drawled, "I allow a delightful involvement. For as long as it lasts."

"That's a loathsome, shallow attitude," she said, her voice thick in her throat.

"You think it would be more commendable for me to make all kinds of promises to women that I didn't intend to fulfill?" Very deliberately he strode across to Rex's photograph and laid it facedown. "Your marriage is over and done with, so for heaven's sake cut your losses! You're a free agent now. Forget Rex, and start living again without any morbid feelings of guilt."

"What made you like this, Jason?" she asked, bewildered by the terrible chaos of her thoughts.

"It's simply a matter of common sense, springing from hard-won experience."

Shelley hesitated. "You said something in the car last night about seeing the light before you made a complete hash of your life. Was that over a woman?"

He laughed without humor. "Not very hard to guess. *Cherchez la femme!*"

"You were badly hurt?" she found herself saying.

"I'd put it rather differently. I'm immensely grateful to the lady in question for getting me on the right track."

"How long ago did this happen?"

Jason shrugged. "Seven years . . . eight."

"And all this time you've let yourself be embittered over one woman?"

"If you like to think of it as being embittered. I prefer to see it as taking a balanced, realistic view of life. And that's what you should do . . . now that you know what a mistake you made in your marriage."

"Oh, no," she protested vehemently. "I don't intend to become a total cynic, the way you are, on account of making a bad marriage."

"You prefer to remain a starry-eyed romantic? Grow up, Shelley!"

"I don't care for your definition of growing up," she cried with passion. "Going in for a series of casual relationships! Using those relationships coldly and calculatingly to grub for business." A dark shadow flitted across Jason's craggy face, and Shelley realized she had touched a vulnerable spot. She pursued her advantage recklessly. "Why waste your valuable time on *me?* You'd do much better looking for another wealthy tycoon's daughter who'd fall for your line. You might even get accused of not performing your managing director's role properly if you miss out on any possible chance of swinging new accounts to P & L. Your affair with Naomi Waterton can surely be repeated *ad nauseam?*"

His eyes blazed with anger and he grasped her

roughly by the shoulders. "Cut that out, Shelley! We're talking about you and me!"

"And I thought I'd made my position crystal clear," she flung at him. "There's *nothing* between you and me. Nothing!" Just the touch of his fingers —even though they were digging into her flesh painfully—was having the most alarming effect. Dear heaven, she thought despairingly, she must be totally out of her mind. For even now, despite all the bitterness there was between them, she still longed for Jason to take her in his arms again. She couldn't stop herself from trembling violently, and perhaps Jason misread that as sheer terror. He let go of her abruptly.

"For God's sake!" he muttered, his nostrils flaring. "I'm not planning to rape you."

Somehow Shelley found her voice. "Thanks for nothing! Do you really expect credit for not actually using physical force on me?"

Jason's jaw clenched savagely as he took hold of himself. When he spoke, his tone was coolly neutral, without any trace of emotion. "We'd better stop slanging at each other like this. We've got to work together at the office."

"Only because you insist on it," she reminded him.

For a moment Shelley wondered if he was finally going to tell her that she could quit the executive suite and go back to her old job. She felt a strange thudding of her heart while she waited, unsure whether or not she really wanted that now. But instead, he said autocratically, "Yes, I do insist on it, Shelley, and I'll continue to do so. I'm damned if I'm going to let you prove me wrong about *that!*"

"It would be unimaginable, wouldn't it, for the

great Jason Steele to be proved wrong—about *anything?*"

He gave her a hard, intent look. *"Was* I wrong about choosing you for the advisory job? Do you consider yourself incapable of handling the responsibility?"

"I didn't say that." Shelley hesitated, then added slowly, deliberately, "My career is very important to me."

"And mine to me. So that makes us two of a kind."

She shuddered. "No, never! I don't share anything with you," she denied wildly.

"Aren't you getting a bit hysterical, Shelley?" he asked in a suddenly gentler tone. "Haven't you let this blow up out of all proportion?"

She shook her head, staring at him in numb misery. For long moments neither of them spoke. Jason's dark eyes were vividly intent as he gazed down at her. Shelley was aware, drowningly, of her desperate longing for him to hold her again, to kiss her again, to make passionate love to her . . .

Was she crazy to deny herself this burning need? But she couldn't face the thought of being taken in contempt, as just another willing conquest. All Jason was offering her was a casual sexual encounter. A brief affair, with no strings, no commitments, no promise of fidelity even for the short period they were together.

Or perhaps, it came to Shelley with a stab of pain, it was just a one-night stand that Jason wanted. Perhaps he felt no more desire for her than the urge to complete a little matter of unfinished business. Maybe he regarded her at this moment as a challenge—a challenge which, once overcome, would no longer hold the slightest interest for him. The thought of that was beyond bearing.

"I would be grateful," she said in a husky whisper, "if you'd leave now."

"Very well, if you insist. It's obvious that you're in no state to listen to reason at present."

"And I never will be! Not your kind of reason."

Jason shrugged. "Right, then, I'll see you in the morning" At the doorway he hesitated, giving her a steady, penetrating look that sent a shiver of emotion jarring through her. It seemed an immeasurable span of time before he finally turned away.

Shelley heard his footsteps going down the stairs, heard the street door click shut behind him. She still waited, frozen with misery, until she heard his car start up and drive off into the night.

With faltering steps she went to the TV and picked up Rex's photograph from where Jason had laid it down. She steeled herself to look at the face of her dead husband, to meet his eyes, and she felt no emotion beyond despair. About to set the frame standing upright again, she paused, then crossed to the writing desk and slid the photograph out of sight at the back of a drawer.

# Chapter Six

The despairing sound of a woman sobbing gradually seeped through into Shelley's consciousness while she hovered somewhere between waking and sleeping. In the end, she roused herself and switched on the bedside lamp. A few minutes to four A.M. Probably the sound that had disturbed her was only a river gull rustling sleepily on the slate roof, or water lapping the stone embankment at change of tide. She listened more carefully. No, it came from inside the house. It must be Clare.

Slipping out of bed and dragging on her robe, Shelley crept downstairs.

Where was Nick? she wondered. There was no sound of his voice trying to comfort Clare. Shelley felt a sudden stab of alarm, remembering back to that terrible time six months ago when she had been roused in the middle of the night and told that her husband was dead. Was this history repeating itself? Had the same thing happened to Nick?

Quickly she rang the Roystons' front doorbell. She heard it peal inside, but there was no other sound. Even the sobbing seemed to have stopped now. She tried again, then pushed open the mail flap and called through loudly, "Clare . . . it's me, Shelley. Come and let me in."

There was a long wait; then, just as she was going to call again, a light went on and she heard footsteps padding down the inner stairs. The door was dragged open and Clare stood there silhouetted against the light. Her face was in shadow, but her whole attitude was one of despair.

"Clare, I couldn't help hearing you crying. What is it? What's happened?"

"It's Nick . . . He's gone."

"Gone?" Shelley slipped inside and pushed the door shut behind her. "How do you mean, Clare, he's gone?"

"He's walked out on me, that's what. Left me for that stupid little blond model he's been running around with. Patti Fairfax." A sob caught in her throat. "Oh, Shelley, what am I going to do?"

Shelley's fears for Nick's safety were instantly replaced by a flood of anger against him—and a feeling of deep compassion for Clare. Slipping an arm around her friend's shoulders, she led her into the living room. Clare was shivering violently, and Shelley switched on an electric heater for extra warmth.

"How about me making some coffee?" she suggested. "I expect we could both use a cup."

Clare nodded bleakly. When Shelley returned with a tray, she was sitting slumped on the sofa, staring blankly into space.

"Here, drink this," said Shelley, putting the mug into Clare's hands.

She was shocked by Clare's appearance. She suddenly seemed much thinner, more fragile, the hollows of her face so extreme that she had a gaunt, skeletal look. Clare was still fully dressed, her elegant silk caftan rumpled and creased from lying on the bed for all those wretched hours. Shelley had heard no sound of her and Nick quarreling, so the final flare-up between them must have taken place before she arrived home with Jason.

"Do you want to talk about it, Clare?" she asked gently.

"What's the use? Nick's gone, and that's an end of everything. You probably think I'm stupid, Shelley, but I love him so much. I've never really loved anyone else but Nick. And now . . . it seems like there's nothing left for me. I . . . I just wish I was dead."

"No, you mustn't talk like that! You mustn't even *think* that way." Shelley hesitated, then said tentatively, "I can't believe that Nick intends to leave you for good. He loves you too, really. I'm sure of it."

Clare shook her head hopelessly, scooping back a strand of her dark hair. "No, it's Patti who matters to him now. He told me so straight out. He said that he can't take any more . . . that he's sick to death of the way I'm always picking on him for being untidy and forgetful . . . things like that. But I'm not really a nagger, Shelley, I only keep on at him when I *have* to." She took a shuddering breath. "Nick said tonight that he was through with me and that he was going to someone who properly appreciates him. But how can a little birdbrain like that girl *appreciate* him? He's not a shallow person like her, Shelley; he likes to talk about things that really matter . . . have meaningful conversations. Patti couldn't even begin to give him that sort of companionship. It's just . . . just a sexual attraction as far as Nick's concerned, and she's only throwing herself at him because she thinks his influence will get her into big-time modeling."

"It won't last," Shelley predicted. "Nick will soon come to his senses and see what a stupid mistake he's made. He'll be back in no time, begging you to forgive him."

"Do you really think so?"

Clare sounded pathetically eager, and Shelley realized that Nick wouldn't have to beg forgiveness. Clare would snatch at the chance to have him back on almost any terms. In the past, she had struck Shelley as a very poised, self-assured sort of person, and it was a shock to discover that beneath the outer layer of sophistication she was intensely vulnerable —where her husband was concerned, at any rate. It just proved that you could never judge from outward appearances.

"If Nick would only give me another chance," Clare went on, her eyes glinting through her tears, "I'd make everything different. Honestly I would. He'd never again have any reason to complain about my being a nagger. Oh, Shelley, it used to be so good between us, and now . . . I just don't know what I'm going to do without him." She bit hard on her knuckles, choking back a sob. "If I really thought it would be any use, I . . . I'd go down on my knees and beg him to come back to me. But he wouldn't listen! He'll never come back to me now, not after the things we said to each other tonight."

"What happened?" prompted Shelley gently, guessing that Clare had a burning need to spill out her misery. "I'd realized that things weren't going too well for the two of you recently, but how did it all come to a head tonight?"

"Well, Nick went off directly after we'd finished lunch, with some feeble story about having a Sunday photo session booked. But I knew what he was up to . . . who he was going to see. He was out all day and didn't get home until nearly ten. I asked him what the hell he thought he was playing at, had he completely lost his mind or something. And he said . . ." She broke off, catching her breath raggedly, and it was a few moments before she could continue. "Nick said that I'd got it the wrong way round, and that he was only just realizing what a crazy fool he'd been to try to keep our marriage going when he and Patti were in love and just wanted to be together all the time. I was so hurt and angry that I let fly at him and said he was a fool to let himself be conned by a little tart like her. Then he started calling me names back, and we ended up having a real slanging match, saying the most hateful things to each other." Clare pressed her hands to her face. "If only I'd held my tongue . . . if I hadn't lashed out at Nick like that, then I might have persuaded him to stay and try to make things work for us again. But it's too late now. He just flung a few clothes into a suitcase and went off back to Patti's place."

Desperately searching for words of comfort, Shelley said, "If you're really convinced that there's no hope of Nick coming back to you, Clare, then maybe it's best things happened the way they did. I mean . . . suddenly. A clean cut! Rather that than dragging on for weeks or months. . . ."

It was entirely the wrong approach. Clare broke in furiously, "Haven't you been listening to me? I was miserable before, heaven knows, because I knew that Nick was seeing that girl. But at least he came back to me each night. I could have kept on like that, which would have been a million times better than losing him altogether. I'd give anything, Shelley, anything in the world, to take back the awful things I said to him this evening."

"Perhaps," said Shelley somberly, "you would merely have postponed the inevitable."

"No, I can't buy that. As long as Nick and I stayed together, I'd have been in there with a fighting chance."

"But, Clare, surely you couldn't have gone on accepting the fact that Nick was having an affair with another woman?"

"Not gone on accepting the fact? Look who's talking!" Clare gave a harsh, bitter laugh. "Okay, when you're fool enough to fall in love with a man—God help you!—you want him all to yourself. Every woman does, it's only natural. But if you can only have a part of him, then you settle for the most you can get. Anything is better than nothing. You ought to know that, Shelley!"

So Clare took it for granted that she had known all about Rex and his other women. It wasn't as simple as that, of course. But it would take a shrink to sort out the complicated tangle of her thoughts and explain everything to Clare. Maybe their two cases weren't all that dissimilar. She herself, in a fervent attempt to preserve her marriage, had clung to a highly romanticized image of her husband; while Clare, for precisely the same reason, was ready to openly swallow her husband's infidelity.

"Hush, Clare, try not to think about it." Shelley put a sympathetic hand on her arm. "I know it must hurt now, but gradually the pain will pass. You must believe that."

Clare shuddered. "I can't face going back to the office. Not with all the gossip there'll be, and the risk of running into Nick any moment."

"But you *must,*" Shelley protested in dismay. "Somehow or other you've got to make yourself face up to the office. I know it's tough, Clare, but you have to be practical. You'll still need to earn your living, won't you?"

"I could always get another job."

"But *could* you? A job that's as good as this one? Things aren't too rosy on the employment front just now, and you'd be insane to throw away what you've worked so hard for. J.S. has a very high opinion of your talents, you know."

"I *can't* go back to P&L," Clare reiterated.

"Yes, you can! You mustn't let Nick drive you out of a job that you enjoy, Clare. Another thing, it's a mentally demanding sort of job, and that's exactly what you need right now to help take your mind off Nick."

"Nothing will do that!" Clare said bleakly.

"At least it'll be a help," Shelley insisted. "Promise me, Clare, that you won't quit your job. Stick it out at P&L for a few weeks, anyway, and then see how you feel."

For what was left of the night, Shelley remained downstairs with Clare. They didn't attempt to go to bed, but just curled up with blankets on the sofa until slowly their eyelids drooped and finally sleep took over.

A bleak, drizzling morning greeted them when they awoke, and a clammy gray mist was swirling across the river. Shelley had her work cut out to make Clare stir herself. After going upstairs to her own flat to get dressed and ready, she returned to find Clare gazing listlessly out the window.

The rain meant that the buses were extra full and extra slow. In the end, Shelley arrived at the office more than ten minutes late. This was a heinous crime in the eyes of the super-efficient Beth Kirby, to judge from her censorious look. And, Shelley discovered, in Jason's eyes too. Though he'd probably been engrossed in paperwork since eight-thirty, she reflected sourly, some kind of second sight had prompted him to get up from his desk and come through to the outer office just at the very moment she was slipping out of her raincoat.

"So you finally made it!" he observed in a curt voice.

"Sorry I'm late," she mumbled resentfully. "But . . . things happened."

Jason grunted. "There's a pile of stuff there on your desk that I want you to study and report on. I'm going to be tied up all morning with Barney Moffat, who's just got back from Spain. It looks like that sherry account we've been pitching is in the bag."

"Oh, that's great." Shelley marveled at the cool, impersonal way they were discussing work. Almost as if the weekend had never happened.

Halfway back through the door of his office, though, Jason halted and gave her a shrewdly assessing glance. "You look rough this morning, Shelley."

"I feel rough! I didn't get too much sleep last night." Then, before he could pride himself that it was on his account, she added hastily, "Clare was very upset. She and Nick have split up. He walked out on her yesterday."

"I see. Pity. Let me know if there's anything I can do."

When Jason had closed his door, Beth asked in an overcasual voice, "What was that about Nick walking out on Clare?"

The story would be all over the agency in no time flat, but Shelley didn't see that it was her function to spread gossip. Pointedly applying herself to one of the folders on her desk, she murmured something about their having had a bit of a row.

Beth wouldn't leave it there. "I could see this coming, of course. For weeks and weeks now, every single chance he had, Nick has been booking that little blond model Patti Whatever-her-name-is. He's obviously besotted with her. Clare is a fool not to have nipped it in the bud." Getting no response from Shelley, she added with heavy emphasis, "It always astonishes me the way some wives just close their eyes to their husbands' fun and games. They seem to hope the problem will just go away of its own accord. It never does, though, it just gets worse."

Shelley bent lower over the folder and scrawled a marginal note. She wasn't going to give Beth the pleasure of knowing how much her barb had stung.

A few minutes later Jason's deputy, Barney Moffat, came through from his office next door. Shelley knew him only slightly. As the financial wizard of the agency, he wasn't much involved with the copy room or other creative departments. Barney was well into his forties and, clad in a formal pinstripe suit and sober tie, he looked more like a conventional City type than an advertising executive.

"Hello, Shelley," he greeted her pleasantly. "I heard you were coming back to us. How are things?"

"Okay, thanks, Barney."

"Settling in all right? Jason isn't overworking you, I hope?"

"No more than I can handle. Being kept busy is the way I like things." And that was true, she thought with a start of surprise. The pile of project folders which Jason had dumped on her presented a welcome challenge.

"There'll be plenty of work for everyone all round when this thing breaks," said Barney, patting the briefcase under his arm.

"The new sherry account, you mean?"

"Not just that. The whole setup with—"

From behind them, Beth's voice warned, "J.S. is waiting for you Barney."

"Oh, yes. Well, see you about, Shelley."

All that day and through that week, Shelley had very little contact with Jason. There were lots of comings and goings of the agency's top management, and working lunches most days of coffee and sandwiches sent out for by Beth. Carl Rossiter, the creative director, was constantly in and out, and also Jason's successor as chief of the media department, Frank Darby. While it was a relief to Shelley to be spared the embarrassment of tête-à-tête sessions with Jason in his office, she felt miffed that he virtually ignored her. Like it or not, she was a member of his personal executive team, but he was treating her like a piece of office furniture.

At home on Thursday evening she settled down to watch TV, more from a feeling of wanting company than any real interest. Clare was now staying with her sister and brother-in-law in Hampstead because she couldn't face being alone in the apartment with Nick gone.

Around eight o'clock, Shelley heard a door slam in the Roystons' apartment. For a moment she froze, then realized that it must be Clare come to collect some more clothes and things. Switching off the TV, she went downstairs and rang the doorbell. To her surprise, it was Nick who answered.

"I'm sorry," she stammered, embarrassed. "When I heard a noise, I thought it must be Clare."

"You got it wrong, then, didn't you? I just looked in to collect some of my LP's and cassettes."

"How come you didn't bring a truck?" Shelley asked sarcastically. "You could've carted away the furniture while you were at it."

Nick's face blazed red and sparks of anger glittered in his eyes. "What business is it of yours, Shelley?"

"It's my business," she retorted, "because Clare happens to be a friend of mine. Anything that makes her unhappy, I'm concerned about."

"Meaning that I'm not?"

"You do make a person wonder! You and Clare had something really good going, Nick. But then you ditch her like a worn-out old shoe, and go running off to live with some kid who's hardly finished high school."

Still scowling angrily, Nick stood aside. It wasn't really an invitation to come in, yet somehow he seemed to expect it of her. In the living room, he said in a less aggressive tone, "Can't you understand, Shelley, that marriages run out of steam sometimes?"

"Sure I understand that! But you and Clare . . . it seems a shame. How come you two couldn't have straightened out your problems one way or another? Did you really need to break up completely?"

Nick shrugged his shoulders. "Our marriage went off the tracks somewhere along the line, and that's all there is to it."

Shelley felt a sense of helplessness. She realized that she should never have gotten herself into this, yet some inner compulsion drove her on. "You've really broken Clare in two. She was in a dreadful state on Sunday after you walked out on her. I had to stay the night with her."

Nick shrugged again, uneasily. "Yeah . . . well, I know she's a bit cut up at the moment, and I'm sorry about that. Okay? But Clare's a strong person, she always has been, and she'll soon get over it."

"How callous can you get?" Shelley blazed at him. "There's no suffering involved for you, Nick, right? You're cozily shacked up with that little blond model. It beats me why some men totally lose their heads when they see a girl with a sexy body, and never mind whether she's got any brains in her head. It's pathetic! I'd have thought you had the intelligence to see that Clare is worth a dozen of someone like her."

Nick thrust his hands into the pockets of his suede jacket. "You're so darned naive, Shelley, you just don't have a clue what it's all about. When you were with Rex you must have been living in cloud-cuckooland."

"If I was," she tossed back, concealing the stab of pain, "not anymore! Anyhow, it's you and Clare we're talking about, not me and Rex."

Nick glared at her with narrowed eyes. "Listen, Shelley, why don't you just go back upstairs and I'll be out of here in ten minutes. No need to worry, I'm not going to pinch the knives and forks or whatever." He touched the trailing leaves of a tradescantia. "This plant looks a bit sickly. I'll give them all a spot of water before I go."

Shelley made one last try, knowing in her heart that it was pointless. With a gesture around the living room, she asked. "How can you bring yourself to walk out on all this? Clare has made a really lovely home for you. Okay, so she sometimes gets after you for being untidy and all that, but it doesn't mean anything. Clare loves you, Nick, she loves you very deeply. She told me so."

"She *would* claim that, wouldn't she? To put *me* in the wrong."

"But it's true. You know it's true."

"Keep out of it, Shelley," he snapped. "Stop meddling in what's my business."

"Will Clare know that you've been here this evening?"

He reddened. "I'm entitled to come whenever I bloody well choose. I pay the rent!"

"Okay! I'm sorry." As a parting shot, Shelley threw at him, "I'll keep on hoping, Nick. Maybe someday you'll come back and have the sense to stay."

# Chapter Seven

$\mathcal{F}$ riday morning Shelley had to attend a brainstorming meeting of second-echelon personnel concerning various minor accounts. Shelley contributed a little, but learned a lot.

As Ben Caster, the group director's assistant, was winding up the meeting, he commented, "Whatever it is they're pitching upstairs, it's obviously something pretty big. Come on, Shelley, you can drop us a little hint."

"Sorry, Ben, I don't know any more than you do." This was greeted with a groan of disbelief. "Honestly, I don't know a thing," she reiterated. "J.S. is playing this one very close to his chest, and I'm not one of the favored few."

Ben grinned as he got to his feet, gathering together the various papers spread across the table. "Okay, I believe you, Shelley. Thousands wouldn't."

Clare Royston was also at the meeting. Since Clare had gone to stay with her sister in Hampstead, Shelley had met up with her once or twice around the building, but never for more than a few brief moments. Now, in the general exodus from the conference room, Clare came over and asked if there was any chance of their having lunch together.

"Sure, that would be nice," Shelley agreed with a smile.

"I'll meet you downstairs, okay? One o'clock? There's a little Greek taverna in Shepherds Market we could go to."

"Great!"

When Shelley got back to the twelfth floor, Beth announced, "J.S. wants to see you."

Despondently Shelley wondered what she'd done now—or hadn't done soon enough to please his lordship. But this time it wasn't a criticism. As she went through to his office, Jason held up the type-written report she'd sent in to him earlier that morning which concerned a proposed TV com-mercial for a washing powder called Bubblo. The scenario depicted two little girls, twins, trying on identical party frocks. Then one of the frocks was deliberately soiled. But after being washed in gentle Bubblo suds, the garment was shown to be com-pletely indistinguishable from the one worn by the other sister at their birthday party—proof positive of the magical restorative qualities of Bubblo. Shelley had argued that this was based on bad psychology. Men might consider the experiment a legitimate way of making a forceful sales point, but to women it might seem both foolish and even offensive to wan-tonly despoil a pristine new frock.

*Why not make it a calamity instead?* she'd sug-gested in her report. *Little girl in her excitement about wearing the new frock upsets a glass of orange juice or whatever all down the front. But after the frock is washed in Bubblo . . . presto, all radiant smiles at the party.*

"You've made a good point here," Jason commented. "This is precisely the sort of thing I was relying on you for, Shelley. A shrewd analysis of the feminine way of looking at things."

Shelley felt herself flush with pleasure. But she had qualms about accepting praise from Jason and passed the compliment off with a careless shrug. "It's very simple, really. While men involve themselves in abstract logic, women see things from the human, personal point of view. To us, the world is all about people, not ideas."

Jason nodded thoughtfully, an odd expression on his face. "All the same," he said, "I still think it's safer to stick to ideas in the abstract."

"To treat people as mere objects, you mean?" she flashed, and cursed herself at once for making the smart retort. Throughout these past few days she had been discovering that despite all the conflict that lay between them, it was possible to work under Jason's command in a job that she found highly interesting and rewarding. It would be much safer, she warned herself, much less hazardous to the delicate balance of her emotions, to keep their relationship on a strictly boss-and-assistant level.

"It can be a big mistake to let oneself become personally involved," Jason remarked slowly, his glance coming to rest on her face. Then he seemed to contradict himself by going on, "You told me that you like jazz, Shelley. There's a club in London called Ronnie Scott's. We could go there one evening."

"No!" It came out as a strangled protest. The

thought of accepting a date with Jason filled her with dread—dread that was redoubled because she knew in her heart how much she wanted to accept.

"Why not?" he demanded coldly.

"Because . . . oh, I've got too many things to do."

"You're saying that every minute of your leisure time is preempted?" Jason sounded bitterly sarcastic. "Tell me, who are these lucky men?"

"I . . . I didn't say anything about men."

Jason raised his eyebrows. "I'd be fascinated to hear more about these social engagements of yours, in which men don't feature."

"You're twisting my words!" she retorted, taking refuge in losing her temper. "In any case, what I do in my free time is none of your concern."

He stood up and came around the desk, towering over her as he met her eyes in a long, intent look. "Shelley, there's no point in our quarreling."

"I couldn't agree more! And we needn't . . . so long as you leave my private life strictly alone."

"Shelley—" he began in a low, coaxing voice, but she cut across him hastily. "Is that all you wanted to see me about, J.S.?"

Jason's mouth went taut. His tone was brittle. "I don't appear to have got the Starglow file back yet."

"But you only gave it to me late yesterday afternoon," she gasped. "There's hours of work collating all those dealer questionnaires."

"Well, hurry it up! We can't sit on our backsides in the ad business."

Shelley left his office boiling with anger. Jason had played the heavy boss merely because she'd refused him a date. The man was insufferably arrogant to imagine that despite all that had gone before, he could still charm away her resistance. How dare he? But then, with a shudder of self-disgust, she remembered again what good reason Jason Steele had for thinking that she could be coaxed into bed. If only that shameful embrace after Rex's death had never happened, Shelley agonized for the thousandth time, unaware of the curious glances that Beth was shooting at her. Or if only *she* had been the one to cut it short.

The Helios Taverna was off the beaten track, and Shelley had never been there before. A small place with little two-seater tables divided by trellised greenery, it was packed at this time of day. But luckily she and Clare were able to grab a table. They both ordered *moussaka,* and while waiting for it they chatted about Clare's sister's family.

"Rita is so lucky," said Clare moodily. "She has an adoring husband and two lovely kids—one of each."

"How old are they?" asked Shelley.

"Stevie's just had his sixth birthday, and Fiona is three and a half." Clare gave a sigh. "Staying there has been a help, but I can't dump myself on them forever, can I? I suppose I've got to make up my mind to come back to Putney sometime soon."

"It won't be soon enough for me," said Shelley. "It's gloomy being all on my own in the house."

"Yes, I know," said Clare apologetically. "I feel a bit guilty about it. But . . . somehow, I just had to escape for a while from that empty flat, to get myself sort of . . . you know, Shelley. It's a bit like your rushing off back to New York when Rex was killed."

But it hadn't been like that at all, Shelley reflected. She had been fleeing, not from grief and loneliness, but from a new and terrifying discovery about herself. That sudden, impetuous kiss in the penthouse apartment and the intensity of feeling it aroused in her went far beyond a search for comfort and solace. She knew now, and she must have been subconsciously aware of it even then, that Jason Steele was a threat to her emotional equilibrium. Had been a threat even while Rex was still alive. Almost from the day she first met Jason, intangible threads of attraction had been drawing her to him. No wonder she had fled to New York, putting the Atlantic Ocean between them.

"I've learned a lot about myself since then, Clare, and about my marriage," she said in a steady, even tone. "If I'd known at the beginning what I know now, I'd never have married someone like Rex."

Clare nodded. "Everyone was surprised when he brought you back from New York with him."

"Yes, it was crazy. I'd been steering clear of romance while I concentrated on my career, and then I must have dropped my guard with Rex and fallen for him headlong. But I think I started seeing through him almost from the beginning." She met Clare's eyes across the narrow table. "How well did you know Rex?"

"Come again?"

"All I've got to go on is hints . . . rumors. It's like I know but I don't know. I'd prefer to have the whole truth, straight and square."

Clare was obviously embarrassed. "Look, there's no point in your getting in a twist about something that was over and done with before you married Rex."

"Don't try to kid me, Clare. I know it carried on after we were married."

"But I'm telling you the truth," Clare insisted, her

face flooding with color. "It was *years* ago that Rex and I . . ."

At that instant their *moussaka* arrived. Shelley waited in numb silence as the waitress set down the plates, staring at Clare in a horror of understanding.

"You mean . . . *you* and Rex were . . . ?" she gasped faintly, the moment the girl departed.

"Didn't you know? I thought that's what you were getting at." Clare sounded utterly appalled. Suddenly she was talking quickly, urgently. "You've got to believe me . . . it happened so long ago, and it only lasted a week or two anyway. It was all over and done with before Nick joined P&L and he and I started dating. There was no one else for me after that. I'm sorry, Shelley, I wouldn't have had this happen for the world. But I really thought that's what you were talking about. Otherwise I'd have kept my big mouth shut."

Shelley felt shocked and shaken. But that was utterly irrational, she told herself angrily. It was something that might happen to any wife—even one who was blissfully happy in her marriage—to come face to face with an old flame from her husband's past.

"Forget it Clare," she muttered, fighting back tears of humiliation. "I suppose there must have been several other women at P&L, too?"

Clare didn't answer at once. She held her fork poised for a moment, then dropped it back on her plate with a clatter. "I hate men!" she said vehemently. "They treat us like dirt and we let them get away with it."

"You might as well tell me who they were. I mean, which ones . . . after Rex and I were married."

Clare moodily dug into her *moussaka*. "My advice to you, Shelley, is to put all this right out of your mind. Remember the good times with Rex. Nothing else really matters."

"Nothing else matters?" Shelley echoed with bitter irony. "I'm not to let it bother me that my husband was sleeping around the whole time we were married?" She glared at Clare challengingly. "That's not the way you feel about Nick's extramarital activities, is it?"

"That's not fair," Clare protested, flushing. "It's altogether different with Nick. I mean, he's still alive."

"So, like you told me the other night, if only you could get Nick to come back, you'd overlook his sleeping with Patti Fairfax as long as he kept living with you? Let me tell you, Clare, that I'd never have stood for it with Rex if I'd known about it at the time. Really known, I mean. Who . . . and when . . . " Her voice trailed off. What was the difference, really, between knowing the specifics, as Clare did, and having known "enough to know," as she had done? Had she been so very different from Clare? Clinging to what little remained of her ignorance and hoping for the future?

Suddenly, as if she'd had to brace herself to ask, Clare changed the subject and burst out, "Have you seen anything of Nick round the house?"

Shelley nodded. "As a matter of fact, he was there last night. I heard him moving about, and I went down. I thought it must be you."

"Did you speak to him?"

"Well, I had to. I mean, having rung your doorbell . . ."

"What did he say?"

"That he'd come to collect some of his LP's and cassettes."

"Is that all? Didn't he say anything about *me* . . . about *us?*"

"I tried to tackle him, to ask him *why*. But he refused to talk about it."

"So you just left it at that?" There was a sting of reproach in Clare's voice.

"I had no choice," said Shelley defensively. "Nick told me in no uncertain terms to mind my own business. I'm afraid there's nothing I can do to help, Clare. If you want to salvage your marriage, it's entirely up to you."

"What chance do I stand?" With a snort of self-hatred, Clare turned to a mirror on the wall beside them and studied her face. "Look at me! And then think of *her*. You've seen from her pictures what a fantastic looker she is."

"But Nick doesn't love Patti Fairfax. He can't."

Clare's mouth twisted into an ugly grimace. "What do men know about *love?* All they ever think about is a good time in bed. Sex is the be-all and end-all of life to them."

For something to say, because she could think of nothing else, Shelley muttered, "Nick watered your plants while he was there."

She watched the pathetic eagerness flare for a moment in Clare's eyes, then die away. "Just habit. It was one of the jobs Nick often did. I forgot all about the plants myself in the rush of leaving for Rita's, but so what? I don't care if the whole darn lot die on me now."

For the past couple of days Shelley had been working on a report that Jason wanted for corporate headquarters in New York. Prescott and Lieder-mann over there were in the running for a new account for a problem-hair shampoo, with a mid-size advertising budget attached to it. They had asked London to check for any possible conflicts of interest.

As things stood, there was no difficulty. But Shelley had to ascertain from each group account director whether there were any prospects on the horizon that might be jeopardized if the American parent company was already handling a direct competitor. It was a tricky matter of having to weigh the pros and cons. Should the Americans turn down this new shampoo account because London was hopefully in line for something even bigger? If that subsequently failed to materialize, then the P&L organization would lose out all around.

Five-thirty Friday came and went. Beth departed, but Shelley stuck at her desk, preparing the final draft of her report. She could have left it until Monday, but she had nothing better to do this evening. As for the weekend ahead, it promised to be very painful. Sunday was the anniversary of her wedding day. It would have been much better, she thought despondently, for it to have fallen on an ordinary weekday, when the pressure of work would have helped keep her from reliving the haunting memories.

Apart from the soft clatter of her typewriter it was very quiet in the office, with only the faintest hum of homegoing traffic floating up from the streets. She was alone in the executive suite, both Jason and Barney Moffat having gone off earlier in the afternoon to a meeting at the bank. Hearing footsteps in the corridor outside, Shelley guessed that it would be the security man making his first round of the night. But instead, it turned out to be Jason.

"Still here?" he commented, his dark brows lifted in surprise.

"I thought I'd get this report finished rather than leave it over. I wasn't expecting you back today."

"Or you wouldn't have stayed?"

"I didn't say that."

"You didn't need to say it. The expression on your face spoke volumes." Jason gave her a deliberate, challenging look. "I'm only surprised that your multiplicity of social engagements permitted you to stay late at the office."

"As it happens," she lied, "I'm not doing anything until later on this evening."

"So you're giving P&L the benefit of an odd couple of hours free from the usual hectic round? I'm grateful!" He gave her a brisk nod, "Right, then. Let me have that report when you've finished typing it and I'll take it home to study over the weekend."

With that Jason went through to his own office and closed the door. Twenty minutes later she took the report in to him and laid it on his desk.

"Thanks," he said briefly. Then, as she stood wavering, he looked up and inquired, "Was there anything else, Shelley?"

"Well, yes, I sort of wanted to ask you something . . . about Rex. You've already made it clear that you didn't have a very high opinion of him, so . . ."

When she dried up, Jason leaned slowly back in his chair and looked at her. He picked his words with obvious care. "Rex was a damned good advertising man, in his own particular field. He held some of his clients in the palm of his hand like no other account director I've ever encountered. And—"

"You don't need to tell me that sort of thing," she

broke in impatiently. "I meant . . . your opinion of him as a man."

"I don't know that I had any particular opinion of him as a man."

"That's not true!" Shelley flashed. "You've made one or two snide comments about him since I've been back in England." With a catch of breath, she added, "The other night . . . you said something then. Remember?"

"I remember," Jason agreed. "I remember every word that was said between us the other night." He rose to his feet and moved across to the windows that overlooked Hyde Park, standing with his back to her. "I wish I knew exactly what you were driving at."

Shelley scarcely knew herself, and she was wishing to heaven now that she'd never started on this perilous line of questioning. But she had been goaded by an urge to know everything there was to know about Rex.

"I keep hearing more and more things about Rex and other women," she faltered.

"Ah, so that's it! You should ignore that sort of talk, Shelley."

"I can't!"

Jason turned slowly. He gave her a long, penetrating look, as if trying to see into her mind. "When you were here before . . . when you and Rex were married, you didn't have the least idea, did you? Not the slightest?"

Color flamed her cheeks. "I guess I knew eventually, but I wouldn't let myself admit it. I *did* love Rex. I guess you think I was terribly stupid and gullible."

Jason shook his head. "Whatever I think of you,

Shelley, it's certainly not that. I know only too well
how easy it is to see people as you *want* to see them.
I suppose it's a lesson we all have to learn the hard
way."

"To be a cynic, you mean?" she challenged. "The
way you are."

"To be clearheaded and see life for what it is. Not
through rose-tinted glasses." Quickly he moved
across to her and Shelley felt the familiar engulfing
awareness of him. "You've got to face up to things
squarely, Shelley, and not run away from the truth,"
he finished.

"What truth?" she said, trembling.

"The truth about yourself." He slowly raised his
hand, and she felt herself go rigidly tense. With one
finger he touched a strand of her rich chestnut hair,
scooping it back across her forehead.

"What . . . what is the truth about myself?" she
stammered.

His eyes burned into her. "You know the answer
to that, Shelley."

She knew one truth, and it was the only truth that
really counted. She knew that she wanted this man,
yearned for him with a fearful intensity that robbed
her of breath. With a little helpless gasp she went
into Jason's open arms, letting him draw her close,
and lifted her face eagerly to meet his possessive
mouth. She was lost now in a wild betrayal of the
senses, while his lips covered her face with little
lingering kisses and slid down the soft curve of her
throat. Her body became pliant and fluid as she
pressed herself against him, feeling with a thrilling
stab of excitement the swift, pulsing stir of his
arousal. Each moment brought a new throb of
pleasure that made her moan aloud as Jason's hands

gently caressed her through her clothes, seeking and finding the tender, sensitive spots that made her dizzy with delight.

The shrilling of the telephone made them freeze. "Curse the thing!" Jason muttered savagely.

Shelley drew back from him, invaded by a sudden chill. "You . . . you'd better answer it."

Jason hesitated a moment, then took two paces to his desk and snatched up the phone. "Hello . . . yes, I'm still here. I'll be tied up for some time yet. . . .No, I can't. I'm involved in something tricky that will take a while to get sorted out. I'll see you tomorrow, as we fixed."

Naomi Waterton! The way Jason was speaking, intimately yet evasively, confirmed this without a shadow of a doubt. Shelley felt a wave of sickness wash over her. A moment ago she had been deliriously happy, and now she was brutally reminded yet again of the fact that to Jason Steele she was just another available woman. A little light diversion from the mainstream of his sex life.

She turned quickly to the door, grasping the handle and jerking it open. Jason at once broke off what he was saying to call her back. But Shelley ignored him, hurrying through the outer office to the cloakroom, where she dragged on her raincoat. As she slipped back to snatch up her handbag from her desk, Jason came through.

"Where are you going in such a hurry?" he demanded, his brow knitted in an angry frown.

"I want to get home. I've stayed here much too long already."

"Shelley . . . I know the phone rang at just the wrong moment, but there's no reason for you to be upset."

She threw him a challenging glance. "It was Naomi Waterton, wasn't it?"

"So?"

"If Naomi wants to see you this evening," Shelley choked bitterly, "I'd advise you to go running."

"It doesn't happen to fit in with my plans," he said calmly. "Come on, I'll drive you home."

"No!" she said, shuddering. "I'm going by bus."

"When my car is right here in the basement?"

She said desperately, "You'd be going way out of your way, taking me to Putney."

"That's true," he agreed. "So you might show a little gratitude, instead of making idiotic objections. Now, come on!"

The elevator took them straight down to the basement car park. In Jason's Mercedes she sat as far away from him as possible, thankful that at least the busy traffic demanded most of his attention.

"So you've got a busy weekend ahead of you," Jason said, suddenly breaking the silence between them.

"Er . . . yes."

"No free time at all? Not so much as a spare half-hour on Sunday?"

"I guess I'll be pretty occupied."

Jason swung the car past a red double-decker bus. "Okay, if you say so. But just make sure that you keep *next* weekend clear."

"Listen," she protested furiously, "on my own time, I figure that . . ."

"There's no such thing as your own time in an executive-level job," he interrupted curtly. "Next weekend is business."

"What business?" she asked suspiciously.

"There's a big new Cleveland account in the

offing, for which we shall be making our presentation. That's what we've been so busy on recently. A team of P&L top executives and their wives will be going to stay over at Sir Mortimer's place at Windsor. It's the way he likes these things done. I need you to be there, Shelley."

"But . . ."

"No buts."

What was he up to? Shelley wondered wretchedly. What purpose would be served by thrusting her and Naomi together? The prospect filled her with dread. Was it Jason's way of demonstrating that no woman could ever touch his heart? He knows how I respond to him, she thought with a rising sense of panic, and he's spelling it out that I mustn't get any foolish ideas about him. Pleasure without involvement, that seemed to be Jason Steele's creed.

"I'm afraid that it won't be possible for me to go to Windsor next weekend," she declared.

Jason flicked her a hostile glance. "If you refuse to go without having a sound, valid reason, you'll be finished with me," he warned. "And with P&L, both here and in New York. You'd better believe it."

"But that . . . that's blackmail."

"It's nothing of the sort. You'd be proving yourself unfit to hold down a responsible executive job. It would, of course, point to a serious error of judgment on my part in choosing you for promotion, but I'd survive that. You wouldn't, though, Shelley."

"What possible use will I be at Windsor?" she burst out furiously. "You've kept this new Cleveland thing so much under wraps that I know nothing whatever about it."

"You'll be briefed in plenty of time."

"Who will be there on the other side?" Shelley asked. "Sir Mortimer is a widower, isn't he?"

Jason nodded. "There'll be his advertising manager, Gregory Wayne, and the Cleveland group's chief accountant. And several lesser mortals."

"And Naomi Waterton?"

"Naturally. Naomi plays a big part in the running of her father's companies nowadays."

"So I've heard!"

"For once what you've heard is true."

"I'm surprised that you dared turn her down this evening," Shelley said.

"I suggest that you leave me to worry about Naomi," Jason said in a chilling voice.

They were crossing Putney Bridge now, almost home. Shelley was afraid that Jason would want to come in, and she screwed herself up to refusing point-blank. But when they stopped outside the house a minute later, he remained sitting behind the wheel.

"I hope," he said, with a questioning look in his charcoal-gray eyes, "that you're not finding it too depressing, being alone here in an otherwise empty house. I originally saw this place as ideal for you, because you would have someone you already knew as a downstairs neighbor."

"So you've heard about Clare going to stay at her sister's?"

"Beth keeps me well informed," he replied dryly.

Shelley sighed. "It's all very sad about Clare and Nick."

"Yes, I'm sorry too. I like them both. Still, at least there are no children to complicate matters."

"I just can't begin to understand Nick," Shelley burst out, a sense of helpless fury welling up in her. "It's nothing short of ridiculous, breaking up a perfectly workable marriage because of that teenage model."

"Patti Fairfax is a very sexy girl," Jason observed.

"So that means it's okay? You men make me sick to the stomach the way you hang together and back each other up. If a man gets bored with his wife, it's always *her* fault for not holding him. Never *his* fault for treating her so shabbily. Any sort of rotten behavior is justified. No man must ever be blamed for indulging his sexual urges. Being unfaithful is treated as trivial and unimportant—just a bit of harmless amusement on the side." Her angry voice choked into silence against the hopeless futility of everything. Men were all the same, all as bad. Nick, Rex . . . Jason.

He said quietly, placatingly, "Try to keep things in perspective, Shelley. Life isn't all roses. This isn't the happy-ever-after world that you'd like it to be, and you've got to accept that fact. Otherwise you're going to get hurt again and again."

There was sincerity in his eyes, gentleness in his voice. But the words conveyed a warning to her. A warning never to dream foolish dreams where he was concerned.

As she groped blindly for the door handle, Jason began, "Shelley, about Sunday . . ."

"I told you," she muttered, "I'll be busy all day."

She had the car door open now and she jumped out hastily. Without a backward glance she hurried to her front door, fumbling in her shoulder bag for the latchkey. Once the door was firmly slammed shut behind her, it seemed like a barrier against invasion. Or a prison gate.

# *Chapter Eight*

$\int$aturday morning, the feeling of emptiness in the house was oppressive and Shelley set out early to shop. Walking back with her few purchases, she idled along the embankment, killing time.

Back home, she found that the mailman had come. A bulky envelope from Prescott & Liedermann in New York lay on the mat. She'd made arrangements with Marge Cohen, Ed Braine's secretary, to send over anything that arrived for her there, plus any letters that were redirected to her at the Madison Avenue office by the new tenant of her West Side apartment.

She scanned the scribbled note from Marge while she made herself a cup of coffee—newsy bits and pieces about her ex-colleagues, nothing world-shattering. Then she took her coffee through to the living room and glanced at the enclosures. A laundry bill she'd overlooked, a letter from a high-school classmate who was married now and living in Seattle. And, puzzlingly, a small envelope postmarked London which seemed to have taken weeks and weeks getting to New York by sea mail. Shelley slit it open. The heading on the sheet of blue-tinted notepaper was a shock—the address of the Knightsbridge penthouse apartment where she'd lived with Rex. The letter was signed Flora McGregor, who with her husband had taken over the lease in the deal negotiated by Jason. It was very brief.

Dear Mrs. Armitage,
    I came across the enclosed at the back of a drawer, and I've been meaning to send it to you for ages. I always think that receipts for valuables are best kept as proof to the insurance people in case of loss. I do trust you are settling down to life in New York again.

A flimsy, crumpled slip of paper was clipped to the letter. A bill, Shelley saw, from a Bond Street jeweler. It was dated September 16, a month before Rex had been killed. The writing was rather a scrawl, but she deciphered the words "Silver 'Dragon' Bracelet." Shelley caught her breath in outrage. Aside from the silver bracelet set with diamonds and sapphires, Rex had given her a gold charm bracelet and a couple of cheaper pieces. But none of them fitted this description. She looked at the scrawl again and made out the words "engraved '*R. to B. with love.*'"

Who, she wondered wretchedly, was B.? Then, sending a cold shiver down her spine, the truth crashed in upon her. B for Blanche. No wild stabbing guess—Shelley knew with absolute conviction.

She had seen this bracelet on Blanche Farleigh's wrist, had actually admired it.

Convulsively, Shelley crushed the slip of paper in her fist and flung it from her. But moments later she was smoothing it out again and searching for some possibility that she was mistaken. No question! The receipt was made out to "R. Armitage, Esq.," the date fitted, the scrawled handwriting could be forced into no other meaning.

In a sudden burst of activity, she got out the vacuum cleaner and started in on the living room. Angrily she told herself that she shouldn't let it hurt her so much. Rex wasn't worth all this anguish and heartache! She had known for a long time that Rex hadn't been a faithful husband, so what difference did it make now that she knew the name of one of his women? But try as she might to convince herself otherwise, it *did* matter.

Her wedding aniversay tomorrow was going to be one hell of a day to live through!

Sunday mocked her with a brilliant, cloudless morning. Outside, the sunlit waters of the Thames glittered under the soft blue sky. Once again Shelley flung herself into a fever of chores around the flat, then suddenly abandoned them half-done. In old slacks and a yellow T-shirt, she padded around restlessly, pausing to stare out at the river, turning back to flick on the radio, then finding the burst of pop music jarring to her nerves.

Around ten o'clock the doorbell pealed. Glancing down from the window, she saw Jason's blue Mercedes parked outside. Dear heaven, what had brought him here? Of all the people in the whole wide world, he was the last person she could face seeing today.

The bell rang again, and still she made no move to answer it. But after the third time she decided furiously that she'd better go down and send Jason packing.

"Hello, Shelley!" he greeted her cheerfully. He looked so devastatingly attractive in fawn corded jeans which accentuated the long muscular length of his legs and a suede jacket that tapered from his broad shoulders to his slim waist that she felt her bones melt. "I've come to take you out. It's such a lovely day."

"But . . . but I can't possibly . . ."

"Of course you can." Pushing her firmly aside, Jason stepped in and closed the front door. "Now, go upstairs and get changed. Something fairly casual, I'd suggest."

"Look here—" Shelley began desperately. But he cut across her. "Upstairs, I said, and don't argue."

The familiar feeling of helplessness swamped her. However fervently she wished him gone, the effort of sending him away seemed beyond her. Perhaps it might be better, her treacherous mind pleaded, for her to be out and about with Jason somewhere than cooped up in the flat all day, alone with her inner torment.

While Jason waited for her in the living room, Shelley went through to the bedroom to get ready. She chose pale blue linen jeans and her navy blazer, with a white cotton jersey beneath it. Having brushed out and arranged her chestnut hair into soft, loose waves about her slender shoulders, she changed her mind and instead twisted it into a chignon, pinning it securely at the crown of her head.

When she returned to the living room, Jason looked her up and down in slow appraisal, his dark eyes lingering appreciatively on her slender, shapely figure. "You'll do very nicely! Come on."

"Where are we going?"

"Sightseeing. Ever been to Runnymede?"

"No."

"Hampton Court Palace?"

Shelley shook her head.

"Right, that's the itinerary, then."

In the car, she sat taut and trembling, as much on guard against herself as against Jason. There must be no weakening! If he wanted to waste his Sunday taking her around, that was his business. But he'd better not expect anything in return!

While driving, Jason enlarged on his plans for the day in a chatty way. Shelley's interest was caught, and she found herself gradually relaxing, despite herself. The first scheduled stop was to be Runny-mede, a place on the River Thames some miles farther up than Putney.

"There's a small island at that point which is supposedly the spot where the Magna Carta received the royal seal in 1215. The fifteenth of June, actually, and it was a very significant day in British history. King John has the distinction of being just about the worst monarch ever to sit on the English throne. He was a selfish, greedy, quarrelsome chap who pillaged and plundered and massacred his way around his realm, and was faithful to no one. Eventually the barons got so fed up with him that they banded together and forced John to sign this Great Charter, which guaranteed them some rights, at least."

"You seem to be very well-informed," Shelley commented.

Jason grinned. "One thing I learned early on in the advertising game was the importance of doing one's homework properly. That way, you don't get thrown when a client fires awkward questions at you."

"So you boned up on your history for my benefit, huh?"

"In the encyclopedia," he agreed. "A busy ten minutes before I came to collect you."

They both laughed, and the mood between them was suddenly much more relaxed.

The lush green meadows at Runnymede were crowded with family parties. There was a pleasantly tranquil atmosphere that seeped through to Shelley as she strolled with Jason to view the two memorials. The first, marking the Magna Carta, had been erected, curiously enough, by the American Bar Association. Nearby was a massive memorial in Portland stone commemorating John F. Kennedy.

Afterward they drove on to a waterside pub, where they lunched in an oak-paneled barroom. Reflections of sunlight on the river danced across the low ceiling. Shelley realized to her surprise that she was eating the tender roast lamb and mint sauce with a keen appetite.

Unexpectedly, not quite knowing why, she found herself saying, "Today is my wedding anniversary."

Jason nodded as he raised his pewter tankard of ale.

"You *knew?*" she gasped in astonishment.

"I knew that you were married the day before you arrived in England last year. So it wasn't hard to calculate."

"But you remembered!"

He shrugged dismissively. "It's not such a big deal."

Shelley felt a lump form in her throat. "And that's the reason you came this morning to take me out?"

"I figured that it wasn't such a good day for you to be on your own. It would have been easier for you if your anniversary hadn't fallen on a Sunday."

"But . . . I told you I had things to do on the weekend."

Jason regarded her across the table, a faint smile curving his lips. "Lucky I didn't believe you, isn't it?"

His gaze lingered, meeting and holding her eyes. Shelley felt a warm glow of happiness steal over her. It was a feeling that stayed with her until after they left the pub and took a roundabout route to Hampton Court, Jason pointing out various places of historical interest on the way—Datchet Mead, where Falstaff received a ducking in Shakespeare's *Merry Wives;* and a bridge from which Sir Izaak Walton was known to have fished. Then Shelley noticed a signpost to Windsor, and a shadow darkened her mood. Windsor might be world-famous for its royal castle, but it was also where Naomi Waterton lived with her father. Was that where Jason had been with Naomi last night? Shelley wondered desolately, remembering the phone call he had received at the office Friday evening. Or had they been together at his mews flat in Chelsea? What difference, though? The pain was the same.

Hampton Court Palace, its splendid facade of red brick glowing a warm rosy color in the afternoon sunlight, had attracted large crowds on this lovely spring Sunday. Shelley and Jason took a tour of the magnificent state apartments, hung with fine paintings and tapestries. They passed through the Haunted Gallery, where the ghost of poor Catherine Howard, last but one of King Henry VIII's six wives, was reputed to walk; she, like Anne Boleyn before her, had been neatly disposed of in Bluff King Hal's charming way by the simple expedient of cutting off her head.

But Shelley's interest was never really gripped as it had been at Runnymede that morning. Her thoughts kept drifting back to Naomi Waterton and her relationship with Jason—two hard-bitten people who were using one another in a sordid amalgam of sex and business.

When they emerged from the Tudor Kitchens into the cloisters of Fountain Court, Jason said, "There's still plenty more to see on this tour . . . the Orangery, the Great Vine and the famous Maze. But maybe some other time? You look a bit tired, Shelley."

"Yes, I guess it's been a more emotional day than I'd realized." True enough, but she'd leave him to conclude that it was on account of Rex. "Will you take me home now, please? I'd like to be on my own."

Jason looked disappointed. "I was thinking we'd have dinner somewhere later on."

Dinner, and then what? The battle was raging within her once again. . . . She despised Jason Steele, yet her treacherous heart still wanted him. Just the touch of his hand at her elbow as he steered a course among the exiting sightseers had whipped the heat through her body.

To hold him at bay, she resorted to irony. "Listen, you don't have to feel obligated to fill every last second of my time today. It was nice of you to think of taking me out, and I'm grateful. But enough is enough."

A hurt look flitted across his lean, craggy face. "If that's how you feel . . ."

"That's how I feel!"

Jason drove her home by way of Richmond Park, where herds of tame red and fallow deer roamed freely, heedless of the human activity all around them. After sitting silent and brooding for a while, he said abruptly, "Tomorrow I'm calling an executive meeting to brief everyone about the new Cleveland account. From then on we'll all be working flat out knocking our presentation into shape for next weekend."

"Why the heavy cloak of secrecy on this account?" Shelley demanded petulantly. "Everyone at P&L has known for days that something big is about to break. Also that the sherry account Barney went to Spain for is somehow linked with it."

"The secrecy was unavoidable. Cleveland Enterprises had some loose financial ends to tie up before anything could be allowed to leak out. But I can tell you about it now, Shelley. I was given the all-clear last night. Sir Mortimer has bought out two big nationwide chains of wine stores—Marlborough Cellars and the Trusty Vintners. He's going to restructure them into a single company, Cleveland Wines, which will run a number of exclusive brand names. Eldorado Sherry is to be the first."

Jason had been given the all-clear *last night*. Pillow talk? Shelley's temples began to throb, and she had to fight hard to keep her tone even. "I presume the account is already in the bag? That the presentation next weekend is a mere formality?"

"What gives you that idea?" Jason's voice had a dangerous undertone.

"Well, I mean . . . the way you were in the know when the whole project was still under wraps."

"P&L's existing association with the Cleveland group has given us an edge over our competitors," he agreed. "But we still have to sell ourselves to Sir Mortimer on the strength of the ideas we put forward."

141

"You mean," she said, letting her disbelief blaze through, "that there's a possibility P&L *won't* get this account?"

"Anything is possible in the ad business."

"I guess you can't have any serious doubts, though? Not with the sort of contact you've got."

Jason swerved the car to the side of the unfenced parkland road and braked hard. "You'd better spell that out."

Shelley colored violently, wishing that she'd kept quiet. With a defiant shrug she said, "I meant that you have an especially close personal relationship with Naomi Waterton."

Jason's dark eyes narrowed. "So?"

"Of course," she back-pedaled, "it's not really any of my business . . ."

"How right you are!"

Shelley would have found some sort of comeback, but at that moment a park patrolman waved them to get moving. Stopping at the roadside in the royal park was not permitted. Jason slid the car into gear and drove off. Ten minutes later, neither of them having spoken another word, he drew up outside the house at Putney and cut the engine.

It was Shelley's cue for saying, "Thanks, see you tomorrow." But something held her there. She sat and watched a small boy wobble past them on a bicycle that was too large for him. An elderly couple, the woman in a flower-bedecked straw hat, strolled by the river railings enjoying the warm afternoon, benign smiles on their time-worn faces.

"Shelley?"

Just the one word, just her name. But there was such a depth of meaning in Jason's voice that she was shot through with terror. How fatally easy it would be to let him take her into his arms! How fatally easy

142

to go back on her resolve and invite him to come in and have a cup of tea. To stay on for supper. To stay the night.

Shelley closed her eyes, fighting off temptation. Last night Jason was with Naomi Waterton, she reminded herself scornfully, and tonight he's hoping to score with me. Did he really imagine that she was such a pushover? She had to prove him wrong, totally and utterly wrong.

When she felt the touch of Jason's fingers on her arm, she reacted convulsively. Flinging open the car door, she jumped out and ran to the house. When the front door banged shut behind her, she stood for a few moments leaning back against it, gasping for breath, her heart thudding wildly.

# Chapter Nine

At ten o'clock Monday morning Shelley's internal phone buzzed and it was Clare.

"I've got to talk to you," she said. "Can you come downstairs?"

"You mean now?"

"Yes, I won't keep you long."

Shelley felt dismayed. Ever since she had arrived at 8:45 this morning she'd been in and out of Jason's office, receiving a string of rapped-out instructions concerning the strategy behind P&L's presentation for the Cleveland Wines account. Now she had a pile of work on her desk and was frantically translating it all into memos for the agency's various departments. Jason had been so remote, so coldly overbearing this morning, that the last thing she needed was to give him any justification for griping at her.

"I'm up to my eyes right now, Clare," she explained. "Can't it wait till midday?"

Clare instantly took offense. "If you're not willing to spare me a lousy few minutes, forget it!"

"Listen, I didn't mean . . ."

"I just thought that you were someone I could talk to. But apparently I thought wrong."

There was a fraying edge to Clare's voice that worried Shelley. Some things were more important than the work load, regardless of sparking Jason's wrath.

"Okay, I'll come right on down," she said. "Where do I see you?"

"In reception. We can talk privately there." Clare sounded very relieved. "Thanks a lot, Shelley."

In the spacious reception area on the seventh floor, she found Clare pacing around agitatedly. Her usual slick, sophisticated image was gone. Instead she looked a bit sickly, the strong cherry-red of her turtleneck sweater seeming to drain her face of all color.

"What's this all about?" Shelley asked as they sat down together on one of the padded leather banquettes.

Clare made a helpless, shrugging gesture. "Of all the awful pieces of timing! My husband has just walked out on me to go and live with someone else, and now I discover that I'm pregnant."

"Oh! Are you certain, Clare?"

"Positive. I suspected it last week, and I had a test done. I've just this minute phoned and got the result."

"How do you feel about it?" Shelley queried warily. "Are you glad?"

"Glad? I don't know *what* I think, and that's the honest truth, Shelley. It's something Nick and I have been trying like mad for these past three or four years, so in one way I'm thrilled to bits. But

145

why did it have to happen now? It's too damned late!"

"Have you told Nick that you suspected you were pregnant?"

"Not likely! In any case, he and I haven't spoken to each other since the night he walked out on me. Not one single word."

"Then you must tell him right away. It might make all the difference."

Clare shook her head unhappily. "You don't know how stubborn Nick can be."

"But he has a right to know. He *is* your husband."

"Pity he doesn't act like it, then!" Clare's defiance crumbled and a despairing look came into her eyes. "I wish I could believe that it would make a difference, Shelley. But the way things are, it's likely to turn Nick all the more against me."

This time the facile phrases about Nick loving her really, deep down, refused to come to Shelley's lips. She was totally disillusioned now about men and their twisted ideas concerning love and loving. Maybe, she thought cynically, Clare would be better off without Nick after all, even with all the problems of bringing up a child on her own. A baby would at least give her an outlet for her thwarted emotions.

"Nick will get to know in the end, of course, whether or not you tell him," Shelley pointed out. "What do you propose to do, Clare . . . I mean, you will *have* the baby, won't you?"

"Sure I will—given the chance! Things went wrong for me before, but the obstetrician said there was no reason why it shouldn't be okay another time."

"I didn't realize that you'd ever been pregnant before."

"That was why Nick and I got married when we

did—I mean, in a bit of a rush. But then I miscarried, so we took the opportunity to get a decent home together before we launched into a family. Only, the irony was, when we started trying, it wouldn't work! And from then on everything seemed to go sour on us." She sighed despondently. "If only this could have happened a month ago."

Furtively Shelley took a peek at her watch. She'd been away from her desk for twenty minutes already. "What will your sister say about your being pregnant?" she asked gently.

Clare shuddered. "I won't tell Rita, not yet. And you mustn't breathe a word to anyone, Shelley. That's why I've told *you* . . . because I just had to tell somebody, and I trust you to keep your mouth shut."

"You can rely on that."

As Shelley reentered the office a few minutes later, Beth jerked her thumb at Jason's door and said with unconcealed relish, "J.S. wants you. Pronto!"

She was blasted by Jason's anger the moment she went in. "Where the devil have you been, disappearing like that without a word to anyone? We're pushed for time, and you choose to take a half-hour out."

"Sorry. But Clare Royston wanted to see me."

"What was wrong with lunchtime?"

Shelley shrugged. "She was in rather a state. I didn't think I'd be gone so long."

"What's Clare in a state about?"

"Oh, something private."

"Well, if it's so private," he snapped, "it can wait till outside office hours. Right? Remember that in the future."

Her own anger flared. "I'm supposed to be in a responsible executive-level job here. But you insist on treating me like some junior kid just out of college."

"Act responsibly, then, and it won't be necessary." He switched the subject with finality. "Now, have you completed those departmental memos yet?"

"I have not! They'll take the rest of the morning."

Shelley was dismissed with a brusque wave of his hand. Going out, she closed the door with a protesting bang and pointedly avoided Beth's gloating eyes. Back at her desk, she shuffled the various papers around mutinously. Jason was being totally unreasonable! Was he mad at her because she hadn't fallen into his arms yesterday? Or was his anger more against himself for having let her escape him? There was no doubt in Shelley's mind that if she hadn't panicked and fled into the house she and Jason would be lovers by now.

*Lovers!* What a mockery! There would be no love involved on his part. Shelley wished now that she had never come back to England . . . wished that she had never met Jason Steele . . . wished again that she'd never allowed Rex to rush her into marriage. She'd been right in her original plan, determining to steer well clear of romance and build up a career for herself. Marriage should have come later, years later, when she had gleaned enough experience to know that falling in love was nothing but a booby trap. At that stage she could have made a practical kind of marriage that would have suited both partners equally, based on mutual liking and admiration, not the heart-bruising emotion of romantic love.

Along with a couple of dozen others, Shelley attended the staff briefing directly after lunch. It ran, with a fifteen-minute break for refreshments, until nearly nine P.M. For most of that time Jason presided, putting everybody in the picture about exactly what was required. Shelley had to admit that it was a masterly performance. He allowed everyone freedom to put forward ideas and suggestions, yet he retained total control.

Tuesday was almost as busy. Beth knocked off soon after her normal time, but Shelley stuck at her desk. She was dissecting a recently published national survey of women's shopping habits and preferences to extract whatever references there might be to liquor buying.

Jason emerged from his office around six-thirty. He stood silently looking down at her for so long that Shelley felt her cheeks growing warm with embarrassment. She was afraid to meet his questioning gaze.

"It's time you quit work, Shelley," he said at last. "You look pretty well done in. I'll drive you home again."

"There's no need!"

"Don't be silly. Get your coat."

"No, I want to stay and finish this." When Jason looked like persisting, she added quickly, "In any case, I'm not going straight home."

"Oh?"

"I'm seeing someone first."

"Who's that?"

Shelley felt like blasting that it was none of his darned business. Instead, she responded with icy sarcasm, "Should I have sent in a memo to you about it? Do you expect a detailed report of every prospective date?"

His jaw set in a hard, dangerous line, and Shelley was almost afraid that he might seize her and shake her violently. But then he said neutrally, "Just so long as you're not staying on here. Overwork can act like a narcotic. Before you know where you are, you're hooked on it."

"Like you are?" she suggested, gesturing at the briefcase he was carrying.

Jason shook his head, smiling grimly. "There's no danger of that with me. Once I realize that I've reached the limit of my effectiveness, I completely dismiss work from my mind."

"How very convenient," she mocked, "to be so totally in command of oneself that there is no risk of ever falling prey to human weakness. You sound like an efficient, well-maintained robot."

His dark eyes glinted. "I am anything but a robot, Shelley. Surely you must have reached that conclusion by now?" Without giving her a chance to think of a riposte, he strode to the outer door. "I'll be off, then. Good night."

Ten minutes later, ten minutes of sitting staring into space, Shelley realized that she wasn't going to get another stroke of work done. To use Jason's term, she had reached the limit of her effectiveness. She had no further excuse for postponing her plan of action. This evening she intended to draw the final line under the balance sheet of her marriage. All the misery and heartache she'd suffered over Rex must be written off against the value of the experience she'd gained.

As she went down in the elevator and left the building, she was sorely tempted to change her mind and go straight home after all. It was a stupid scheme. She would learn nothing that she didn't know already, and there was no way she could alleviate her bitter hurt over Rex. Yet she still felt compelled to go through with her plan. Uncertain of the route, she hailed a cruising taxi, instructing the driver to take her to Cheyne Walk.

The rush-hour traffic was thinning, and quite soon they were cruising along the Chelsea street that was so renowned for its historic literary connections. Now many of the gracious red-brick Georgian houses were the homes of well-known artists and stage stars. Nervously she told the driver to pull up outside one whose immaculate garden was fenced with handsome wrought-iron railings. She paid him off and stood looking up at the house for a few moments, gathering her courage.

Blanche Farleigh opened the door herself, looking fabulous in a white linen leisure suit. Her glorious wavy red hair, which she claimed was entirely untouched by hairdressers' hands, tumbled softly about her slender shoulders.

"Good heavens!" she exclaimed, staring at Shelley in astonishment. "What brings you here?"

Shelley hadn't really expected a welcome. "May I come in, Blanche? I want to talk to you."

"It's devilishly inconvenient. Why didn't you phone me first?"

"What I have to say won't take long."

Grudgingly Blanche stood aside. "I suppose I can give you a few minutes. We'd better go in here." She led the way into a small study on the ground floor. Without asking Shelley to sit down, she demanded impatiently, "Well, what is it?"

Shelley produced the crumpled slip of paper she'd slipped into her shoulder bag that morning. "I think you should have this. I imagine that it refers to something which is your property."

"Really?" Blanche looked puzzled as she took it. "A receipt, isn't it?"

"Exactly. A jeweler's receipt for a bracelet. An

expensive gold bracelet, engraved with your initial."
Maddeningly, Shelley was unable to keep a betraying tremble from her voice.

"Oh, yes . . . Rex's birthday present," drawled Blanche, understanding dawning in her green-gold eyes. She glanced at the receipt again interestedly. "Is that how much he spent on me? Silly man, it wasn't necessary. But Rex was always generous to a fault, as you well know."

"So you admit that my husband gave you a gold bracelet?"

"Why not? What would be the point of denying it?"

Shelley swallowed back the shocked protest that sprang to her lips. Though her specific purpose in coming here this evening was none too clear in her head, it certainly wasn't to give Blanche the pleasure of seeing how raw and ragged her emotions were. In what she hoped was a coolly crisp voice, she said, "You seem to be taking a positive delight in throwing it in my face that you and Rex had a filthy little affair."

"Filthy?" Blanche's silvery laugh tinkled out. "Believe me, little innocent, it wasn't like that at all. Rex and I had something really special going—on and off—for several years. I miss him quite a lot, I don't mind admitting it."

Somehow, Shelley thought desperately, she had to get under the skin of this woman. She said, with intended viciousness, "There was nothing *special* about your affair, Blanche. You were just one of many in Rex's life."

"Correction! I was *the* one. Oh, I don't deny that Rex slept around. I certainly didn't begrudge him any of those other women. Not even you, Shelley! It didn't really bother me when he amazed us all by arriving back from his New York trip with a wife in tow. But one single glance at you was enough for me to see that Rex had made a mistake. It was so typical of him to act on impulse and regret it later."

Shelley knew that it was crazy to have come here, and crazier still to stay for any more of this. Yet she couldn't stop herself from going on. "Rex never had any reason to regret marrying me," she asserted in a steady, defiant tone.

"You're kidding yourself, my dear Shelley. I don't pretend to know how you managed to nobble Rex into marriage in the first place, but I'll tell you this for free—he was round here knocking on my door again within a week of arriving in London with you. Think about it!"

Shelley gasped, unable to hide her shock and mortification.

"Before you can ever hope to hang on to a man," Blanche continued victoriously, "you'll have to learn a few things about what makes them tick, Shelley. Rex used to say to me that you were quite a sweet little thing, and that you meant well, but . . . And believe me, Shelley, it was a very big but. It wasn't conversation that Rex came to me for."

Shelley felt herself trembling in every limb. She had to get out of this polluted atmosphere before she lost the last shreds of her self-control. "I think it's high time I went," she said stiffly.

"I can't think why you came in the first place," Blanche retorted. "I suppose you were hoping to have me break down and confess my shame . . . beg your wifely forgiveness and so forth. But you've been disappointed, haven't you? Still, cheer up, Shelley. You can at least console yourself that you had a good time for those few months with Rex." Blanche preceded her along the hall as she spoke, and opened the front door. With a sweetly savage smile, she said, as a parting shot, "Have a nice evening."

Those hard, derisively smiling eyes stayed in Shelley's mind as she walked away from the house and began to wander aimlessly through the quiet evening streets of Chelsea. How Blanche had enjoyed passing on Rex's dissatisfaction with her performance in bed. It wasn't true, she sobbed in silent misery, it surely couldn't be true. And yet . . . had sexual incompatibility been the real cause of the failure of their marriage? Was the responsibility for the problems she had barely admitted more hers than Rex's?

This shocking, mind-torturing thought stayed with her no matter how she tried to dodge the issue. She'd known when she first met Rex, she'd fully accepted the fact, that he was a man with wide sexual experience. While she . . . It had been her choice, her conscious decision, to avoid serious emotional entanglements while she was in the process of building her career. Maybe, though, she lacked genuine, uninhibited passion. It could be that she just didn't have the ability to satisfy a normal, hot-blooded man.

Shelley came to a sudden halt. A thought had darted into her mind which caused her to catch her breath with a gasp. There was one sure way of establishing the truth.

Jason lived only a short distance from here, somewhere in this maze of Chelsea streets. He was a virile man who found her attractive, and he had made it abundantly obvious that he wanted to make love to her. So why not go to him now and indicate that she was available? Then she would be left in no doubt about herself, one way or the other.

Quickly, before she could reject the idea as totally

outrageous, she started walking on again with purpose in her footsteps.

Jason's exact address? It was right there in her
brain, Shelley realized with surprise, just waiting to
be dug out . . . subconsciously memorized, she
guessed, from the time when she had started to
phone him to cancel the trip to Cheltenham. This
time, with a very different plan in mind, she
wouldn't let her courage fail her.

Only now did it occur to her that she wasn't
exactly dressed for the scene she had in mind. Her
casual skirt and jersey outfit was somewhat crumpled after a busy day at the office. But no matter, it
would have to do.

Gratton Mews was a narrow, cobbled roadway
flanked with the converted stables and coach houses
of the formerly elegant terraced mansions onto
which they backed. Nowadays, with their bow-front
windows, bright paintwork, and polished brass
coach lanterns, they were more fashionable than the
big houses themselves. Even if she had not known
the number, Jason's could be identified by his blue
Mercedes parked outside.

At the last moment Shelley hung back, shrinking
with nerves. But by now Jason might easily have
spotted her through the window. When she rang his
doorbell he answered almost at once. He had
changed, and was now wearing fawn slacks and a
casual cream shirt open at the neck. His peat-dark
hair looked almost black, still damp from a recent
shower.

"Hi!" she said with forced gaiety. "I realized that
I was almost on your doorstep, so I thought I'd drop
by to make sure you didn't carry on working too
late."

Jason masked his surprise with a welcoming smile

and stood aside for her to enter. "How nice, Shelley!" He helped her off with her raincoat. "As a matter of fact, I packed in work about a half-hour ago, and I was just fixing myself some supper. You'll have eaten by this time, I imagine?"

The thought of food simply hadn't crossed her mind. She walked ahead of him into his spacious living room, which was furnished with a sort of Spartan luxury; the walls were pristine white, the carpet, curtains and cushions subtle tones of gray and green, with here and there a splash of color. There were several modern paintings, and ceiling-high bookshelves all along one wall. A stereo unit was softly playing Mozart's *Eine Kleine Nachtmusik*. By the front window a small round table was laid with a bowl of salad—crisp lettuce and tomato, cucumber and bright red radishes—and some pâté, a cheese board, and a long French loaf and butter. A tall green bottle of Rhine wine was misting in the warm air.

Without directly answering Jason's question, she remarked, "Hey, you don't do too badly for yourself."

"Perhaps you could manage a morsel?" he suggested, and immediately fetched another setting.

"I might at that. It all looks very mouth-watering." Eating would help to break the ice, Shelley thought. She sat down at the place he had set for her, feeling quite sick with nerves. She was thankful when Jason immediately poured wine and handed her a glass.

"I guess you must be feeling pretty tired by now," she said, forcing herself to make conversation.

Jason smiled at her slowly and sipped his wine before replying. "Never too tired to entertain a beautiful woman."

Oh, cut it out, for heaven's sake, Shelley wanted to say. But she stifled the thought. Raising her own glass, she looked back at him over its rim, using her eyes provocatively. In her nervousness she swallowed half her wine in the first sip, and it made her gulp. Besides which, the alcohol on her empty stomach had an instant effect.

Jason's dark eyes were regarding her curiously, as if he was trying to sum up her mood. He sliced the crusty bread, and pushed the dish of pâté in her direction.

"Try some of this," he invited. "It's very good."

They were fencing around, and it was obvious that Jason knew it as well as she did. Outside, the daylight was fading, and in the lamplit room they were very much on view to the occasional passerby. Jason rose and drew across the long green curtains, and immediately the atmosphere changed. There was an electric tension between them now. But outwardly Jason revealed nothing, calmly helping himself to salad and a wedge of Camembert cheese. Shelley accepted more wine—a mistake, she knew. The small quantity of food she'd managed to swallow wouldn't counterbalance the effect of the alcohol.

When Jason went to make coffee, Shelley sat in a deep armchair beside the writing desk on which evidence of his evening's work still lay strewn. Then, with a change of mind, she moved to the huge white sofa and took a seat there, leaning back and crossing her long slim legs.

Returning from the kitchen, Jason set the tray down on a low table in front of her and went to the armchair she had just vacated. Shelley knew that she had to make a definite tactical move soon, and in her sudden panic it seemed a choice of now or never.

She forced her stiff facial muscles into an enticing pout.

"Must you sit so far away, Jason?"

He didn't get up, but sat regarding her with a wary expression in his charcoal-gray eyes. "Shelley, why have you come here this evening?"

"I told you . . ."

"I know what you told me. I'm still asking."

"You're not making me feel very welcome." Was this really her voice, lightly teasing and flirtatious? "Do you want me to leave?"

Jason stirred restlessly in his chair. "It might be wisest—for us both. But, no, I don't want you to leave, Shelley."

She leaned forward to pour the coffee, only half-filling the cups because her hand was shaking so much. Rising, she carried his cup over to him, and when he took it, she perched herself on the wide arm of his chair.

"So . . . you want me to stay?"

Jason put his coffee aside and gave her a long, probing look. "Something has happened to you since we talked at the office. You said you had to see somebody. Who was it?"

"Oh, no one important."

"Somebody living in this neighborhood, presumably. That is, if it's true about you finding yourself almost on my doorstep."

Shelley felt frantic. What was the matter with the wretched man? Previously he had shown himself so eager, so impatient to make love to her. Yet now that he had the opportunity, now that she was virtually throwing herself into his arms, he was holding back. She wished to heaven that she'd never embarked on this reckless experiment. But to fail now would condemn her to living with the bitter knowledge that she truly was inadequate as a woman. Desperation making her feel awkward and clumsy, she leaned forward and lightly trailed her fingertip across Jason's lower lip.

"Why should you care about who it was I went to see?" she murmured. "What matters now is that I'm *here*. Right?"

Jason didn't move away from her caressing finger, but neither did he attempt to touch her in response. "What matters, Shelley, is *why* you're here. Exactly what prompted this visit?"

"Just listen to the man!" she exclaimed on a rippling laugh. "Am I on trial or something?"

His reply came slowly, thoughtfully. "In a curious way, I get the feeling that you are. You're putting yourself on trial. Testing yourself."

He was too shrewd, too perceptive. But perceptive or no, surely he wasn't going to refuse a woman he fancied when she offered herself to him on a plate?

Shelley made one last, despairing try, sliding her other hand up the back of his neck with little circular movements and tangling her fingers into the crisp luxuriance of his dark hair. Jason's resistance snapped, and with a gasp he responded by pulling her down on top of him and clasping his arms around her. Shelley felt a wave of relief—but a shiver of fear, too. There was no going back now. Nor, sweet heaven, did she want to go back when Jason's mouth covered hers in a fiercely passionate kiss that set her blood dancing. No longer was she consciously acting the temptress. She was caught up irresistibly in the rising tide of mutual excitement. With a drowning sense of joy she felt the quivering probe of his tongue as he explored the intimacy of her mouth, while his hands slid over the soft warm curves of her body. Clinging to Jason, pressing herself close against him, Shelley could feel the fierce, urgent throb of his desire.

Presently, after long moments of such delirious delight, Jason murmured into her ear, "Let's make ourselves more comfortable, shall we?"

"Yes," she whispered almost inaudibly.

Shelley felt him lift her in his arms as though she weighed less than nothing and carry her upstairs to his bedroom. She lay with her cheek snugly pressed against his broad shoulder, feeling the rapid thud of his heartbeat, intoxicated by the warm, musky male scent of him.

"Stay right there, just as you are," he said softly, setting her down on the bed. Through a swirling mist she was aware of him moving about the room, drawing the curtains and switching on a shaded lamp. Vaguely she noticed that his bedroom was furnished with the same kind of plain, almost austere luxury as the living room downstairs.

Jason came back and stood at the bedside, gazing down at her slender form with appreciative, desirous eyes. With a muttered exclamation he sat down beside her and bent to kiss her once more. Shelley welcomed him eagerly, opening her mouth to receive the warm thrust of his tongue. Jason's hand slid up beneath her jersey to caress her breast, and she felt the nipple swell and stiffen to a peak of longing under the tender torture of his fingers. Then Jason was undressing her, deftly removing each garment and casting it aside. His dark eyes were like smoldering fires as they feasted on her naked beauty.

"Shelley . . ." His voice was husky, ragged with the intensity of his desire. "Shelley, you're so lovely . . . so exquisite!"

With urgent impatience Jason stood up and

stripped off his own clothes. She caught just a brief glimpse of his fine naked body, the smooth skin bronze in the muted lamplight, a faint hazing of dark hair on his broad, contoured chest. Then he was upon her, crushing her into the feathered softness of the quilt with his hard masculine weight. His lips and hands were everywhere, smoothing, stroking, kissing, caressing, suffusing her with the most rapturous sensations until she was frantic with wanting. She moaned in ecstasy, drawing him closer, raking his thick dark hair with trembling fingers, soft whimpers of delight escaping from deep in her throat.

Time had no meaning, nor the world beyond this softly lamplit bedroom. Her wretchedness and misery, her wild plan to prove herself a real woman before another night had passed—all were forgotten in this maelstrom of passion. She gasped aloud as Jason took complete possession of her and the flames of longing within her soared to new heights, meeting and matching the hard thrust of his desire. For Shelley knew now that she loved Jason—loved him far more deeply, more intensely than she had ever loved Rex. This was the most tumultuous experience of her life, the gateway to ecstatic fulfillment.

"You little witch, Shelley, keeping me waiting so long," he breathed hoarsely, his lips against her tumbled hair. "I've never wanted a woman so much in all my life as I've wanted you."

Shelley went rigid, his words freezing her like an ice-cold shower. What for her was a unique, miraculous expression of love was for Jason merely one more act of sex. She was no more to him than just another woman, another notch on his scoreboard.

"No, don't," she moaned in anguish. But Jason ignored her protest. His movements quickened to a wild frenzy till, with a convulsive explosion, he cried out and was still.

Shelley lay beneath him, feeling the thudding of his heartbeat, the long breaths hissing in his throat. Tears of despair flowed from her eyes and rolled down her cheeks to dampen the pillow.

After a few moments Jason raised himself on his elbows and looked down at her. "What is it, Shelley?" he asked huskily. "Why are you crying?"

She shook her head wretchedly, unable to think clearly enough to invent a plausible explanation.

"It was what you wanted, wasn't it?" he said.

"No . . . no!" Her voice emerged as a distraught, choked whisper.

"No? But this was your idea, not mine," he pointed out. "You came here of your own accord and virtually threw yourself at me."

"That's . . . cruel."

"It's true!"

How could she deny it? She muttered weakly, "Please, let me go now."

But Jason made no attempt to move, holding her pinned to the bed beneath the warm weight of his body. With his right hand he held her chin, forcing her to look at him.

"You wanted me, Shelley. You wanted me all the way, right up until the very last moment. Tonight you were completely different from other times, as if you couldn't wait for me to get you to bed. And then, all of a sudden you went ice-cold on me. What's it all about, for pity's sake? Why did you come here and act the way you did if you weren't prepared to go through with it?"

"What are you complaining about?" she cried bitterly. "You got what you were after."

"Did I?"

"What's that supposed to mean?" she lashed out, wanting to hurt him as she had been hurt herself. "Is your ego dented because I didn't play hard-to-get?"

"There might be a grain of truth in that," he admitted. "Most men prefer to do the running."

"Don't tell me that you have to do the running with Naomi Waterton," she cried half-hysterically.

Momentarily Jason's grip on her tightened in fury. Then he rolled away and got up from the bed, collecting his scattered clothes.

"Come downstairs when you're ready," he said grimly, "and I'll drive you home."

Shelley heard him on the stairs. Heard faintly, from below, a clink of glass as he poured himself a drink, and then the opening strains of a violin sonata. For long minutes she lay there limp and trembling, engulfed by dark waves of pain, until she was suddenly galvanized into action and started dragging on her clothes. She wanted only to get away from here, to banish this evening's bitterly shaming events from her mind. Yet she knew with a terrible certainty that she would never be able to forget.

When she went downstairs, Jason was standing with his back to the curtained window, a glass in his hand. Hearing her footsteps, he seemed to jerk himself out of an abstracted reverie. His gaze was hard, unyielding. "D'you want anything before we leave, Shelley? A drink . . . coffee?"

"Nothing. And I'd rather you didn't drive me home, Jason. I'll take a taxi."

His eyes flared. "There's no cause for you to be like that."

"No?"

She heard him take a quick, angry breath. "Why are you so intent on punishing me, Shelley?"

"I'm not!" she said, knowing that it was a lie. "But I'd much prefer you to call me a taxi."

He shrugged. "If that's how you feel . . ."

"Yes, it is."

Jason picked up the phone, quickly stabbing out a number. He spoke briefly, giving the address in clipped tones. "Five minutes," he told her, and hung up.

It seemed like five hours. Each time he started to say something, Shelley cut him short, making it clear that she wanted no further discussion. At the sound of a vehicle turning into the mews, she was at the front door before the taxi had pulled up. Jason followed her outside, but she scarcely glanced at him as she jumped in and told the driver where to go. In a trice they were speeding away through the night-lit streets of London.

Back home, Shelley huddled on the sofa, nursing a mug of coffee with both hands. When the phone rang, she let it ring on and on. But the caller was determined. In the end she got to her feet and walked stiffly into the bedroom.

"Hello?"

"Shelley! You took your time answering. I was just checking that you got home okay."

"Of course I did! Why shouldn't I have?"

"You're not . . . too upset?"

"For heaven's sake!" she exploded. "Can't you leave me alone? We've said all there is to say, and in the future I'd prefer it if we kept strictly to an office relationship. Okay?"

"Have it your way, Shelley!" Jason's voice, concerned until now, was suddenly granite-hard. "Good night, then!"

There was a click, and the dial tone buzzed in her ear. In some odd way, Shelley felt bereft.

# Chapter Ten

$A$lmost the instant Shelley arrived at the executive suite on Wednesday morning, she was summoned to Jason's office. Her heart plummeted as she gathered up her notebook and ball-point. What now? Was it going to be a continuation of last night's bitter encounter at his flat? Or was Jason having one of his spells of cold hostility, when the only words he spoke to her were rapped-out instructions? As it turned out, she found his briskly cheerful attitude slightly unnerving.

"'Morning, Shelley," he greeted her. "I've got some stuff on the Cleveland Wines presentation that I want you to look at."

"You mean these?" she queried, peering upside down at a number of photographs spread out on his desk.

"Come round here," he instructed, "where you can see them properly."

Reluctantly Shelley did so, and found herself starting to tremble. It was ridiculous, she reproved herself. She had stood as close as this to Jason scores of times during these past weeks, studying artwork and layouts with him. Yet this morning she was infinitely more aware of his vibrant, blood-stirring masculinity. By contrast, Jason himself seemed quite unperturbed, as though last night had never happened.

"Nick Royston sent these pictures straight to me this morning," he explained, "instead of going through the usual departmental channels. I don't blame him for that, of course. Initiative is the name of the game. I gather he's been working all hours to get them hustled through in time."

Shelley saw that each photograph featured Patti Fairfax in a different pose. Some were blown-up mug shots, but mostly they showed off her sexy figure. There were three or four of her in a provocatively scanty bikini, lazing at the poolside with a drink at hand, and others in a daringly revealing black evening gown. Another range depicted her as pertly demure in a shop assistant's overall, smilingly handing a bottle across the counter.

"Well," demanded Jason, "what do you think of *her* as the Cleveland Girl?"

Shelley stared at him in astonishment. "You've got to be joking!"

"I don't joke about work," he said coldly. "You ought to know that by now, Shelley. Your job is to give me a considered opinion on whatever issue I put to you, and that's what I expect from you now."

"Okay then . . . the answer is that it's a ridiculous suggestion." Shelley felt a surge of indignation on Clare's behalf. How could Nick be so totally insensitive as to put this forward as a serious proposition? And how dare Jason *receive* it seriously? The idea of creating a "Cleveland girl" had already been accepted as one of the main features in P&L's proposals, and the hunt was on to find the right model even before the presentation to Sir Mortimer this weekend. Nick Royston had cut corners by putting forward his own candidate direct to the boss man, a piece of cool cheek of which the boss man clearly approved.

"What I'm still waiting for," said Jason, splinters of ice in his voice, "is a sound, reasoned judgment from you, Shelley. Not an emotional outburst."

"Very well, I'll give you a reasoned judgment. Nick Royston is just trying to promote his girlfriend, that's what. He's aiming to make her a star model overnight by using her in a publicity campaign that would put her picture in every newspaper and on every TV screen in the country. I don't know how you can give the idea a moment's serious consideration."

"In the advertising game," Jason observed dryly, "an idea is an idea is an idea."

"Even when there's an ulterior motive behind it?"

"I judge everything purely on its merits, Shelley. Is it basically a *good* idea? Can it be made to work? Will it further P&L's interests? The fact that in this particular case Nick Royston hopes to give his girlfriend's modeling career a big boost is in no way relevant."

"It is to me!" said Shelley defiantly. "I can't help letting a thing like that affect my viewpoint."

Jason gathered together the spread-out photographs and slid them into a file. "If that were really true, then you'd be no damn good to me in this job.

But I don't believe it *is* true, Shelley, or I'd never have chosen you. In my opinion, you're capable of rising above such side issues."

"Rising above!" she echoed scornfully. "Sinking below, you mean."

Jason gave her a look of weary impatience. "What you're really saying amounts to this. Even if Patti Fairfax was considered perfect as the Cleveland Girl, we still shouldn't use her! Even if everyone were to agree that she'd do a superb promotional job for the client—to his and our mutual advantage—P&L should nevertheless reject the whole idea of using her because we don't happen to approve of her boyfriend's morals."

At bay, Shelley stared back at him challengingly. "Don't tell me that *you* think the girl is the right choice?"

"I'm not saying whether I do or not. You might be influenced by what I think . . . for whatever reason."

"What do you mean—'for whatever reason'?"

"You might tend to support my judgment simply because I'm the boss. Or—more likely with you!—you might go against it out of sheer perversity." He thrust the file into her hands. "Take this away and think it over."

Shelley didn't budge. "Why are you doing this to me, Jason?"

"Why? Because it happens to be what you collect your salary check for." His voice hardened. "I've no more time to argue with you, Shelley. *Out!*"

Back at her desk, Shelley was in too much turmoil of mind to give a thought to the Cleveland Girl issue. She was wondering wretchedly, as she'd wondered most of the previous night, whether she could possibly carry on in this job after the disastrous episode at Jason's flat.

"So J.S. has thrown Nick Royston's sexy little playmate into your lap," Beth commented dryly, glancing up from her typewriter.

"You know about that?"

"I certainly do! Nick was lurking in wait for me when I arrived this morning. Asked me to make sure that J.S. saw the photos right away. He's got quite a nerve, I must say."

"That's more or less what I told J.S."

"Not to much avail, it seems."

"Meaning?"

"The fact that you've brought the file out with you indicates to me that Patti Fairfax is being seriously considered. Or am I wrong?"

Shelley shrugged, then surprised herself by asking, "What do you think of the idea, Beth?"

"Me? Fortunately it's not my job to give opinions," she responded loftily. "But it doesn't take much to know what Clare will think about it."

Shelley nodded gloomy agreement as she bent over her desk. She was to learn Clare's views on the matter all too soon, when, five minutes later, she answered the phone and Clare was on the line.

"Shelley? Listen, there's a rumor going round that Nick is trying to clinch the Cleveland Girl job for Patti. It's not true, is it?"

"Well, yes, it is."

"Oh, no, I could kill him! Shelley, please. . . they say that J.S. listens to you. Can't you put a stop to it?"

"I'm sorry, Clare, it's not that easy."

"I thought you were on my side."

"I am . . . I am! But . . ." Oh, darn it, Shelley

thought resentfully. Why should I be in the middle, shot at from all sides when all I want is out? It was something of a relief that just then Jason buzzed for Beth to go in, so she was able to talk less guardedly. "You've got to understand this, Clare . . . my job is to make a careful evaluation of the merits of each and every situation from the woman's point of view. Jason has laid it on the line that I mustn't ever allow my personal feelings to cloud the issue."

"You're saying that Patti Fairfax gets your vote?" Clare sounded coldly incredulous.

"No, I'm not saying that. I've just this minute had the photos thrown at me. I haven't had any time to think about it yet."

"But it's perfectly possible that you'll decide to give her the thumbs-up?"

"It's . . . *possible.*"

"I see. Well, thanks for nothing, pal!"

"Don't hang up, Clare." Shelley hated being at loggerheads with her like this. "How are things? I mean, are you okay?"

Clare's laugh was heavily sarcastic. "Me? Oh, I'm fine . . . just fine and dandy! My husband has walked out on me for a tarty young model he's dead set on turning into the country's newest upcoming sex kitten. And I'm left to cope on my own with a kid on the way."

"I still think you ought to tell Nick about it," said Shelley bluntly. "He's got to know sometime, and the sooner the better."

In reply, Clare gave a noncommittal grunt and hung up.

"What has Nick got to know sometime?"

Shelley was startled. She hadn't heard Beth reenter the office. "Oh . . . nothing."

"Sounds intriguing, though. There's one thing

. . . it seems to me that if this idea of Nick's gets the official stamp of approval we can forget him and Clare ever getting back together. Don't you think?"

"What I think," said Shelley pointedly, "is that Nick and Clare would stand a much better chance of saving their marriage if people didn't gossip about them all the time."

Beth's face was tight with anger as she sat down at her desk. Oh, hell, Shelley thought dismally, now I've put her back up against me even more. I've made a real enemy of her when what I badly need right now in this organization is a friend to talk things over with.

She thought suddenly of Barney Moffat. He was nice—sincere and trustworthy. A chat with Barney wouldn't do any harm at all. On an impulse, she jumped up and went to the door, telling Beth where she could be found if needed.

Barney's office was a few yards along the corridor, and he looked up with a smile of welcome as Shelley went in.

"Hi! What can I do for you this bright and sunny morning?"

"A favor, Barney. I want you to lend me your ears."

"As friend, Roman or countryman? To rephrase —is it about ad business or personal?"

"A bit of both, actually."

Barney pulled a wry face. "That's the worst kind of problem. Look, why don't you and I have a spot of lunch together, Shelley? It's time we did."

"I don't want to impose on you," she said doubtfully.

"Since when has lunching with a beautiful gal been an imposition?"

"Thanks for the ego boost! But that's no way for a happily married guy to talk."

"It's high time Suzy had something to feel jealous about." He grinned. "That wife of mine is getting altogether too complacent about me."

"She's entitled. It's public knowledge around P&L that you're nuts about her."

"Maybe I am at that, but not a word to Suzy." He looked across the desk at Shelley, his head tilted speculatively. "Whatever's bothering you can wait till one o'clock, can't it?"

"Yes, sure. See you then, Barney."

She could well have done without having to run the gauntlet of Nick himself that morning. But other work couldn't be allowed to stop just because there was a hustle on the Cleveland Wines presentation. She had to go down to the studio three floors below to see George Turner about the revised artwork for the Heyday Holidays campaign, passing on some minor criticisms Jason had made. As she was leaving, Nick beckoned her over to his desk.

"What's the verdict, Shelley?"

"Verdict?" she parried.

"About using Patti as the Cleveland Girl."

"J.S. hasn't reached a decision yet. There'll be other suggestions to consider."

Nick scowled as if he hadn't reckoned on there being any competition. "Patti is dead right for the job," he contended. "I've never come across any other model who's as photogenic as she is."

"That girl seems to have been 'dead right' for just about every campaign you've had a hand in lately," Shelley pointed out ironically.

He shrugged. "You said it yourself, Shelley, about those Slikfit photos. Patti is terrific. She'd be sensational as the Cleveland Girl."

"And that opinion is completely unbiased, I suppose?"

"Okay," he acknowledged sullenly, "I'm not trying to say that it wouldn't be marvelous for Patti to get the job. She'd be over the moon. But that doesn't alter the fact that she's the right choice."

"And what's poor Clare supposed to think if she sees Patti's face and figure plastered over every newspaper? If she can't switch on the TV without being forced to look at her?"

"It's none of Clare's business. She and I are finished."

"Just like that? After being married all those years, you see a young kid with a fabulously sexy figure, and that's enough to make you cut loose from your responsibilities?"

"We've been through all this before," he said angrily. "You just keep out of my life, Shelley; it's no business of yours."

"I only wish I could," she retorted. "Unfortunately, though, J.S. is waiting for my assessment on the question of using Patti." Shelley spun on her heel and marched off across the studio. But Nick came after her and caught hold of her arm.

"Listen . . . you won't let your personal feelings about me and Clare make any difference, will you? I mean, just because you've got a downer on me, it wouldn't be fair to spoil Patti's chances. Please, Shelley . . ."

Jerking her arm free, she looked at him with contempt. "If you want to crawl, Nick, go crawl to Clare."

With that she strode out, leaving Nick standing. She was boiling with rage and felt in a mood to storm straight into Jason's office and announce that she'd come to the conclusion that Patti was totally wrong for the Cleveland campaign. But she knew that he would demolish any justifications she might think up and expose the fact that she was still letting her emotions rule her brain.

Barney took her to the grillroom of a hotel tower in Park Lane. If he had mentioned the place beforehand, Shelley would have opted out, for this had been a favorite haunt of Rex's. Artificial sunlight bathed them through a tinted glass ceiling, and a pink marble fountain of nymphs and dolphins tinkled coolly. The tall, princely majordomo was the same man she remembered, but fortunately he didn't recognize her.

From behind the two square feet of menu, Barney ruminated, "After all those sandwich lunches I've been swallowing down at my desk lately, I feel like having a square meal. Rump steak, I wonder . . . or roast veal?"

"Something light for me," said Shelley.

"Fish, then? How about sole *bonne femme?*"

"Sure, that sounds great. And a salad."

They elected to skip wine, with another busy afternoon ahead of them, and ordered iced mineral water instead. When they'd been served with chilled cantaloupe to start with, Barney asked, "So what's on your mind, Shelley?"

She gestured apologetically with her spoon. "It was stupid, I guess, running to you this morning. I just needed someone to talk to."

"If the boss wouldn't suit your purpose," he conjectured, "the problem must concern him. Yes?"

"No!" said Shelley instinctively. Then, "Well . . . in a way. It's to do with Cleveland Wines. You probably haven't heard, but Nick Royston has put up a crazy scheme for using that model Patti Fairfax as the Cleveland Girl."

"His little dolly bird!" Barney smiled. "I had heard, Shelley. How has that turned into a problem between you and Jason?"

"Well, when he first showed me Nick's photographs of Patti, my immediate reaction was that there was no way we could use that girl."

"Why so?"

"I'd have thought that was obvious. Or are all you men totally devoid of decent feelings?"

Barney smiled at her amiably. "I'm with you now, Shelley. The old conflict of loyalty to the organization versus loyalty to one's friends. And what, as if I couldn't guess, did J.S. have to say about your reaction?"

"He said that Nick's motivation didn't come into it. That I had to judge the issue only on its merits as a creative proposition." When Barney nodded his head approvingly, Shelley burst out, "So you're just as bad! You're every bit as cold-blooded and ruthless as he is."

"No, you've got us wrong, love. I've known J.S. a long time now, and I'd say that if it could conceivably help Clare for us to turn down Patti Fairfax, *his* gut reaction would be to look for reasons for doing just that. But it wouldn't help Clare, beyond satisfying her sense of revenge. That being so, we have to consider the matter from a stricly neutral viewpoint."

Shelley regarded him with dismay. "So what you're saying is that I've got to go along with Nick's choice? Give it my backing?"

"Not at all."

"What, then?"

Barney sighed. "Balance the pros and cons, Shelley; consider them calmly and analytically. Then give J.S. your verdict . . . for or against."

"But it's not so darned easy to clear your mind of personal feelings."

"J.S. and I have to do it constantly," Barney returned with a smile. "Every single day. Come to that, he did it in your case."

The waiter arrived with their food, serving them with well-practiced ease.

"What do you mean," Shelley demanded as the man departed, "he did it in my case?"

"It's like this. J.S. has always maintained that women were underrepresented in the higher echelons at P&L, and since he took over as managing director he's been aiming to rectify the situation. When he heard you wanted to return to London, Shelley, he reckoned that you were ideal material for the sort of promotion he had in mind. But . . ."

"But he wasn't exactly overboard about me personally. Right?"

The amiable Barney looked discomfited. "Put it this way . . . he and Rex weren't exactly great buddies."

"That's the understatement of the year!" Shelley moodily prodded her fish with her fork. "So you mean that, despite believing I was the right person for the job, Jason was tempted to let his personal prejudices sway his judgment?"

"That's just what I don't mean. Being the man he is, J.S. would never be tempted that way."

"You make him sound like a pious automaton."

"No, not that either. Don't be too tough on J.S. He's tough enough on himself without other people joining in."

"*Me* tough on *him?* That's a laugh!"

"Well, aren't you? All this indignation . . . calling him cold-blooded and ruthless and devoid of decent feelings."

"He'd probably take that as a compliment."

Barney laughed. "No comment!"

As if by tacit consent, they switched off the topic of Jason and started discussing the Roystons. She half-wished she could tell Barney about Clare being pregnant. His kindly, unflappable approach carried a sort of moral authority in the organization, and he might be just the person to bring Nick to his senses. But she had promised Clare to keep her mouth shut.

Lunching with Barney was pleasantly relaxing, and she was sorry to notice that the time had flown by. "I don't know about you," she said with a rueful sigh, "but I'll have to hustle. I don't dare be late getting back."

Barney looked amused. "J.S. has got you well trained." He signed the bill and rose. "Let's go."

They walked back along Upper Grosvenor Street, and as they entered the building, Jason was just behind them.

"I thought it was about time I stood Shelley a lunch," Barney explained as the three of them stepped into the elevator.

"How nice." Jason's voice was cold and clipped. "I've got to be out with Carl Rossiter all afternoon, Shelley, but I'll be back later. I shall want your comments about the Cleveland Girl before you leave."

"Right." She hoped she sounded sure of herself, because she certainly didn't feel it.

With Jason safely out of the office all afternoon, Shelley felt less pressured. Nevertheless, the question of Patti Fairfax hung over her like a sword of Damocles, however resolutely she tried to focus her attention on something else. By four o'clock she had concluded that, in order to satisfy Jason that she was being truly impartial, she had better give a thumbs-up to Patti Fairfax. But ten minutes later, her conscience rebelled. Her job was to give a frank, honest opinion, and all her instincts were screaming that Patti Fairfax was the wrong choice. No matter what Jason thought, however much he might penalize her for it, she refused to compromise her professional judgment.

Now that she had finally decided, waiting for Jason was an agony. She longed for his return so she could get the dreaded confrontation over with. Five-thirty came, and Beth cleared her desk and left, bidding Shelley a tight-lipped good night. As the door closed behind her, Shelley gave up all pretense of working and just sat and stared at the clock on the wall ticking off the seconds.

It was 5:57 when she heard the whine of the elevator. Hastily she shuffled papers and bent over the desk to give a semblance of being occupied. Jason strode in briskly, throwing her just a cursory glance as he clipped, "Right, Shelley, come on through, will you?"

In his own office he tossed down his briefcase and looked at Shelley across the wide desk.

"Well?"

"About Patti Fairfax?"

"What else?"

The script she had been rehearsing came out clumsily. "She's quite hopeless. It would be madness to use her. If we put her forward in the presentation this weekend, I'm sure that Sir Mortimer would be shrewd enough to see that P&L had made a ghastly blunder. And his daughter, too, come to that."

"So much for your opinion. Now I want some reasons to justify it."

"Okay." She took a deep breath. "Much as I hate to admit it, Patti is perfect for some campaigns . . . Slikfit jeans, for one. I said it at the time, before I ever knew that Nick was involved with her. She's pert, slick and very sexy . . . the perfect image for kids who buy that sort of jeans to identify with. But when it comes to promoting a chain of wine stores, you're appealing to a broad spectrum of citizens. Okay, I'll accept the fact that Patti would make an instant eye-catcher for most men. But even with the men, I doubt if she'd convey the image we're after for the Cleveland stores—that of a respectable, high-toned business, not a string of cheapjack shops. As for the women . . . Remember that the research findings indicate that more often than not it's the housewife who buys the bottle of wine to go with the evening meal, the housewife who replaces the sherry and so on when supplies get low. For them Patti would rate lower than zero. Definitely a negative factor." Jason's deadpan expression was so unnerving that Shelley broke off and looked at him questioningly.

"Well, go on," he said. "I'm listening."

She took another breath. "We want a completely different sort of model for the Cleveland Girl. Older, for one thing. I'd say the image should be of a married woman in her mid to late twenties. Attractive, outgoing, vital, but not blatantly sexy. Intelligent, too. The kind of person everyone would be glad to know."

Jason nodded and reached for his briefcase. Opening it, he extracted a large envelope from which he flipped out a photograph.

"Someone like her, would you say?"

The face that looked back at Shelley was of a beautiful girl of about her own age. Brunette, her hair fell in soft waves about her delicately molded cheekbones. She was smiling serenely, but in her golden-brown eyes there was a hint of hidden fires . . . of a sensuality that could be aroused by the right man. Her figure, too, was ideal; not too thin, like so many models', but gently rounded in all the right places. It gave Shelley quite a shock to be confronted like this with precisely the woman she'd been visualizing.

"Oh, yes!" she exclaimed. "Someone like her would be fantastic. Who is she?"

Jason smiled. "Her name is Diana Saxby. She's the model we've selected to be the Cleveland Girl."

*"What?"*

"Carl Rossiter and I have been doing the rounds of the model agencies all afternoon, sorting through what they have to offer. We decided that this girl is just about perfect in every way."

Shelley blazed at him in an upsurge of fury. "You mean to tell me that you've kept me worried frantic over this, when all along you'd already decided that Patti Fairfax was no good?"

"Correct."

"For heaven's sake, *why*? Do you enjoy forcing me to make a decision like that, when what I say doesn't even matter?"

"It shouldn't have been so difficult," he countered relentlessly. "You can't seriously have believed that I'd settle for using that kid Patti?"

"What else was I to think after the way you bawled me out when I said it was a ridiculous suggestion?"

"For the wrong reasons, though. As I thought I'd made clear, Shelley. I told you to go away and consider Nick's proposal from square one. You finally arrived at the right conclusion, but it took you a long time. Too long!"

"I was right from the very start," she cried passionately. "I would never have thought twice about using Patti—from any point of view—if you hadn't gotten me all screwed up. I guess it must be your way of punishing me for . . . for . . ."

"You're still allowing your personal life to interfere with your job," he said in a low, dangerous tone.

"And the great Jason Steele never does," she flung at him recklessly. "What sort of a man are you if you can blatantly carry on an affair with Naomi Waterton and still claim to be acting impartially? You must be cold as ice, ruthlessly calculating, and . . ."

"Do *you* think I'm cold as ice, Shelley?" he demanded, his dark eyes burning into her.

"I'm talking about you and Naomi Waterton."

"And I," he retorted, "am talking about me and *you!*"

At least, Shelley thought with a hollow feeling of triumph, he had handed her a weapon to strike him with. "Aren't you doing the very thing you tell me I mustn't do, Jason? We're at the office, remember."

He gestured impatiently. "How I regard you personally, Shelley, and how I regard you business-wise are entirely separate."

"It would have been better," she said bitterly, "if you had followed your natural inclinations and not given me this job on your personal staff. Or if you had refused to accept me on the London staff at all."

Jason gave her a strange, long look that she found hard to read. He knew that Barney must have filled her in, but he didn't seem to object.

"My belief in your talent has been fully vindicated. When you are forced to look at the essentials of a situation, your judgment is very sound. Very shrewd and perceptive." He paused, tapping the desktop with his fingertips. "It's a pity, though, that you can't translate that ability into your private life and not let emotional issues sidetrack you."

She gazed back at him in numb despair while, faintly, the siren of a police car could be heard as it streaked past in the street below. "May I go now, please?" she muttered at length.

"No, wait a minute." Jason came around the desk and stood before her. "Shelley, we've got to talk."

"Isn't that what we've just been doing?"

"About last night."

"Last night," she said huskily, "is in a separate category. And the file is closed. Do you hear?"

He went on as if she hadn't spoken. "I was surprised when I answered my front door and found you standing there. You were very uptight, I could see that. I was hoping that after a glass of wine and something to eat you'd relax a bit and I'd get to learn what it was all about. But instead . . ."

"Let's forget it, please."

"I can't forget it, Shelley. And I don't think you can, either. Attempting to plaster over the memory won't work. So let's have things out in the open and try to talk it through."

"No!" She turned to the door. "I'm leaving right now."

But Jason caught her by the arm and jerked her around to face him. His grip was harsh and implacable. "Why do you always run away from me?"

"I'm not running away!"

"Yes, you are. You've done it time after time. Twice when I've driven you home you've jumped out of the car and rushed into the house like a scalded cat. Then last night you ran out on me— that's what it amounted to. And now again!"

Shelley felt the prickle of unshed tears. "What would be the point of staying here to argue? We've said all there is to say."

"We've only just begun," he replied, his eyes vividly intent. "You say we should forget last night, and I say that's impossible. But okay, let's put it behind us and start over again. Let's take it slowly this time, go out to dinner, do a show. That jazz club I was talking about, maybe, or some nightspot with dancing. You name it, Shelley."

"No!"

"Why are you so insanely stubborn?" he demanded with a flash of impatience. "You enjoyed Sunday . . . you actually managed to force yourself to admit that you'd had a good day. Once or twice you even smiled at me."

"It was good of you to take me out on my anniversary," Shelley said reluctantly. "I appreciated that."

"And because you couldn't bear to feel obligated to me, even to such a minimal extent, you decided to drop in on me at home last night and square the debt. Is that it?"

"That's a lousy thing to suggest."

"So what *is* the explanation of your surprise visit?"

Shelley said nothing, and turned her eyes away from the hostile challenge of his dark gaze. The moments stretched. Suddenly Jason's patience seemed to snap, and with a muttered cry he drew her tightly against him, locking her slender body to the hard lean length of his. Her gasp of protest was stifled when his lips claimed hers possessively, and Shelley was at once flooded with a marvelous, beautiful, tingling elation. Her struggles ceased and her arms slid up across his muscled shoulders as she let herself melt against him. Jason's hands, no longer needing to hold her captive, began to roam over her soft body slowly and caressingly, moving down the channel of her spine and over the warm curve of her hips. With a little moan of arousal Shelley felt his tongue thrust in between her parted lips to taste the inner sweetness, felt her own desire soar and leap to match his mounting passion. She wanted him, heaven help her! She wanted him so much.

Jason drew back a little and looked at her with searching intensity. "Let's go, Shelley," he breathed hoarsely. "Let's go to my place, and . . ."

The magic was broken and Shelley came back to reality with a shudder. What a crazy fool she was, begging to be humiliated all over again.

"What is it?" Jason asked huskily, his dark eyes narrowing.

"Let go of me!" Her voice surprised Shelley herself—it was so crisp and decisive. Jason continued to hold her tightly, but her body was stiff, hard and unyielding. With a muttered curse, he released her.

"Have it your way!"

Suddenly free, Shelley found that her legs were weak and trembly and they almost buckled beneath her weight. But she forced herself to stand upright, glaring back at him with loathing and fury.

"Does it make you feel good to take advantage of me like that? I guess you had it all planned out beforehand. That was why you told me to wait for you, and only came back to the office when everyone else had gone. Isn't that right?"

"You can think what you damned well like," Jason retorted with savage indifference. He began shoving things into his briefcase. "Right, then—I'll leave you in splendid isolation. I won't offer to drive you home, or you'd be sure to suspect my motives."

He was gone, leaving Shelley standing there alone in his office. What was wrong with her, she wondered bleakly, that after her disastrous experience with Rex she had to go and fall in love with another man who was every bit as untrustworthy?

# *Chapter Eleven*

*W*ork at the office built up in a crescendo of activity with preparations for the weekend at Windsor. The hard, exacting schedule had one important plus factor for Shelley. It allowed her no time to brood. When she finally arrived home Thursday night, it was almost 10:45. She just fixed herself a grilled cheese and coffee, and flopped thankfully into bed.

Friday afternoon, when she was in Jason's office checking out a few last-minute details, he ended up by saying, "By the way, Shelley, I've been meaning to tell you that the weekend will be fairly formal. Sir Mortimer favors dressing for dinner, for instance."

"Thanks for bothering to tell me," she flared. "What am I supposed to do about it at this late date?"

"Simmer down!" he said airily. "How about that outfit you wore at the Cosmos conference?"

"I guess it will do," she mumbled.

"It will more than do! And you'd better toss in a swimsuit while you're about it."

"How about my polo gear, shall I be needing that? And maybe a floppy hat for croquet on the lawn?"

"Scrub the sarcasm, Shelley. Be ready tomorrow morning at ten-thirty. I'll be round to collect you."

His proposal filled her with dismay. "I'd planned to get to Windsor by train," she said stiffly. "I'd prefer that."

"And I'm telling you that you'll be getting there in my car! Everyone else but you has their own transport, and I'm not having a member of my staff dumped on Sir Mortimer's doorstep by the local taxi, baggage in hand."

Shelley gave a sullen shrug. "Okay, you're the boss."

"An admission you seem to make grudgingly," he observed. "Right, back to work, Shelley. I'm sure you've still got plenty to do."

The temperature rose to sultry heights on Friday night, and London wakened to a blazing heat wave. The brilliant weather brought the crowds out, and the river embankment was humming with activity when Shelley and Jason set off. The rowing eights practicing in their narrow rowboats were stripped to their shorts, a harmony of rhythmic muscular movement as they dipped and pulled on their oars.

"It takes me back," Jason observed. "I used to row for Oxford."

"Really?" Shelley couldn't resist a jibe. "It's kind of hard to imagine you as just one member of a team. Taking orders with the rest, instead of dishing them out."

"Nobody can give orders effectively," said Jason, "who hasn't first learned how to take them."

Shelley fell silent, wondering how she was going to get through this journey. They could hardly spend the entire time sniping at one another, and she was scared of embarking on any topic that might veer toward the personal. Somehow she had to try to stay calm and placid, but it was going to be difficult in the confined intimacy of Jason's car.

She found herself constantly studying his chiseled profile, studying the broad, long-fingered hands that lightly gripped the steering wheel. The bronzed skin glinted with tiny golden hairs where the sun struck through the windshield. When Jason moved one hand suddenly in her direction, Shelley couldn't help flinching away, afraid that he was going to touch her. But it was only to flip a cassette into the slot.

"Er . . . shouldn't we be talking about the presentation?" she finally asked to break the silence.

"What for?" he asked.

"Well, to make sure that we're adequately prepared in every possible way."

Jason didn't even flick an eye at her. "We already *are* adequately prepared. In every possible way. Relax, Shelley."

Relax, the man said, when her nerves were stretched to snapping point. Once at Chithurst Manor, she mused consolingly, she could lose herself among the gathering guests and wouldn't be so devastatingly aware of Jason's nearness. He'd be totally occupied with Naomi, no doubt. And that was a darned good thing, she told herself sternly. It would show Jason for the calculating womanizer he really was, and help her to flush him right out of her system.

Yet she couldn't fool herself. It hurt quite desperately to think of Jason and Naomi Waterton together. She despised Naomi, and yet she envied her with all her heart . . .

"There it is!" said Jason suddenly.

Shelley jumped, startled out of her brooding. "We're there already?"

"No, you weren't listening, Shelley. Windsor Castle—over there. Residence of the English sovereign for nigh on nine hundred years. It's the largest inhabited castle in the world. I was hoping you might be a tiny bit impressed."

"I am!" It was a truly majestic sight, ethereal in the misty blue haze of this hot summer morning. The castle stood proudly atop a chalk cliff, its great round tower and stone bastions rising out of the skirting of trees, with the River Thames flowing at its foot. "Nine hundred years, huh? It sounds as if you've been doing your homework again."

"No need this time. I do remember a little about my country's history." He pointed in a fresh direction. "That's Eton College, the famous boys' school. Can you see it . . . the red brick buildings?"

Shelley nodded. "I guess that's not as old as the castle."

"Not nearly." Jason grinned. "A mere five hundred years, I think."

"Was that where you went to school?"

"Hardly! My father couldn't have run to Eton's fancy fees on his income as a vet. My education was rather more practically commercial. Which is why I'm managing director of an advertising agency and not a diplomat in the foreign office or whatever."

"Do you ever regret that?" Shelley queried.

"Why should I? I know what my talents are."

They had left the main road and were driving more slowly along a winding country lane where foxgloves and pink campions grew lushly on the grass shoulder, and birds flitted among the hedge-tops.

"Nearly there now," said Jason. "This high stone wall completely surrounds Chithurst Manor. We'll reach the main gates in another half-mile."

"It's a mighty big place."

"Sir Mortimer's a mighty big man."

The entrance could now be seen, and Jason slowed to take the turn. Ornamental wrought-iron gates stood open between huge stone pillars that were topped with sculptured griffins. As they drove through, the gateman standing at the doorway of his little circular lodge touched his cap to them. The driveway swept in a series of gentle curves across rolling parkland that was dotted with stately trees—oak and ash, great spreading cedars and the late-leafing beech. Away to the right stretched a long lake shaped like a silver-blue scimitar.

The house came into view, still some distance off, its hundred or more windows glittering reflections of the morning sunlight. It was a gracious mansion built of warm, honey-colored stone, with terraced gardens on all sides.

"It's really beautiful!" Shelley exclaimed. "Are the Clevelands an ancient family?"

"Only in the sense that we all have ancestors. Sir Mortimer's father was a humble jobbing gardener, and Sir Mortimer made his first hundred pounds by borrowing his dad's tools and cleaning up cottage gardens. He told me once that his first million came a lot more easily."

"He sounds like a determined man."

"He's that, all right! Sir Mortimer knows what he wants, and he expects to get it."

They pulled up before the columned portico. Two menservants appeared at once and hastened down the apron of shallow steps. One of them, bowing deeply, opened the car door for Shelley.

"Good morning, madam. Good morning, Mr. Steele. If you will give Barker your keys, please, he will attend to the luggage and put the car away."

They followed the dignified, black-garbed figure up the steps and into the house. The main entrance hall was a splendor of pale, rosy-gray marble, the walls hung with a number of massive oil paintings. A wide, gilt-balustered staircase rose at the far end to a gallery on the upper floor.

"Sir Mortimer's instructions," the manservant intoned, "are that drinks will be served on the south terrace at noon."

"We'll be there," said Jason easily. He glanced at his wristwatch. "Right, Shelley. I'll meet you here in the hall in fifteen minutes."

The room allocated to Shelley was large and stately, containing every modern comfort. It had thick carpeting and a well-sprung bed, velvet boudoir chairs, and long brocade draperies at the two huge windows, which were thrown open to a view of emerald-green lawns stretching down to the lake. The decor was a harmony of pink and gold, contrasting with the adjoining bathroom in varied tones of blue.

Her suitcase had already been brought up, and Shelley took out a few things, leaving the rest of the unpacking until later. She freshened herself and went down to join Jason.

To reach the south terrace they descended an elegant flight of stone steps, set at intervals with Grecian urns of white marble containing bright red geraniums and trailing greenery. Beyond was a magnificent view of the wooded Thames valley, with the river a twisting silver ribbon running through it.

The terrace was thronged with people. Jason led her straight across to Sir Mortimer. Shelley remembered the tall, well-preserved man with a sleek head of white hair and neat Vandyke beard from when she'd met him once before with Rex. Not surprisingly, he didn't remember her.

"Mrs. Armitage," he mused. "You are from America, I gather. Do you like it in this country?"

She had a part to play, and she'd play it as best she knew how. "It's great, Sir Mortimer. And I certainly envy you this beautiful home."

"Jason, *darling!*" The sultry voice of Naomi Waterton floated across the terrace. Shelley glanced around to see Sir Mortimer's daughter bearing down on them, her arms outstretched in welcome. Wearing a slinky, sexy white jumpsuit, with a tumbled mass of chunky ethnic jewelry draped around her neck and wrists, she looked quite devastating. She greeted Jason with a kiss full on the lips. Totally ignoring Shelley, she slid an arm through his and drew him away. Sir Mortimer watched them go, a benign smile on his face. The blindly doting father, thought Shelley sourly, who never in a million years would see his daughter for what she really was.

A white-jacketed manservant sidled up and Shelley took a drink from the silver tray, not caring what it might be. Sir Mortimer proceeded to introduce her to various members of the Cleveland Enterprises staff. Being well-briefed, she was able to match the new faces to familiar names. After a few moments Sir Mortimer excused himself, leaving her with a tall, stoutish man named Jim Bellamy, the group's chief accountant, together with his plump wife.

"Our Naomi has latched onto Jason in double-quick time," this lady observed, much amused.

"Didn't she, though!" said Shelley.

With no more than this brief exchange, they were buddies. "A tiny piece of advice," murmured the older woman. "Watch Naomi's claws. They're most dangerous when she's purring loudest."

"Gwen!" her husband said warningly, with an anxious glance over his shoulder.

"Oh, don't be silly, Jim." She laughed, unconcerned. "Shelley isn't going to tell on me, are you, dear?"

"Of course not!"

Barney and Suzy Moffat strolled over to join them, and they all chatted together until luncheon was announced. Naomi had carried Jason off somewhere, and only now did they reappear, her arm still linked possessively with his. The meal was an alfresco buffet served from long tables on the patio. Delicious cold meats arranged on huge platters, a side of smoked salmon being carved into wafer-thin slices by a man in a chef's tall white hat. Dishes of crab and lobster, puffy little bite-size *vol-au-vents,* and all kinds of savory quiches and salads. There was a great bowl of trifle, a mountain of strawberries, and crystal jugs of rich yellow cream.

Shelley loaded her plate with delicacies and strolled to the balustrade where she could sit on a sculptured stone seat and look over the terraced grounds to the magnificent countryside beyond. A gurgle of familiar laughter made her turn her head. A few yards off to the right, Naomi was teasingly feeding Jason tidbits. Shelley felt the censorious weight of his gaze come to rest on her—because, she assumed, she wasn't socializing. She rose hastily to her feet and joined a threesome standing by the steps.

The first business session was scheduled for four o'clock, to finish at seven for dinner at eight. The swimming pool seemed enticing on this hot afternoon, so when people dispersed after lunch, Shelley decided to have a dip. Returning to her room, she collected her black one-piece swimsuit and headed for the lower terrace.

Surprisingly, the pool was deserted. After changing in one of the chalets, Shelley stretched herself out on a lounge chair, enjoying the feel of the sun on her bare skin. The sumptuous meal, added to the lethargic warmth of the summer afternoon, made her eyelids droop, but they snapped open again at the sound of voices.

Jason and Naomi were emerging from a changing chalet at the far end of the line. They were stripped for swimming, he in red briefs and Naomi in a daringly sexy white bikini. How blatant they were, she thought with a stab of misery. How totally uncaring that the nature of their relationship was laid bare to everyone.

Naomi, she had to concede, possessed a stunning figure. But Shelley's gaze was held by Jason, the sight of his virile, masculine perfection causing the blood to race in her veins. From his thick peat-dark hair down the length of his tautly muscled body and long, powerful legs, he was in superb physical shape.

Shelley felt quite certain they must have seen her, but for the moment Naomi was looking away, playfully pretending to be scared of the water.

"Promise, Jason, darling, that you won't throw me in like you did last time?" She giggled. Only then did she allow herself to acknowledge Shelley's presence. "Ah! We have company, I see! The ubiquitous

Mrs. . . . er, Armitage, isn't it? Are you waiting for someone?" Naomi asked sweetly, coming nearer. "Not one of the other women's husbands, I hope?"

"Don't worry, I'm not desperate for a man. I was merely enjoying a peaceful sunbath—until now."

Naomi raised ironic eyebrows. "And we're disturbing you? Isn't that a shame, Jason, darling? Never mind, Mrs. Armitage, we'll have our swim and leave you in peace."

She went to the pool's edge and stood poised, making—as she was well aware—a very provocative picture with her long, slender legs and lissome body. But Jason didn't at once follow her.

"Aren't you coming in too, Shelley?" he asked.

She avoided meeting his eyes. "No, thanks, I prefer my own company."

She watched his retreating figure as he went to join Naomi without another word. They stood side by side, arms raised, then launched themselves in a simultaneous dive, cleaving the water at the same instant like two swift arrows.

For several painful minutes Shelley stuck it out, sitting there and listening to the sounds of their splashing and laughter from the pool. Then she got to her feet and went back to the chalet to dress. Naomi, she knew to her seething fury, had scored a victory.

The library at Chithurst Manor was the site of the presentation, and by four o'clock everyone was gathered there. Easels had been set up for the demonstrations, and there was also a large-screen video player and a slide projector.

Sir Mortimer opened the proceedings with a little speech of welcome to the representatives of Prescott and Liedermann, for whose collective talent he expressed the greatest respect. He laid it on the line, however, that just because the agency handled several other of his advertising accounts, it didn't mean they were guaranteed to handle Cleveland Wines.

Shelley caught an exchange of glances between Naomi and Jason. Sir Mortimer's daughter, it was obvious, chose to disassociate herself from that last remark.

When Sir Mortimer finished speaking, Jason stood up and introduced the first item on the agenda, a ten-minute videotape of the P&L organization in action.

After the film, Carl Rossiter outlined the advertising campaign proposed for the launch and promotion of Cleveland Wines. Shelley stood at one of the easels and turned the pages of a huge portfolio for him while Carl commented on each ad in turn, explaining the exact nature of its objectives. The idea of a Cleveland Girl, together with photographs of the model suggested, was greeted with distinct murmurs of approval from the assembled Cleveland personnel.

There were no hitches, and the time flew by. A number of slides were shown suggesting shopfront and interior design to give the new chain the desired corporate identity. Finally they came to the matter of expenditure. Enormous sums were tossed off by Barney Moffat as if pounds were peanuts.

Just before seven o'clock Sir Mortimer rose again to wind up the session.

"Thank you, gentlemen . . . and Mrs. Armitage," he added with a little bob of his head. "You've given us a lot to think about, a lot to digest. And now we will relax for the remainder of the evening. Tomorrow morning we shall meet here again for a question-and-answer session."

The P&L staff, insofar as they could gather together for a quiet word without danger of being overheard, seemed of the opinion that all had gone well.

"Mind you," said Frank Darby on a quick, nervous laugh, "J.S. is by far our biggest asset. All the clever advertising ideas in the world wouldn't help us unless we had Naomi Waterton's vote."

Shelley escaped to her room, sick at heart. Dressing for dinner, she wondered how she was going to get through the evening ahead. How, if Naomi deliberately needled her, would she hold back from giving as good as she got, which would undoubtedly make Jason blow his top.

Downstairs, the sight of Naomi spreading herself all over Jason sent Shelley's despair plummeting to new depths. Why did she let jealousy get to her like this?

Jason looked incredibly attractive wearing, like all the men, a black tuxedo. The women were in their most lavish evening dresses. Naomi, clearly braless, was wearing a halter-neck gown in black crepe de chine. Its understated plainness put all the other women's outfits totally in the shade, including Shelley's own Java-print dress that she'd felt so happily confident in at Cheltenham.

When dinner was announced, Sir Mortimer led a procession into the formal dining room with Carl Rossiter's wife on his arm, Jason and Naomi following. The rest formed twos as best they could, and Shelley found herself escorted by Frank Darby. Sir Mortimer and Naomi took their places at either end of the long banqueting table, with Jason on Naomi's right hand. Shelley, from her seat a few places along, watched them laughing together with a gnawing sense of pain.

The evening proved one long ordeal for Shelley,

and she earned Jason's disapproval several times by responding to Naomi's thinly veiled insults with barbs of her own. It came as a relief to learn that Sir Mortimer had strongly held views about bedtime. Around eleven o'clock he made it plain that, in his opinion, it was time they all retired. His guests meekly took the hint and said their good nights.

Up in her room, Shelley knew that she wouldn't get to sleep for a long while, if at all. However much she tried to keep a tight rein on her thoughts, they always jumped back into the same painful groove—Jason and Naomi. In which room had they joined company by now? she anguished. Doubtless they would stay together until the early morning, separating just before the servants were likely to be about. Or would Naomi even care about that?

After the blazing heat of the day, the night seemed breathless. There was a balcony to her room, and Shelley opened the long window and stepped out. But even here it felt unrelentingly sultry. She went back inside and undressed and showered; then, slipping into her nightdress and a thin cotton robe, she returned to the balcony once more.

She remained standing there, her hands resting on the cool stone of the balustrade as the minutes slowly dragged on. She had even less inclination, though, to lie feverishly tossing in bed, tormented by images of another bed just a few rooms from hers, where a man and a woman would be engaged in passionate lovemaking.

Presently Shelley heard a faint tapping sound. At first she dismissed it as no more than the creak of branches disturbed by some unfelt breeze. But when the sound came again, she realized that someone was knocking at her door.

She went back inside and asked warily, "Who is it?"

"Jason! Let me in." It was a whisper, just loud enough for her to hear.

"What do you want?" she asked nervously, opening the door a mere crack. "You . . . you can't come in."

She might have saved her breath. Jason pushed the door wider and came right inside, closing it quietly behind him. He was wearing a thigh-length silk dressing robe . . . and nothing else, it seemed.

"You and I have got to have a talk," he said grimly, "before you do any more damage."

"I don't get you."

"Oh, yes, you do! Just what the hell did you think you were playing at tonight? Naomi isn't a woman to cross swords with, Shelley. She's out of your league."

"Very much in yours, though."

"I can handle Naomi, but that's another issue. I won't stand for a member of my staff deliberately going out of her way to needle a client. Particularly an employee I've picked out as being potential executive material."

"And I'm the sort of person who won't stand for being sniped at without shooting back. So it just proves what a big mistake you made in picking me for the job. Agreed?"

His eyes were stern under his strongly marked brows. "I didn't make a mistake about you, Shelley. You're perfectly capable of keeping a check on your temper when it suits you. So I can only conclude that trying to get under Naomi's skin is a piece of deliberate sabotage."

"That's a crazy thing to suggest."

"Is it? Then give me another explanation."

Shelley stared back at him helplessly. How could she admit to Jason the true cause of her hostility toward Naomi—that the sight of the two of them together and Naomi's smugly possessive attitude goaded her to a frenzy of jealousy. That since the fateful episode at his flat on Tuesday evening her thoughts had dwelt on him to the exclusion of everything else. That she loved him, loved him quite desperately.

"If Naomi needles me," she said mutinously, "then I've got the right to needle her back."

"Not as long as you're working for P&L, you haven't."

"Then I guess I'd better quit working for P&L."

Jason took a quick stride toward her, causing the dressing robe to swing apart and expose the full muscled length of his thigh. Shelly shivered involuntarily and backed away. She mustn't, she simply *must not,* allow him to touch her. Just imagining his fingers on her skin brought a torment of wanting. The potent aura of his masculinity, pulsing across the two feet of space between them, seemed to tug at her like a powerful magnet. All her clamoring instincts urged her to go into his arms. But that way she was doomed. At all events she had to resist Jason's hypnotic spell, even at the cost of quitting her job and never seeing him again.

"That's stupid talk," Jason grated harshly. "What I require of you is very simple, Shelley. You only have to divorce your private feelings from the demands of your job. Whether or not you dislike Naomi is totally beside the point. She is the daughter of one of our major clients and I demand that you show her due respect."

"And what you show her is respect, too, I suppose?" Shelley spoke with icy sarcasm, though she felt like weeping instead.

"That is also beside the point," he rapped. "We're talking about *you*. So tomorrow morning, Shelley, you will keep your claws sheathed as far as Naomi is concerned. Understood?"

"You'd better tell Naomi to keep off my back, then!" she riposted. "I can't see you doing that, though—no way! You have to watch your P's and Q's, don't you? It has to be 'Yes, Naomi, no, Naomi, three bags full, Naomi!' "

Anger flamed in his face. "Cut that out, Shelley!"

But she was past holding back. "It would be fascinating to know what kind of deal you struck with Naomi. Is it a watertight contract drawn up by our legal department? Bedroom services traded against business favors? Do you reckon so many thousands of pounds spent on advertising in exchange for . . . for . . ."

Her flood of bitter taunts was brought to a sudden halt when Jason caught hold of her by the shoulders. His grip was fierce and unrelenting, his fingers digging cruelly into her flesh. "I told you to cut that out, Shelley. You're getting hysterical."

Her tempestuous fury dissolved at his touch, swept away by a torrent of emotion that made her feel dizzy. Yet some tattered remnants of her will to resist him remained, and she struggled to escape his grasp, but in vain. Jason held her captive with contemptuous ease.

"Let me go!" she sobbed.

"Not till you give me your promise to act sensibly toward Naomi in future. That tomorrow you'll keep a tight curb on your tongue."

Rebelliously Shelley drew breath for yet another

jibe, but before she could get the words out, Jason checked her by the effective method of clamping his mouth over hers. At the achingly familiar contact of his warm lips, Shelley felt engulfed by a flood tide of yearning. She seemed in some strange way to become two people, one half of her standing aside in helpless agony and watching her alter ego being swept away to drowning destruction. She had to struggle; she had to fight! And yet, how was she to resist Jason when every nerve in her body screamed for the rapturous enchantment of his lovemaking?

Jason's lips were demanding now, his tongue probing through to meet and curl sweetly against her own. His hands slid over her body, her cotton nightgown and robe offering only the flimsiest barrier. She was elatedly aware through Jason's thin silk robe of the throbbing arousal of his own desire. She wanted this man, longed to abandon all common sense and decency and let him take possession of her right here and now in a tumultuous explosion of mutual passion. This man who had come straight from another woman's bed, and would be returning to it.

Shelley gasped aloud as she felt him press her backward as though to lay her on the bed, and her fingertips dug convulsively into the hard, rippling flesh of his chest where the robe gaped open. But her other self, the passive witness of her drowning, finally summoned the determination to fight. With a superhuman surge of strength she pushed herself back from Jason, dragging her mouth away from his kiss.

"Stop this! You . . . you sicken me."

He gave a grim laugh from deep in his throat. "I hardly think that's true, Shelley."

"It is! It is!"

"You mean you *wish* it were true?" he suggested. "For some obscure reason you wish that you could prevent yourself from falling prey to my fatal attraction."

With another angry thrust Shelley almost broke free. "You have one hell of an opinion of yourself, don't you?"

"I never make the mistake of underrating myself." Jason held her wrist purposefully, making it impossible for her to twist away. "Let's get this thing straightened out, Shelley. I find you extremely attractive, infinitely desirable, and I don't mind admitting it. But you . . . Though it's clear you feel the same way about me, you fight like crazy to deny it. Why, for heaven's sake? Why not admit it openly, joyfully? It can be wonderfully good between a man and a woman who want each other, and between you and me it could be sensational. The potential was there the other night, but then you suddenly went cold on me at the very last moment."

"Must you remind me of that?" she protested, bitter loathing in her voice. "It was horrible!"

"Not horrible. Disappointing, I agree. Very far short of what it should have been." His grip tightened and he began to draw her to him again. "Let me show you now, Shelley."

"No!" she cried, on the edge of panic.

Jason paid no heed, wrapping her in his arms once more, and at once the ice in her body melted in a blaze of longing. His fingertips drew a shivering snake of delight down her spine; then with both hands he cupped her softly rounded flesh to draw her closer against him so that she could feel the thrust of his resurgent passion. Sliding his hands up to her shoulders, he pushed off her flimsy cotton robe so that it slithered to the floor in a tumbled heap. He touched his lips to the soft bare skin of her shoulders and laid a burning trail of tiny kisses down to the secret valley between her breasts where the V of her nightdress plunged. Shelley's head fell back and she moaned aloud at the terrifying stab of longing she felt. But somehow she gathered together her last tattered shreds of willpower to resist a total surrender. She forced her body to become rigidly stiff, refusing him the pliant submission he sought.

For moments longer Jason endeavored to arouse her. But at last he gave up and stepped away. His voice was thick and husky. "Why are you like this, Shelley?"

"Why? Because I find you despicable."

"That's nonsense, and you know it."

"Can't you get it into your skull that I don't want there to be anything between us? I've begged you over and over to leave me alone and let me get on with my job. You just won't listen, though. If you insist on keeping me on your personal staff . . . okay, I'll do the work as well as I can. But nothing more, Jason. That's as far as it goes!"

"I can't accept that."

Shelley stared at him bravely, though her eyes were misty with blinked-back tears. "Don't my wishes count with you at all?"

"Your wishes? Can you put your hand on your heart, Shelley, and swear that anything I've done has been against your *true* wishes?"

Not answering that, she said, "My wish at this moment is for you to leave my bedroom. Besides," she taunted, "isn't it time you went to Naomi's room? She must be getting impatient by now."

Jason's dark eyes glittered dangerously for a moment; then he turned and walked to the door. With his hand on the knob, he shot her a glance over his shoulder. "Just you remember what I said about you and Naomi. Cut out the sniping."

"I'd be a whole lot happier," Shelley retorted, "if I never had to say another word to Naomi Waterton."

When Jason had gone, Shelley gathered up her robe from where it lay in a crumpled heap on the floor and drew it on again. She returned to the balcony, leaning on the balustrade and gazing up at the light of the stars. A faint breeze rustled among the treetops, a melancholy sound that seemed to carry a distant echo of Clare's heartfelt cry on the night Nick walked out on her.

*Okay, when you're fool enough to fall in love with a man—God help you!—you want him all to yourself. But if you can only have a part of him, then you settle for the most you can get. Anything is better than nothing.*

Was she being a fool to spurn what Jason was offering her? No one woman could ever hope to have more than a tiny part of him, because that was all Jason Steele was willing to give of himself. So why not settle for what she *could* get—pathetically little though it was.

Her mind didn't work like Clare's, though. Not about Jason. Maybe she was too selfish, too possessive. But a few nights of sexual passion would be no compensation for the agony of sharing the man she loved with other women.

# Chapter Twelve

The household arrangements at Chithurst Manor were on a scale of Edwardian extravagance. Shelley was given to understand by the maid who brought her early-morning tea that an array of traditional English breakfast dishes would be available in the dining room—bacon and all kinds of eggs, grilled kidneys and sausages, poached haddock. Alternatively, she could opt for a tray in her room. She chose the latter as less of a strain on her nerves, ordering a lightly boiled egg and toast with a pot of tea.

Shortly after the maid withdrew, there was a tap on the door. Or rather, a sharp, authoritative rap. Shelley's heart sank. Surely not Jason back again?

"Who is it?" she called.

In response, Naomi Waterton swept into the room, her raven-black hair swinging loosely about her shoulders. She wore a lacy peach-colored negligee, nipped in with a sash at her slender waist and falling in soft folds to her ankles. Though Naomi had applied light touches of makeup there was a hollow-eyed look about her beautiful face this morning. The legacy, Shelley thought with a pang, of a long night of passionate lovemaking. No doubt she herself also had a hollow-eyed look—the legacy in her case of a long night of sleepless tossing and turning.

"Good morning, Mrs. Waterton," she murmured, steeling herself to be civil. "How can I help you?"

Naomi crossed to the dressing table and sat on the velvet-covered stool, crossing her long legs elegantly. "I think," she began, making a business of examining her fingernails, "that it's high time you and I had a little chat, Mrs. Armitage."

"What about?" asked Shelley. She threw back the covers and slipped out of bed, reaching for her robe. She would feel at less of a disadvantage on her feet.

Naomi treated her to a long, probing gaze from her green-gold eyes before speaking. "Tell me," she said at length, with studied laziness, "do you want Prescott and Liedermann to win the Cleveland Wines account?"

"Naturally I do. I work for them, don't I?"

"Then why," drawled Naomi, "do you act as if it's your dearest wish to see them lose it?"

"What are you talking about?" cried Shelley hotly. "I put in a great deal of hard work this past week preparing for the presentation. Everybody has. So it's crazy to suggest that I don't want my agency to get the account. Perhaps," she muttered through clenched teeth, "you'd better simply tell me what you're talking about. Because I haven't the faintest idea."

"No?" Naomi's lovely eyes narrowed, but her voice retained its ironic lilt. "Surely you aren't going to try to pretend that Jason Steele wasn't in this room last night?"

"So what, Mrs. Waterton?" she retorted, tossing discretion aside. "Are you jealous of me? Are you scared that I might steal him from you?"

Naomi laughed, mocking and self-confident. "Me, jealous of you? That's a joke! If you imagine that you could ever be more to Jason than just a whim of the moment, someone with whom to pass the odd evening when he's got nothing better to do, I advise you to think again. Jason is out of your league, you pathetic little schemer."

Out of his league! It was the same phrase that Jason himself had used. Shelley's eyes pricked with tears at this vitriolic attack, but she faced Naomi with a defiant tilt of her chin as she recklessly flung out words calculated to wound in return.

"If that's how you view the situation, then why should you care? Don't tell me that you're so quaintly old-fashioned that the idea of Jason having a little extracurricular sex with me shocks you? Or can't you bear the idea of sharing your current man, even occasionally?"

Naomi stood up. "I never share a man, Mrs. Armitage. *Never!*"

"You mean," queried Shelley, "that they're expected to remain faithful until you're ready to discard them?" But her sarcasm missed its mark.

"That's exactly right, Mrs. Armitage. If I ever caught a man two-timing me, he'd be finished. And I do mean *finished!*"

Shelley drew in a quick breath. "So shouldn't you be having this conversation with Jason rather than with me? If you plan to hang on to him a while longer, you'd better make sure that he knows the score. Tell him to be a good little boy, or else!"

Before Naomi could find an answer to that, a tap on the door heralded the arrival of Shelley's breakfast. The maid came in and slid the tray onto the bedside table.

The interruption had given Naomi time to control her anger. She strolled over to the window and stood looking out across the sunlit parkland. "For your information, Mrs. Armitage—just so you can't claim that you don't know the score—I may decide to marry Jason. I'm giving the matter serious thought. But whether I do or not, *you* will steer clear of him. Is that understood?"

Naomi *marry* Jason! In her worst fears Shelley had never envisaged this. And yet it made a horrible sort of sense. They were both hard-as-nails, ruthlessly ambitious people . . . That Naomi Waterton should be considering a replacement husband was understandable enough, he would serve as her background, her escort, her obedient, attentive lover. She was apparently planning to buy herself the man of her choice with the lure of her father's vast wealth.

"I asked you a question," said Naomi in a crisp voice. "Do you fully understand the situation?"

She understood all too well! If Naomi Waterton was thwarted in her plans regarding Jason—whatever she finally decided that she wanted from him—she would make use of her far-reaching power to exact vengeance.

"You can do what you damn well like, Mrs. Waterton. You don't scare me."

"Not if it means ruin for the man you love?"

Shelley caught her breath. "What gives you the idea that I'm in love with Jason?"

"One only has to look at your face when he's around. I'd have thought that after going through one marriage you'd have got girlish dreams of great romance out of your system. But not so, it seems."

Shelley wished that she could deny loving Jason flatly and emphatically. But something held her back from uttering the outright lie.

"So just let's get this straight," Naomi continued. "Whatever there is between you and Jason, it must stop right now."

"There isn't anything between us," Shelley faltered wretchedly. Dear heaven, Naomi surely couldn't know—Jason would never have told her—that they had gone to bed together a few nights ago. She plunged on, "I promise you that nothing happened in this room last night. And nothing ever *will* happen between Jason and me. Won't that satisfy you?"

"You'd better mean it," said Naomi ominously. "I'll remind you that there's a lot at stake. Not just the new wine stores' advertising, but all the other Cleveland Enterprises accounts that are presently handled by Prescott and Liedermann. In total, the annual billings come to nearly ten million pounds."

"And you're threatening to take it all away?" gasped Shelley, deeply shocked. "Everything?"

"I hope it won't prove necessary. But if you behave stupidly, I warn you, P&L is going to come a cropper. Losing all the Cleveland business would be a disaster for the agency, and the American bosses would want to see heads rolling. Jason would be the first in line."

It was monstrous . . . blackmail on a massive scale. Shelley felt sick with disgust and fury. But she could not ruin Jason—and how many others of the staff at P&L?—just for the sake of preserving her pride. She would have to give Naomi what she wanted.

"Do you want me to quit working at P&L?" she asked, swamped by a feeling of defeat.

"I don't give a damn whether you quit or not. I'm just telling you this—forget your romantic ideas about Jason Steele. Wipe them out of your mind. If you don't, you've been warned what to expect."

Clearly Naomi knew that she had won. There was a smug smile on her face as she moved across to the door. "Jason and I and a few others are going riding for an hour this morning before the meeting," she said, raking her two hands sensuously through her gleaming, bed-rumpled hair. "You will not be joining us, Mrs. Armitage. Understood?"

Shelley nodded dully. She had no fighting spirit left in her. If Naomi had threatened her personally, she'd have fought back like a tigress, whatever the cost to herself. But by holding Jason's career as hostage, by threatening the livelihood of her colleagues at P&L, Naomi had achieved an easy victory.

Everybody assembled in the library for the second meeting on the dot of eleven-thirty. Sir Mortimer was in the driver's seat this time, with his various executives ranged on either side of him at the long table, Naomi on his right hand.

Sir Mortimer opened with some complimentary remarks about yesterday's presentation by P&L, but he carefully stressed the fact that the situation was still fluid. He himself had several queries he wanted to put, and doubtless his colleagues had questions of their own.

The instant the meeting broke up, Shelley went over to Barney and Suzy Moffat. "You live at Wimbledon, don't you? So Putney wouldn't be far off your route home. Any chance of my cadging a lift?"

"You're more than welcome, love," Barney assured her. "But I thought you'd be returning to town with Jason."

"Oh, no . . ." She could think of no reasonable explanation, so she left it ambiguously vague.

Barney nodded with a friendly smile. "Right, then, I'll tell them to put your case in our car."

There followed yet another sumptuous meal, and the afternoon drifted by in social pleasantries. For Shelley it seemed an endless ordeal. About six o'clock, after tea and dainty cakes had been served, there was at long last a move to go. Cars were brought around to the front portico, and Sir Mortimer and Naomi stood together at the head of the steps to bid their guests good-bye. When it was Shelley's turn, Sir Mortimer took her hand and pressed it warmly. To complicate matters, Jason came up at that instant and took her elbow.

"All set? We'll be off in a minute, then." He grinned at their host disarmingly. "Sir Mortimer likes to keep us guessing, Shelley. It's the client's privilege, and I'm not complaining. But no man who has made his sort of millions could fail to be aware that P&L can do more for Cleveland Wines than any other ad agency in Britain."

Sir Mortimer chuckled. "I like a nice show of confidence in a man. Eh, Naomi?"

But Naomi didn't respond. Doubtless, thought Shelley, she didn't appreciate the way Jason's hand remained on her elbow. Tactfully she tried to ease herself away, but his grip was too firm.

"Thank you again for the splendid hospitality, Sir Mortimer, and I'll be looking forward to getting your call in the next day or so with the verdict."

As Jason turned for a final word with Naomi, Shelley was at last able to pull free. She went over to Barney's black Citroën, wishing that he and Suzy would get a move on. But they were still chatting with Cleveland's chief accountant and his wife. She saw Jason break away and walk lightly down the steps. Spotting Shelley, he changed direction and came across to her.

"What are you doing here?" he asked. "My car's over there."

Shelley stared back at him woodenly, very conscious of Naomi's watchful gaze from the steps. "Barney and Suzy are giving me a lift home. It's more on their way than yours."

"You're coming with me," he said, frowning darkly.

Shelley shook her head. "I'd prefer it this way. Besides, my luggage is already in Barney's car."

"So we'll take it out of Barney's car." Jason called to the Moffats, who were now coming over, "There's been an idiotic mix-up, Barney. Shelley's driving with me."

Suzy, sensing friction in the air, glanced at each of them interestedly. Barney, less aware of nuances, took the situation at face value.

"I must admit, I thought it was a bit odd when Shelley asked us for a lift," he said with a cheerful grin as he took out her suitcase and handed it over to Jason. " 'Bye, then, Shelley . . . J.S. See you both in the morning."

It would have been far better, Shelley thought wretchedly as she settled in Jason's car, not to have gone through that abortive charade. This way, the fact that she was riding with Jason would be doubly underlined for Naomi. She must be livid!

"What the dickens was all that about?" Jason demanded as he swung the car onto the driveway.

"What was what all about?"

"Don't play games with me, Shelley. I'm not in the mood."

She bit her lip. "I thought it would be simpler to ride with Barney and Suzy."

"Simpler? In what way?"

Shelley hesitated, then said, "My relationship with you could be misunderstood."

"As if it mattered—who by?"

"Naomi Waterton, for instance."

"You can leave me to worry about Naomi," he clipped. He drove on in silence for several minutes, then stated, "We'll find somewhere pleasant to stop for dinner."

"No!" she responded in a panic. "I . . . I don't feel in the least bit hungry. We've been stuffed to the eyebrows with food."

"Granted. But we'll need something before the evening's done. Tell you what, I'll drive straight to Putney and you can fix us something at your place."

"I've nothing in the fridge." It was the quickest excuse Shelley could think of.

"You must have a few odds and ends in the larder, even if it's only sardines and crispbread."

Danger sirens were screaming in her head. If she let him come to the flat, suppose Naomi found out? The way Jason was acting, he'd think nothing of casually mentioning it to Naomi himself . . . and then what would be the result? The loss of all the Cleveland accounts . . . the end of Jason Steele as a major figure in advertising! She hadn't a doubt that Naomi's threat had been made in deadly earnest.

"I'm sorry, Jason," she said in a clipped, brittle

voice. "I'm not going to ask you in. Just drive me home and drop me off at the front door."

"There are things we've got to get cleared up, Shelley."

"They can wait till tomorrow at the office. Our working weekend is now at an end."

Jason shook his head. "It's nothing to do with work."

"In that case," she retorted, "there isn't anything for us to talk about."

Jason made no reply, but Shelley had the distinct feeling that he wouldn't leave the matter there. After a minute, he remarked with brisk cheerfulness, "We clinched the Cleveland Wines account; I suppose you realize that?"

"How can you be so certain? Sir Mortimer hasn't yet made a firm decision."

"He will, don't worry."

Shelley swallowed nervously. "And what about Naomi?"

"Oh, we'll have Naomi's support."

Jason wouldn't be so confident, she thought unhappily, if she were to tell him of Naomi's threat. Should she warn him about the precipice that lay ahead? Shelley knew, though, that she would never be able to speak to him of that horrible, humiliating encounter with Naomi that morning. Never!

Jason switched on the radio to catch a news bulletin, but the newscaster's staccato voice flowed over her unheeded. More than ever before in her life she was faced with an impossible decision. In the short while she'd been doing this new job, she had come to revel in its tough challenge—despite her repeated protests to Jason that she'd prefer to work in the copy room. Strictly from the career point of view, P&L offered everything she could wish for. But how could she stay on now, as things were? How could she continue to work so close to Jason when she loved him so desperately and must never let him get the least hint of it?

There was only one answer for her. She would have to quit her job. And the sooner the better.

When they drew up outside the house in Putney there was no question of her jumping out and doing another of her quick disappearing acts. She had to wait for Jason to get her suitcase from the trunk. But instead of passing it over to her, he kept it firmly in his hand.

"Lead the way, Shelley."

"But I said that . . ."

"You're giving me something to eat, remember? As a thank-you for driving you home."

She could hardly make a big scene of it here in the street, with Sunday strollers passing by on the river embankment. Silently seething, she unlocked the front door and led the way upstairs. Once inside her flat, she turned on him in a fury.

"There's no question of my giving you a meal, Jason; I told you that in the car. You want thanks? Okay—thanks! And now, will you please go!"

Jason came closer and stood right before her, not quite touching her. Shelley trembled as she felt the familiar emotional tension flowing between them.

"You've been in an odd mood all day," he said. "What's up?"

"I wish you'd go away," she murmured. "Please!"

"Not until we've sorted this out."

She made a helpless little gesture with her hands. "There's nothing *to* sort out."

"Oh, but there is!" Shelley had been carefully

avoiding his eyes, but Jason put a finger under her chin to make her look at him. "You don't really want me to go, do you?"

"Yes . . . yes, I do!" But her words lacked conviction. The next instant Jason's arms were about her, the imprint of his hands burning into her back. How fatally easy it would be to make her body soft and pliant against his rock hardness and respond to his kisses with wild abandon. Shelley didn't care anymore that making love to her would mean little to Jason. She loved him so ardently, and she yearned for him with such an intense longing, that she was now ready to give herself to him unreservedly.

But the image of Naomi Waterton hung over her like a black cloud. It was bad enough for Naomi to know that Jason was driving her home. But what if she got to hear that he had come inside?

With a sudden determined thrust she pushed away from him, and injected ice into her voice. "Get this straight, Jason, once and for all. I haven't the smallest intention of having a casual affair with you."

"A casual affair," he echoed scornfully. "Why make it sound so trivial? There's something very special between you and me. A unique kind of magnetism. You can't possibly deny it, Shelley."

She took a step back to put a safer distance between them. "I've responded to you, I admit. But I'm not proud of the fact."

"Not proud of being a warm, vibrant, responsive woman?"

"I'm saying I'm not proud of something that's purely physical."

"The enjoyment of sex is nothing to be ashamed of, Shelley."

"Agreed! You talk about sex, though, as an end in itself. The ultimate thing. But sex without love is . . . is shallow and worthless."

Jason looked down at her, the expression on his craggy face one that she couldn't interpret. "And you don't love me . . . could never come to love me?"

Shelley had a sudden almost overwhelming urge to admit the truth—not only that she *could* love him but that she already did. That she had loved him, perhaps, for a long time . . . longer than she cared to acknowledge even to herself. But she dared not admit anything so rash. Jason would be swift to take advantage of her confession, and she would never find the strength of will to resist him.

"No, Jason, I don't love you and I never could," she said in a flat, matter-of-fact voice that cost her a supreme effort. "I like you, I respect and admire your ability as far as work goes. But . . ."

"But I have too many shortcomings in other, more relevant directions?"

"Far too many," she agreed tightly.

There was a pleading look in his dark eyes. "What the devil do you want from me, Shelley? Is it pretty, romantic speeches you're after? A promise of eternal devotion?"

"No," she cried. "I don't want you lying to me. I don't want *anything* from you. Just for you to go away right this minute and leave me in peace."

He regarded her hard and searchingly for long, throbbing moments. "If I were to go away now, Shelley, it wouldn't leave you in peace. You can't wipe me out of your thoughts just like that. Even if you were to quit P&L, you'd not find contentment of mind away from me."

Bitterness welled up in her, exploding in a torrent of angry words. "So *you* believe that the way to achieve peace and contentment of mind is to grab instant sexual gratification every time the fancy takes you? That's not the way for me, Jason. And it never will be, as long as I live."

His voice was low-pitched, very quiet. "I'll tell you what I believe. I believe that some things are altogether too big, too important, to intellectualize about. And it's like that between you and me. There's an inevitability about our coming together, a glorious inevitability. You must have felt it, Shelley, just as I have."

"What about Naomi Waterton?" she flung at him in torment. "Isn't she enough for you?"

"Naomi," he said dismissively, "is totally irrelevant to my relationship with you."

"You have no relationship with me, except at work."

"No relationship? Do I have to remind you that—at your own instigation—you and I have already become lovers?"

"Lovers!" she cried, hating him. "You can describe what happened between us as an act of *love?*"

"Oh, call it what you like," he gritted. "An act of passion, how's that? At least there was nothing cold and calculated about it."

"Unlike your mercenary affair with Naomi," she choked, unable to leave well enough alone.

Jason's chiseled mouth went taut. "Keep Naomi out of this conversation."

"I don't want *any* conversation, Jason," she told him, a beseeching note in her voice. "I just want you to go away."

He hesitated, giving her a strange, long look.

Finally he said, slowly and deliberately, "If I leave now, Shelley, I won't be coming back. You understand what I'm saying?"

She nodded mutely, and the silence stretched.

"I'm not playing games," he added with emphasis, as if he couldn't believe she had grasped the significance of his words.

"For pity's sake, do you think I am?" she exclaimed wretchedly.

His brows knotted in a frown. "I wish I knew, Shelley. I wish to God I knew what it's all about. What I do know, though, without a shadow of doubt, is that you're attracted to me. The spark has been there between us from the very beginning—even when you were married to Rex. I recognized it, and maybe you did, too. I can't be sure. Anyway, whether you recognized it or not, your feelings for me surfaced after Rex was killed. Remember? I could have coaxed you into bed that time, and heaven knows I wanted to. But you were emotionally off-guard, and it would have been taking unfair advantage. I knew you'd have been wretched with guilt about it afterward. Now, though, ever since you've been back in this country, you've been so ambivalent toward me, so blow-hot, blow-cold, that you've kept me guessing. I've asked myself over and over again what prompted you to come to my flat the other night. I had a curious feeling—I said so at the time—that you were using me. Using me in order to prove something to yourself." Jason broke off and studied her face, as if seeking to find the answer there. "No, I *don't* think you're playing games, Shelley. But it would be a relief to know what it is you think you *are* doing."

"I know exactly what I'm doing," she answered

unsteadily. "I've made some stupid mistakes,. I admit that. But not anymore. I want you to leave me alone, Jason. Leave me alone and don't interfere in my life. Is that so much to ask?"

"Yes, it is!" His gaze was steady, unblinking. "Far, far more than you can possibly imagine."

There was such intensity in his voice, such tender emotion, that Shelley was momentarily shaken. But it was nothing more than a cheap ploy to soften her up, she decided angrily.

"You seem to forget," she blazed at him, "that I know you too well to be taken in by that sort of talk. Remember what you said? 'A kiss is a kiss is a kiss.' In your book, sex is just a natural impulse between a man and a woman who find each other attractive."

His eyes hardened. "You're word-perfect, Shelley. So?"

"So you'd better go seek your meaningless instant gratification elsewhere. You'd better go find some other woman to share your bed."

"Perhaps you're right at that."

But Jason made no move, nor did she. They stood looking at one another while the silence pulsed between them. Shelley felt an almost overpowering urge to blurt out the truth of her aching need for him. To abandon her plan and risk everything for the sake of a few ecstatic hours in his arms. But she loved Jason too much to bring disaster crashing down on him. Steeling herself, she kept her face hostile, bitterly accusing.

At long last Jason gave a shrug and turned toward the door. "That's that, then! I'll stay out of your private life from now on, Shelley. You can concentrate one hundred percent on your career, and you'll have a brilliant future. That's for certain. But whether or not a meteoric climb up the corporate ladder will prove enough for you in the long run, you'll have to wait and see.''

When he had gone, Shelley sank down into a chair and pressed trembling hands against her burning cheeks. She should be thankful—thankful to have finally succeeded in driving him away. Naomi Waterton would have no further cause for jealousy, and she herself would no longer be tormented by Jason's ruthless pursuit. Yes, she ought to be thankful.

With sudden determination, she rose to fix herself something to eat. But in the kitchen, breaking eggs for an omelet, she paused and stared vacantly at the view across the rooftops from the little back window.

*Thankful?* she thought. Who am I kidding?

*Chapter Thirteen*

$A$t the office Monday morning, all those who'd been on the Windsor weekend were besieged by eager questioners. It was generally agreed that the Cleveland Wines account was as good as netted. Just one person, apart from Shelley herself, seemed less than happy about the way things had panned out. Nick Royston. When she took some sketches down to the studio for a blowup job Jason wanted done quickly, Nick gave her a dark glower. Luckily, though, his phone rang at that moment and Shelley was able to escape before he could pick a fight.

All day long she was afraid that Jason would mention the scene between them yesterday. But he was brisk and businesslike, as though he really had decided to cut his losses and finally leave her be.

The question now nagging at Shelley's brain, since she'd taken the firm decision to quit P&L, was what she was going to do about finding another job. As she had warned Clare, the prospects weren't currently all that rosy. She could never hope to land anything with such good pay and prospects. At least, she thought with an inward sigh, Jason would probably be glad to see the last of her. He wouldn't want her right there under his nose as a constant, humiliating reminder of his failure to score with her.

Even so, Shelley dreaded telling Jason of her decision to leave. Maybe she'd better hold back just for the moment, just until the Cleveland Wines account was definite. . . .

After the hectic rush of last week, the normal pace of work seemed almost like a vacation. Shelley cleared her desk on the stroke of five-thirty and departed for home. Hitting the peak of the rush hour, she had to stand all the way on the bus. By the time she reached Putney, she felt jaded and limp. There was hardly a breath of breeze on this sultry evening, even when walking along by the river, and she heard the distant rumble of thunder. Upstairs in her flat, she threw open the living-room window and set a small folding table there to eat her dinner salad. Gathering stormclouds darkened the sky, and she felt the oppressive atmosphere bearing down on her like a ton weight.

Later, the sound of a car drawing up outside the house made her go tense with alarm. Not Jason, for heaven's sake? Glancing down from behind the window drapes, she recognized Nick Royston's yellow Ford. Well, she wasn't going to make the same mistake she had made last time he dropped by. She would keep well clear of him.

But that wasn't to be. Within a couple of minutes Nick was ringing her doorbell. Shelley opened up to him reluctantly, not pretending to be surprised.

"What do you want?" she asked ungraciously.

Nick looked embarrassed, as if now that he was here he didn't know quite what to say. "Hi, Shelley. I thought I'd better call round to check that everything's okay downstairs. I heard a rumor that Clare was coming back here."

"It's news to me. Though she did say she couldn't expect to stay at her sister's place indefinitely." Shelley opened the door wider. "You'd better come in, I guess."

In the living room, Nick looked at her with a resentful expression. "Everybody at work is cock-a-hoop about the Cleveland Wines account—and the Cleveland girl. So if you hadn't given Patti the thumbs-down, she'd have been in."

"That's not true," Shelley protested. "Actually, J.S. had already made up his mind not to use Patti."

"So why did he ask you for your opinion?" demanded Nick suspiciously.

"Because, if you must know, it was a sort of test case for me. He wanted to check the value of my judgmental ability."

"Huh! Your judgmental ability isn't much good, then. Patti would have been sensational as the Cleveland Girl."

Shelley shook her head, unconsciously quoting Jason. "You're letting your personal emotions get in the way, Nick. If you level with yourself, you'll have to agree that it was a dumb idea from the outset. She's totally the wrong sort of model for the Cleveland campaign."

"Try telling Patti that!"

"If Patti's miffed about it, then it's your fault for raising her hopes in the first place."

Nick picked up a brass ornament from the mantel-

225

piece and fiddled with it. "Patti had set her heart on getting that Cleveland Girl contract. It would have put her straight into the big time."

"And now she's bawling you out—right?"

The sullen flicker in Nick's eyes was confirmation enough. "So what now, Nick?" she asked impatiently.

"Now?"

"Will you be shoving Patti forward each and every time we need a girl to model for something, never mind whether she's remotely suitable or not? If you try that, you'll come unstuck in a big way. Oh, Nick," she rushed on impetuously, "Patti's no good for you, can't you see that? Okay, it's none of my business, you told me that before. But honestly, I think you're a real dummy to waste your life on that girl when Clare's such a fine person."

Nick threw her a tormented look. "It's easy for you to preach, Shelley. You don't understand the half of it."

"I guess not. But tell me this, Nick . . . you do still feel something for Clare, don't you? I mean, it hasn't *all* gone?"

He sighed deeply. "How could it? I loved her like crazy when we first got together, and to begin with it was marvelous. For the first few years. But then . . ."

"Clare told me about how she got pregnant, way back," Shelley said gently. "It was tough luck about her having a miscarriage." She watched Nick's face carefully, gauging his reaction. "If Clare had ever had a child, I guess you two might never have split up."

"What's the use of talk," Nick snapped with a sharp look of pain. "That time she got pregnant

226

. . . I suppose she underlined the fact that it was a chance in a million?"

"Clare did tell me that you'd been trying hard since then, but no go."

"You mean to say Clare didn't treat you to all the grisly details?"

Shelley shook her head. "Only what I've just said—about your keeping on trying, but no go." She paused a moment, then went on slowly, "Clare feels horribly guilty, Nick, about the way she treated you . . . some of the things she said when you quarreled. She really loves you, even now."

A spark of hope glowed fleetingly in Nick's eyes, then died. "How *can* she love me?"

"I don't know; you certainly don't deserve it. But strangely, she does. She told me so. She thinks that despite everything, she'll always love you, Nick."

He shook his head disbelievingly. "She's got every reason to hate my guts. She always wanted kids; did she tell you that? I married her under false pretenses. Only, I didn't know it at the time."

"Didn't know what?"

Color flamed in Nick's face, and he half-turned away in his embarrassment. Yet Shelley had the feeling that he wanted to go on talking, as if he needed to share a burden of guilt he carried.

"Know what, Nick?" she repeated.

He hesitated, then burst out, "It was entirely *my* fault that Clare never managed to get pregnant again. We had all the checks done and Clare was in the clear. The problem was me."

"Yes?" Shelley prompted, hoping she was doing the right thing in pressing him.

Nick bit his lip. "Clare and I could go on trying for the rest of our lives and she'd probably never get pregnant again. Not by me! I'm all but sterile, Shelley!" He flung it out with bitter resentment. "We lost the one chance we ever had of producing a baby."

Shelley looked at him with compassion. "Nick, I don't know a lot about this . . . just that it happens sometimes. But as I understand it, it doesn't make any difference to a guy as a man . . . as a husband."

"That's a laugh! Clare made it painfully clear when we quarreled that last night what she thought of me in that direction. And the horrible irony of the thing is that you don't *feel* any different. There's just the awful knowledge gnawing at your guts that it's bloody near impossible for you to father a child."

Shelley felt a great lump in her throat. Surely, if ever there was a moment that Nick ought to know about his wife being pregnant, it was right now. In certain circumstances, she told herself, it was even more important to *break* a promise than to keep it.

"You're wrong about that, Nick," she said softly. "You couldn't be more wrong."

"Meaning?" Nick jerked around to stare at her, sensing that her words had some deep significance.

She smiled at him shakily. "Chance in a million or not, Nick, you *are* going to become a father. Clare is pregnant again right now."

He looked dazed. "Is this some kind of sick joke?"

"It's no joke, Nick, not for Clare. She's all mixed up about it . . . happy in one way, yet at the same time miserable because the realization she was pregnant came too late to save your marriage." Shelley looked at him challengingly. "Only, maybe it didn't at that. Would you consider going back to her?"

Nick shook his head, looking despondent. "Clare

wouldn't want me back, not after the way I treated her."

"Think so? You're a prize idiot, Nick. All you've got to do is to go to Clare and tell her you're sorry."

"I'd go down on my knees to her if I thought it would help," he said huskily.

Shelley laughed. "Know something? That's just what Clare said, too. You'd make a fine pair, crawling around the carpet to each other."

Nick was in too emotional a state to share her amusement. "I'll go over to Hampstead to see Clare right away, talk to her," he said, his eyes flooding with hope. "Maybe she'll come back here with me tonight."

"Hey, what about Patti?"

"Patti and I are all washed up," he muttered. "She's been a real little pain over not getting that Cleveland Girl job. She was only into an affair with me for what she could get out of it careerwise, and I've had about enough of her."

"Hadn't you better tell Patti that before you go rushing off to see Clare?"

Nick gave her an impatient look. "You want everything to be so neat and tidy, Shelley. Life isn't like that."

"I guess you're right!" Her sigh was deep and heartfelt. "Okay, Nick, you'd better go off and see Clare."

He hesitated, glancing at Shelley anxiously. "Do you honestly think that she'll listen to me?"

"I think so."

"If we can patch things up between us, Shelley, it'll all be due to you." Nick leaned forward and kissed her on the cheek. "Thanks a million."

Shelley smiled wistfully to herself as he went

bounding off. Then on a sudden thought she ran to the head of the stairs and called down after him, "Leave your front door open, Nick, and I'll pop down and get the place readied up a bit."

He looked back up at her and grinned appreciatively. "Will do! You're a doll, Shelley."

Upstairs again a little while later, Shelley watched TV for a while and finally went to bed. But not to sleep. Her ears were stretched for the sound of Nick's car. She was beginning to have her first uneasy doubts when she heard it draw up outside. She went to the door at the top of the stairs and opened it a crack. Clare was with him! Shelley breathed again and returned to bed. Ten minutes later she heard the faint but unmistakable sound of them laughing together. Her eyes filled with tears. Tears of joy for Clare and Nick, she tried to kid herself. But she knew that the tears were really for the unhappy contrast of her own situation.

Next morning Shelley was sitting over her toast and coffee when her doorbell rang. She opened up to a smiling Clare.

"I'm back, you see! I guess you'll be wanting a lift to work as per usual. . . ." Clare's voice cracked on a sob and she launched herself at Shelley, giving her a fierce hug. "Oh, it's so wonderful, I can't tell you. I'm only just getting used to the idea, and not having to pinch myself every five minutes. And it's all thanks to you."

Shelley gave her friend an affectionate little squeeze before disentangling herself. "Come in and have a cup of coffee, Clare. If Nick can spare you for five minutes, that is."

Clare giggled. "Honestly, he treats me like I was fragile . . . made of precious porcelain or some such."

"And what," laughed Shelley, "is wrong with that?"

"Not a lot!" Clare's eyes met hers, twinkling happily. "To tell you the truth, it's very nice indeed!"

As Beth emerged from Jason's office after dealing with his morning mail, she gave Shelley a more than usually sour look. "J.S. wants you right away."

Each such summons sent Shelley's heart plunging. As she went in, Jason was standing by the window, the sharp, clean lines of his profile catching the light. He wheeled around to face her.

"I gather that Nick and Clare Royston are back together again."

"News certainly travels fast around this place."

"How did they manage to sort themselves out?" he asked.

"Does it matter?" she said, shrugging. "The important thing is that that they're okay now."

Dismissing the Roystons, Jason said, "I had a phone call from Hilary last night."

"Your sister, you mean?"

"Uh-huh." He seemed abstracted. "She told me that she's managed to dig up quite a bit of information about your ancestors. It seems the Bowyers are mentioned in a whole range of old documents stashed away in the county archives and whatever, and once Hilary started delving, she got hooked. Anyway, she suggests that you go down there on the weekend for her to fill you in."

"That's very kind of her," murmured Shelley. But she felt dismayed rather than pleased. Closer contact with Jason's relatives was the last thing she needed. That would make it all the harder to keep the necessary distance between them.

"So I'll drive you down on Friday evening," Jason told her. "That will give us two nights there. Okay?"

"No, it isn't okay! I thought we'd agreed once and for all that any sort of personal relationship is off-limits for us. If I go to Bourton-on-the-Water this weekend, I go on my own."

"But why, when I'll be going anyway, and there's room in my car? It doesn't make sense."

He was being deliberately obtuse. Shelley drew a quick, shaky breath. "If you're going, then I'm afraid you'll have to tell Hilary that I can't accept her invitation. I don't want to be rude to her, Jason, when she's been so kind and gone to so much trouble, but you're giving me no option."

"Don't be ridiculous," he snapped, his voice tight with anger. "For pity's sake, it's not as if I'm suggesting we spend the weekend together at a hotel. We'll be staying under my sister's roof, suitably chaperoned!"

"I don't want to be *anywhere* with you," she said doggedly, "except here at the office."

Jason's charcoal-gray eyes hardened swiftly, but before he could say anything his phone rang. He gestured at Shelley as she left, saying, "We'll talk again later."

Returning to the outer office, Shelley had a suspicion that Beth had intended to eavesdrop on Jason's conversation. She replaced her phone guiltily, but couldn't hold back from saying, "It's Mister Big himself who's calling."

"Sir Mortimer, you mean?" Shelley's pulse was suddenly thudding. "It'll be about the new account."

Beth nodded. "Have we, or haven't we? Well, we'll know the worst in a minute."

They waited together, fleetingly allied in their mutual anxiety while the conversation dragged on for what seemed an interminable length of time. This must, Shelley fretted, be a bad sign. Sir Mortimer must be breaking it to Jason at length that Prescott and Liedermann were not, after all, being awarded the Cleveland Wines account. Perhaps—oh, please no!—Sir Mortimer was even breaking the news that P&L was going to lose Cleveland's other accounts. Was this Naomi's swiftly meted-out revenge for Sunday?

But when the call finally terminated and Jason appeared in the doorway between the two offices, he looked highly gratified, though unsurprised.

"That's it! Another million-plus account signed up, bar the inking in. The old boy was deeply impressed by our presentation, and looks forward to another long and mutually profitable association with P&L. Beth, phone round the glad tidings, will you? And I'll want a call to New York as soon as their morning catches up with ours . . . I think they're as anxious as we were. Shelley, come in now and perhaps we can finish our interrupted conversation."

She couldn't raise an objection in front of Beth, but the moment the door was closed behind her she said decisively, "Our conversation was already finished."

"On the contrary," he rapped, "it had scarcely begun. I want a reason, Shelley, for your refusal to come with me to Hilary's."

"You're only entitled to a reason from me when it's something to do with business," she said coldly.

His face was like stone. "I repeat, Shelley, I want a reason."

"That's crazy!" She turned to leave the room, but Jason's peremptory voice stopped her. "Stay right where you are!" He was close to her in three strides and Shelley felt herself trembling before the bitter brilliance of his eyes. "Whether you like it or not, I *am* entitled to an explanation."

"Whatever reasons I have," she said woodenly, "they're personal."

"Agreed! Very personal."

"I meant . . . personal to me."

"And who else?"

"There doesn't have to be anyone else involved," she parried.

"Oh, yes, there does! It's the only explanation." His dark brows drew together in a puzzled frown. "How you feel about me, how you *genuinely* feel about me, is only too apparent. Yet something—or someone—is preventing you from responding to me naturally. I thought at one point that it was a curious mixed-up sense of loyalty to Rex that inhibited you, and maybe it was at first. But not any longer. So what's it all about?"

Why was he driving her so remorselessly into a corner? She sighed, knowing that the time for her resignation had arrived. Yet the thought of voluntarily quitting, the thought of not being able to see Jason each day, made her feel faint with misery. In a breathless little rush she stammered, "I . . . I want to resign from my job."

"You'll do no such thing." Fury darkened his face, and he gave her a dangerous look. "I won't accept your resignation. Not without a damn good reason."

"You can't refuse," she protested. "The choice is mine."

"Legally, perhaps. Morally, I'm due an explanation. And you know it!"

Shelley hesitated in an agony of indecision. "It . . . it's because I can't trust you to keep your word,

Jason. You agreed that we'd only have an office relationship, and now . . ."

"I didn't lay a finger on you this morning."

"But you're putting pressure on me. All this talk about taking me to Hilary's for the weekend. Where will it all end, if I don't quit?"

"Stay and find out." Suddenly his voice was so tender that her heart missed a beat. "I promise you this, Shelley, and it's been true from the start. Nothing that happens between us will be against your *real* wishes. So the only person you've got to learn to trust is yourself. Stop running away and face up to things instead."

Shelley took a deep, shuddering breath. "Okay, so I'm running away. But that's my privilege. You've left me no option, Jason."

There was a tap on the door and Barney looked in, an excited expression on his amiable face. At once sensing the atmosphere, though, he mumbled apologetically, "Sorry J.S., I didn't realize . . ."

"Give me two minutes, Barney." When the door was closed, Jason glanced at her thoughtfully. "From now on there'll be continual interruptions as the good news gets around the building. We'll have to talk later, Shelley. This evening."

"No," she cried in panic. "Definitely not."

"I insist! I'll come round to your place. We'll be able to have this out properly, in peace."

With Nick and Clare seeing Jason arrive, noting how long he stayed? Without their meaning any harm, it would be a bit of cheerful gossip that would buzz around P&L—and probably get to Naomi's ears!

"You've got to promise me, Jason," she pleaded earnestly, "that you won't come to Putney."

"On one condition."

"Condition?" She met his glance nervously.

"That you come round to my place instead."

Shelley was aghast. Going to his flat would be the greatest insanity of all.

"You can forget that," she said.

"You know the alternative. My place . . . or yours."

"I'll be out," she countered desperately.

"Then I'll wait for you."

"Please, Jason," she begged, "please just let me quit my job and vanish out of your life."

"Don't talk nonsense," he said dismissively. "We're going to have this out and it's up to you to say where."

Frantic thoughts raced through her head as to how she could escape this terrible dilemma. Quit her job this very day? Quit the flat as well? Just disappear? But she knew with a strange fluttering in her heart that Jason would track her down wherever she might run. Staring down at the green-carpeted floor, she mumbled in helpless resignation, "Very well, I'll come."

Jason put his hand beneath her chin and forced her head back so that she was looking directly at him. His dark eyes challenged her. "You mean it? No tricks?"

"I . . . I mean it."

"Eight o'clock," he told her. "Don't be late! Unless you want me to fetch you?"

Panic surged again. "No! I'll get a taxi."

"Very well. Now, tell Barney he can come in."

A steady rain was falling and the evening streets were almost deserted. Traffic lights were mirrored on the wet tarmac like splashes of red, amber and green from an artist's brush.

Shelley's thoughts were in terrible chaos as the taxi whirled along. In only minutes she'd be there, and she was still totally unprepared as to what to say to Jason. She'd been mad to come. Mad! Perhaps, even now, she should tell the driver to turn around and head back to Putney. She was still wavering when the taxi swung into the Gratton mews and drew up outside Jason's door. At once he was there, paying off the driver and ushering her inside.

It was very silent in Jason's living room. The taxi had driven away and there were just the hiss of rain on the cobbled roadway and a dripping from the eaves. After he took her raincoat they stood looking at one another, not touching, not speaking, for what seemed an eternity. Shelley was gripped by the strangest feeling—as if the two of them were frozen like this in an eternal tableau.

Then suddenly the threads of tension snapped and they were in one another's arms. Jason held her tightly and she clung to him, her heart soaring in a joyous tumult of emotion. He kissed her long and deep and tenderly, and it was everything that was wonderful.

After long, lost aeons of time Jason drew back a little, smiling down at her. His breath came raggedly and his voice trembled.

"I think you've given me the only answer that matters, Shelley. But why in heaven's name, love, give me all that crazy talk about quitting your job and vanishing out of my life?"

The breath-robbing, dizzying illusion of happiness fled before this reminder of the cruel, harsh facts. She pushed back from him with what feeble strength she could summon.

"Please let me go, Jason. I only came here tonight because you virtually blackmailed me into it. Why can't you just take *no* for an answer?" she rushed on as he started to speak. "Why can't you believe me when I tell you that . . ." She broke off and stared at him in disbelief. "What . . . what did you say?"

"I said that I love you, Shelley, darling."

The blood in her veins seemed to stop flowing, and her heart froze. "No, it's not true! It can't be true! You're just saying that to try to soften me up. You don't love me, Jason . . . you're incapable of love. You've made that very clear."

"I love you," he repeated gently, slowly, his dark eyes watching her face. "I've known it since . . . oh, God knows when. But, like an idiot, I fought against the knowledge. I'd learned better, I thought; love was just for naive young fools. I told myself that what I wanted from you, Shelley, was exactly what I'd had so many times before from other women— the simple, uncomplicated gratification of desire. And then, that night you came and offered yourself to me, I knew that it wasn't enough . . . would never be enough where you were concerned. I wanted your love, my darling. Your *love!*"

Shelley stared back at him, her amber eyes huge and round with bewilderment. But there was a glimmer of dawning hope. "I don't understand, though, Jason—"

He checked her by putting a tender finger against her lips. "I realize that you must despise me, darling; you have every right to. It must appear as if all I've ever wanted from you is to get you into bed—right from the time when Rex was killed. It must have seemed to you then that on the pretext of helping you through your grief and all the problems you were confronted with, I was just waiting for my chance to take advantage of you."

"I thought that *you* must despise *me* for what

happened then," Shelley whispered on a choked-off sob. "Reacting to you in that abandoned way within just a few days of my husband's death! I've always felt so ashamed."

"There's no need to, my love. You can't be blamed, not in any way. It was a very traumatic time for you, and you were in shock. This feeling between us has always been there, deep down, even when Rex was alive. So it's no wonder that it should have come to the surface, considering the highly vulnerable state you were in."

"I bet that you've always regretted not seizing your chance that day," she stammered, crucifying herself.

"No, Shelley, no! I've always been grateful that I managed to draw back in time, before I committed the unforgivable." There was a pained look in his dark eyes as he went on, "It's really no wonder that you fled back to New York. You must have felt that I was totally untrustworthy; I realize that now, though at the time I was furious with both you and myself! You see, I'd never wanted anyone in my whole life as desperately as I wanted you. You seemed to be the loveliest, most desirable girl I'd ever met, and there was some indefinable quality about you that I couldn't categorize. It brought out feelings of tenderness in me that I hadn't felt for anyone in a long while. Heaven knows what I thought at the time. With Rex only just dead, I didn't have any clear idea of what I wanted for the two of us. I just knew that I needed to stay close to you, Shelley. Only I blew it. I sent you rushing back to New York because you didn't trust me."

His face tautened, the skin stretched tight over the lean bone and muscle. "Anyway, I imagined that with the Atlantic Ocean between us I'd be able to forget about you. But I never could. And I was angry with myself about that, too, Shelley . . . furious that I let you get to me to such a degree. In an effort to put you right out of my mind, I looked elsewhere. . . ."

"To Naomi Waterton?"

Jason nodded somberly. "For some time Naomi had been showing me the green light, and . . . In a way, I suppose, the less respect I had for the woman concerned, the better she suited my purpose."

"You mean you *don't* respect Naomi?"

"Oh, her ability in business I do. She's highly intelligent, too. But she wildly overrates herself as far as her attractions go. She thinks she's just about the greatest thing that ever happened to the entire male sex. So I used her, without a single qualm. I told myself that Naomi Waterton made use of men for her own purposes, so why shouldn't I be the one to turn the tables?"

Shelley met his glance and asked quietly, "What made you so hard and cynical, Jason? You told me once that there had been a woman who was important to you, way back."

He turned away from her and paced across the carpet, then swung back to face her again. "It's true what I said, Shelley; I was an out-and-out romantic when I was young. I went through one or two brief idylls at Oxford, but it wasn't until I started working at P&L that I was hit by something really big. She was incredibly attractive, three or four years older than I was, and she seemed to have fallen for me, too. Me, just a junior space buyer at the time! It went to my head. I was completely besotted by the woman. I'd have laid all my riches at her feet . . . only, I didn't have any riches. One thing I could do, though, was to wangle orders for advertising space in the newspaper she worked on, and Marion seemed so artlessly pleased when I did. So I got in deeper and deeper, just for the delight of seeing a grateful smile on her face. That beautiful, cheating face of hers! It lasted about six months before I finally discovered the truth about her. Do you know, she was living with another man the whole time! She also had several other affairs going with gullible young idiots like me who could push orders her way. When I threw it at her that I'd found her out, she wasn't in the least ashamed. She just laughed in my face, Shelley."

"Oh, Jason!" she said sympathetically, understanding how deep the hurt had gone.

"For so long I was knotted up with bitterness," he said, meeting her eyes with a slow, sad smile, "that I refused to believe a woman could mean anything to me. And then I met you, my darling. I tried to tell myself that I must be out of my mind to feel that way about Shelley Armitage. Mad to worry about your feelings on that fateful evening when I was so stupid as to let our emotions get out of hand. And again, afterward, mad to care that I'd driven you back to New York. So what? I tried to tell myself. You were just another woman . . . another pebble on the beach. But I couldn't stop thinking about you, couldn't stop tormenting myself about you."

Shelley swallowed the lump in her throat. "I don't get it," she said bewilderedly. "That day I lunched with Barney he told me that althought you thought I was the right material for promotion onto your personal staff you reacted against me as an individual. That you didn't want to appoint me."

"Barney got it a bit out of focus," Jason replied

wryly. "Not that one can blame him. I didn't exactly go around wearing my heart on my sleeve."

"And yet you always seemed so hostile toward me."

"Because I was scared of you, Shelley."

*"Scared?"* she echoed, dumbfounded.

"I was scared out of my wits that history was going to repeat itself. That I'd go crazy over you and find out too late that you were as shallow and worthless as all the other women I'd encountered along the way."

"What . . . what changed your mind?" Shelley whispered huskily.

He looked at her with a strange sort of wonderment in his charcoal-gray eyes. "Your sincerity, my darling, your total lack of any sort of feminine guile. You were attracted to me, you wanted me and you didn't try to hide the fact. You even admitted it to me frankly. I could see you weren't just playing hard to get, yet something held you back from committing yourself." Jason reached to take her in his arms again, but Shelley stepped quickly out of range.

"Something still holds you back even now," he said in a voice that carried overtones of reproach. "Even though you know that I love you. Or can't you accept that as the truth?"

With surprise Shelley realized that she had no doubts whatever that Jason truly loved her. Yet her burgeoning sense of happiness was overshadowed by the dark cloud of Naomi Waterton's threats.

"I love you, Shelley, darling," Jason said again in a low, intense voice. "I love you with all my heart. Please say that you believe me."

"I do . . . oh, yes, I do," she gasped breathlessly. "And I love you, Jason. I've loved you for so long. Forever, it seems now."

As his arms closed around her, Shelley was stabbed through with fear. By this open admission of their mutual love they were leaping into a great chasm. A bottomless pit of disaster. She had to warn him. Jason had to be made aware of the terrible risk he was running. In her struggle to find the words to explain, they came out strangled, scarcely audible. "Naomi . . . she won't let you go."

"Naomi?" Puzzlement darkened his rugged face. "What's it to do with Naomi?"

"She warned me to stay away from you . . ." Shelley faltered, pulling back from him. "She told me loud and clear on Sunday morning that I had to stop seeing you—the man she might marry— or else! I guess she was livid about your coming along to see me that night before you went to her room."

Jason stared. "What in the hell do you mean— before I went to her room?"

"I . . . I thought you spent the night with Naomi," Shelley stammered, flushing. "I just took it for granted."

"You got it wrong, then," he said with a quick flash of anger.

Relief gushed up in her like a fountain. "Anyway," she went on, "Naomi knew somehow or other that you'd been in my bedroom."

Jason's brow knotted with concentration. "It figures! I remember hearing a slight noise behind me in the corridor. It must have been her door opening. But never mind how Naomi knew. It's what she *said* . . . about marriage."

"She . . . she said she was considering marrying you."

"Nice of her!" His mouth tightened to a hard, straight line. "The lady would do well to wait and be asked. And Naomi Waterton would wait in vain. She's not my type."

Shelley felt a surge of jealousy. "She's your type enough to . . . to go to bed with!"

"Not even that, lately. Which presumably is why Naomi's feeling so vindictive."

"Since when?" Shelley queried, goaded to indiscretion.

Jason's dark eyes were reproachful as he met her glance. "Since just before you arrived back in this country, if you must know."

"That isn't true, Jason," she said huskily, bitterly hurt that he should lie to her. "It's obvious that you've gone on seeing her—"

"*Seeing* her, yes. She's a client, and she has a right to make demands on my time."

With a numb feeling in her heart, Shelley persisted. "Naomi's whole attitude toward you, at the office and during the weekend at Windsor, showed what your relationship really is."

"What she would like it to be," he corrected.

A swift image of the two of them, wearing only the scantiest swimwear and emerging laughing from the same changing chalet, brought Shelley a sharp stab of pain. In a rush of bitter words, she flung it at him accusingly.

A frown furrowed Jason's brow, and he spoke with reluctance. "Shelley, for heaven's sake, we had our suits on under our clothes. It was no big deal. I'll admit that she took the chance to try to get my interest aroused, and I had to make it clear that I wasn't in the mood. Maybe I should have spelled it out to Naomi in words of one syllable that our relationship was over. But, quite frankly, I didn't want to make heavy weather of it right then. Naomi understands that we're finished; she just doesn't like to admit the fact that she's lost her power over me."

"Can a relationship like that ever be over?" Shelley asked, feeling swamped with misery.

"Oh, yes, very easily—when the two people concerned are in it entirely for their own selfish ends. It was a mutual thing while it lasted; it suited us both. But emotionally Naomi never touched me, any more than I touched her. I don't expect that a person of your nature, Shelley, can understand another woman who can take sex as . . . just sex."

A shudder passed through her. "No, I can't. To me, sex without love is empty, utterly devoid of meaning."

"It's taken me a long time to discover the truth of that," he said, his eyes softly tender. "I look back with a sort of wonder at my wasted life. And yet, that's not wholly true, I suppose. The only life I can envisage ever wanting now is one spent with you, and it seems that I had to wait until now to come to my senses. But there are so many tomorrows ahead of us, Shelley, darling. You and I are going to have a wonderful future together."

Jason would have embraced her again, but she resisted firmly. With pain slashing her heart, she began to tell him, falteringly, of Naomi Waterton's trump card. "You don't understand . . . Naomi's not going to *let* you go. She made that very clear. She told me that if there's anything more between you and me she'll break you, Jason."

"Break me? Just how does Naomi propose to do that?"

"By taking away the Cleveland Enterprises accounts. Not just the new one, but all the others, too. Ten million pounds a year, she told me it comes to.

245

Losing that would ruin the British end of P&L. She said that heads would roll, Jason, and yours would be the first in line."

The strange expression on his chiseled face was one that she couldn't interpret. "Maybe Naomi's right at that," he said. "If I was such an inept managing director as to lose the agency's biggest client. Suppose that should happen, Shelley, darling, would you still be interested in me?"

"You . . . you mean . . . ?"

"If I was fired, I mean. Jettisoned as so much useless scrap. If I had to start again at the bottom of the career ladder, with a reputation as a failure to weigh me down. Would you think I was worth having then?"

Shelley drew back a little to gaze into his eyes, amazed that he should ask such a question. Then she slid her arms around his neck and pressed her cheek against his shoulder. "I love you, don't I?" she murmured. "Wherever you are is where I want to be, Jason. *Whatever* you are, I want to share it with you. I always shall."

"Even if it's nothing?"

"We'd manage, somehow. Just having you, just being able to love you, would be enough for me."

She let Jason kiss her then, a sweet, tender meeting of lips which seemed to fuse them together for all eternity. At long last he gave a soft laugh deep in his throat. "The truth of the matter, darling Shelley, is somewhat less romantic, but a whole lot more comfortable. There isn't the least risk of P&L losing the Cleveland accounts. Nor of my losing my job. Sir Mortimer and I understand one another very well."

"But . . . but Naomi can twist him around her little finger, Jason. Everyone knows that."

"Then everyone is wrong! In many ways he *is* the doting father who gives in to his daughter all along the line. But the determined, thrustful man who created a vast business empire from nothing by the shrewdness of his wits isn't going to put it all at risk on a whim. Even on the whim of his adored daughter. Naomi threatened you, my love, because she knew she couldn't threaten me! Whether or not she comes to hate my guts and wants to destroy me, her father isn't going to listen. He respects my ability far too much, and he knows that the ad agency I control can do a far more effective job for Cleveland Enterprises than any other agency he could appoint."

All Shelley's pent-up anxiety seemed to flood out of her like a river bursting a dam. Her voice shaky with love and happiness, she whispered, "Oh, Jason, you're so wonderfully sure of yourself."

He smiled ruefully. "If you think that, then you've got a lot to learn about me. To stop me expiring from self-doubt, you'll have to tell me every single day how much you love me."

"I will!" she breathed fervently. "Oh, yes, I will!"

"That other time you came here to my flat—" he began, but she cut him short. "It's not fair, Jason, bringing that up."

"You're not still embarrassed about it, are you, my darling?" he asked gently. "You shouldn't be."

The color that had stained her cheeks faded and she looked at him with unashamed commitment. "No, I'm not embarrassed anymore. Though what I did was for all the wrong reasons."

"What made you come here?" he pressed.

Her oval face was serious as she considered his question. "The person I went to see that evening . . . it was Blanche Farleigh. You see, I'd discovered a few days before that *she* was one of Rex's women.

247

But that evening Blanche threw it all at me without holding anything back. How their affair had gone on the whole time Rex and I were married, picking up practically from the moment he got back from New York with me. How Rex used to talk to her about me . . . very disparagingly. It was horrible, Jason."

His arms tightened around her. "You poor darling! And you came to me on the rebound?"

"Sort of. But it's not as simple as that."

Jason waited, but she couldn't go on, choked by the pain of remembering that nightmare time. He smoothed back a strand of her chestnut hair and touched his lips gently to her brow to show that he understood and wouldn't push.

"I could hardly believe it," he said, "when I heard that you were coming back to this country. It seemed like a heaven-sent gift."

"I didn't understand at the time what prompted me to come," she confessed.

"But you do now?"

She nodded, suddenly shy. Again Jason understood without the need for explanations. "I wonder," he said thoughtfully, "how long I'd have been able to hold out before I went to you in New York."

"Would you have?" she asked, her heart suddenly racing. "Would you really?"

"Oh, yes! I had to know, Shelley. Sooner or later I'd have been driven to establish the truth of the situation, one way or the other. I needed to know if it was all just in my imagination . . . if you really felt for me what I *believed* you felt. Not love—that was too much to hope for—but an attraction on which love could be built. Or did I really want that? I was so confused I didn't know what I wanted. Perhaps I was hoping in my secret heart to discover that you were just another worthless woman whom I could use for a brief fling and discard without conscience." With a quick shake of his head he dismissed the past. "When will you marry me, Shelley? How soon?"

Her amber eyes glowed with a radiant joy. "As soon as you want, Jason. But . . . we don't need to wait for wedding bells."

He stood tense and very still, holding her tightly against his lean, sinewy body. She was aware of his heart thudding rapidly through the thinness of his summer shirt, aware of his surging desire. Then, slowly, reverently, he lifted her in his arms and bore her tenderly upstairs.

Shelley stirred and heard the faint hum of the London night around them. In a daze of bliss and fulfillment she gazed at Jason's face on the pillow beside her and saw that he was awake and watching her.

"Tears?" he murmured.

"Silly tears," she said, blinking them back. "Silly, happy tears."

Jason touched his lips to each of her cheeks in turn to kiss the tears away. In the soft lamplight his dark eyes glowed with tenderness. "I love you, Shelley."

"And I love you!"

A long time later they surfaced again and he murmured, "Shall we go to Gloucestershire at the weekend, darling? It will be a good chance to break the news to Hilary."

Shelley nodded. "I'd like that. Only . . . I guess we won't need to tell her, Jason. One look at us will be enough."

"Will it be so obvious?" he queried, smiling.

"Obvious to every woman, anyhow."

He pulled her close again in a fresh surge of passion. "That's good . . . that's great! I want everyone to know that I love you, Shelley, darling. Everyone!"

But right now, other people seemed remote. The two of them were alone together in their own private, wonderful world. This was the first of so many nights of bliss, stretching on and on into an endless future, a whole lifetime of loving.

# If you enjoyed this book...

...you will enjoy a Special Edition Book Club membership even more.

It will bring you each new title, as soon as it is published every month, delivered right to your door.

### 15-Day Free Trial Offer

We will send you 6 new Silhouette Special Editions to keep for 15 days absolutely free! If you decide not to keep them, send them back to us, you pay nothing. But if you enjoy them as much as we think you will, keep them and pay the invoice enclosed with your trial shipment. You will then automatically become a member of the Special Edition Book Club and receive 6 more romances every month. There is no minimum number of books to buy and you can cancel at any time.

# Silhouette Special Edition

## Coming Next Month

### December's Wine by Linda Shaw

Padgett Williams' laughing eyes dared Leigh
Vincent to give herself in love. She felt alive again,
as his tender touch stirred feelings from the
very depths of her soul.

### Northern Lights by Jacqueline Musgrave

Beneath the brilliance of the Northern Lights, Rod
and Jan shared a love warm enough to set the cold
Alaskan nights aflame. He taught her the meaning
of trust, the beauty of a lover's touch, and the
secret of the heart.

### A Flight Of Swallows by Joanna Scott

Karin couldn't believe that Lucas McKay was out
for revenge—not when she matched him touch for
touch, promise for promise, and soared with him
to the land of paradise, the edge of ecstasy.

## Silhouette Special Edition

## Coming Next Month

### All That Glitters by Linda Howard

Jessica had once been involved in a marriage
rocked by scandal, but in Nikolas Constantinos'
arms she found a peace she thought she'd never
know. His lips told her of delights that were to
follow, and his hands led her down a path
of desire and surrender.

### Love's Golden Shadow by Maggi Charles

Guy Medfield's waning sight left him feeling bitter
and alone—until Tracy's healing touch taught him
to live again and to read the promise of their
future in every heartbeat and caress.

### Gamble Of Desire by Diana Dixon

Unhappy with her singing career, Kendra traveled
with Paul to Martinique. In this land of shadowed
forests and scorching sands Paul carried her on
wings of passion and happiness that come
only from true love.

Look for more Special Editions from
**Janet Dailey** and **Brooke Hastings**,
and a new novel from
**Linda Shaw** in future months.

# Silhouette Special Edition

## MORE ROMANCE FOR
## A SPECIAL WAY TO RELAX

### $1.95 each

1 □ TERMS OF SURRENDER
  Janet Dailey

2 □ INTIMATE STRANGERS
  Brooke Hastings

3 □ MEXICAN RHAPSODY
  Diana Dixon

4 □ VALAQUEZ BRIDE
  Donna Vitek

5 □ PARADISE POSTPONED
  Jane Converse

6 □ SEARCH FOR A NEW DAWN
  Billie Douglass

7 □ SILVER MIST
  Sondra Stanford

8 □ KEYS TO DANIEL'S HOUSE
  Carole Halston

9 □ ALL OUR TOMORROWS
  Mary Lynn Baxter

10 □ TEXAS ROSE
  Kathryn Thiels

11 □ LOVE IS SURRENDER
  Carolyn Thornton

12 □ NEVER GIVE YOUR HEART
  Tracy Sinclair

13 □ BITTER VICTORY
  Patti Beckman

14 □ EYE OF THE HURRICANE
  Sarah Keene

15 □ DANGEROUS MAGIC
  Stephanie James

16 □ MAYAN MOON
  Eleni Carr

17 □ SO MANY TOMORROWS
  Nancy John

18 □ A WOMAN'S PLACE
  Lucy Hamilton

---

**SILHOUETTE SPECIAL EDITION,** Department SE/2
1230 Avenue of the Americas
New York, NY 10020

Please send me the books I have checked above. I am enclosing $_____
(please add 50¢ to cover postage and handling. NYS and NYC residents
please add appropriate sales tax). Send check or money order—no cash or
C.O.D.'s please. Allow six weeks for delivery.

NAME _____

ADDRESS _____

CITY _____ STATE/ZIP _____